KING

KING

A Mystery

DAVID S. FALDET

RESOURCE *Publications* · Eugene, Oregon

KING
A Mystery

Resource Publications
An Imprint of Wipf and Stock Publishers
199 W. 8th Ave., Suite 3
Eugene, OR 97401

www.wipfandstock.com

PAPERBACK ISBN: 978-1-5326-7379-5
HARDCOVER ISBN: 978-1-5326-7380-1
EBOOK ISBN: 978-1-5326-7381-8

Manufactured in the U.S.A.   01/28/19

for Marty
(1957–2012)

*Surely the Savior knows her very well.
That is why He loved her more than us.*

GOSPEL OF MARY

Prologue

Most of my life I have believed in what I can see, what I can smell, what I can rub between my thumb and forefinger. I'm writing to set down a record of my brother, Joshua King: what I saw and heard, the effect I saw him have on others.

Sadly, my brother is dead. Some question the story of his life. Others question the reality of his death. I want to give you the facts about Josh—let you decide what's true.

I've got problems with this. First, I'm an archeologist. I have experience writing e-mails. I can write about a potsherd discovered in stratified or disrupted soil, but have no practice putting into words the feelings of the maker of the pot. I can record transactions, facts, reports about inert material, academic theories, but for Joshua I want to use words that give a sense of his life and the lives he touched. In such writing, I'm a novice.

There's also this; my brother was a spiritual person. Josh cared for the life an outside observer cannot see or touch: the life that, as he once told a friend, exists "between the soul and the spirit." As I've already said, what experience do I, trained to work with dried-out bones, broken pots, and charred wood have attending to the world of intention, of feeling, of soul: the life to which my brother pointed as prophet?

My brother is dead. I can't call him back, can't ask him describe his thinking as he returned from his wanderings in Mexico and the western states to the familiar territory of Bremer County, Iowa, or have him put into words what it felt like to have a power pass through his hand as he eased a suffering man's pain. How can I hope to extend, slightly, even a tiny sliver of light into my brother Josh's inner and now-extinguished existence? What Josh cared about he explained with an analogy. The purpose of a tent, he said, is not the canvas, not the thin outer fabric you easily see and feel, but the kind of space the tent fabric creates *inside*.

So too with the Spirit. My brother, Josh, attuned as he was to the Spirit, was remarkably aware of the true, large inner shape of human lives. He recognized that we are not what we seem to one another. Josh lived with the conviction that our invisible inner life has a purpose he respected, a purpose he lived to see.

How do I come to terms with my brother's commitment to that invisible life? I do it by reminding myself that the world in which we breathe and scuff our knees, the measurable spectrum of energy, that until less than a year ago, was my chief focus, is maybe 5 percent of the whole universe. The other 95 percent is hidden: dark energy and dark material that only clues us to its presence by the measurable bend it puts on the arc of travel of what we *can* see and detect. As with the universe of energy and matter, so with Josh. I watched my brother swim and run and butter his bread. I heard him mumble in his sleep. I listened when he spoke. But I could not climb into his skin. When Josh sensed the presence of the Spirit, I could not feel her tug on his pulse or the illuminations she cast into his brain. I could only observe her trace effects, the ones I plan to report. Even though I feel I scarcely knew my brother, I would like you to know him better, to know his message, to know how the light he carried lives on, even after his passing.

To do that, I'll use my field skills. I have asked questions about the thought and feeling of the security guard who found my brother as he died. I have talked to the woman who eased that security guard's back of its pain, and who, you will come to find, knew my brother well. I've also got my own memories of Josh. By triangulating between those three known bearings, security guard, friend, and the Josh I knew, I hope to give you some sense of Josh's life and what took it.

But I've got to publish those experiences through the medium of language, choosing which words to write, which to leave out. Better to ask me to give birth to a child or to dance the lead in the Russian National Ballet.

Be patient. Be kind.

CHAPTER I

ARNIE MIKESH GOT TO know my brother only for a few minutes, in the small hours of a Saturday morning in March.

His work shift behind him, Mikesh drove, banging the dash to remind the struggling heater of his aging Chevy pickup to blow warm air against his windshield. The blacktop was almost erased by mist. Disoriented, Mikesh kept his brain clear by singing with Gregg Allman's "All Night Train." Above the beat of Allman's Hammond, Warren Haynes's slide on the tight-wound strings of his Gibson dived and caught, like a bird of prey on a speed pill, and twitched and looped around the fuzzy alto melody of Dickey Betts's guitar.

The Allmans rocked on. Mikesh's truck edged forward at the floor of a white pool of fog covering half of two states. Mikesh was nearly invisible in a cab lit only by the deep-ocean-fish glow of his dashboard. No one waited at home for him. No one sat up late, staring at their phone, toying with the idea of giving Mikesh a call. The ghostly slide of Warren Haynes's guitar was Arnie Mikesh's only company as he decompressed from another round in his nocturnal life. "Ride!" he sang off-key with the chorus, "Ride!"

Mikesh had a good memory for weather, but he couldn't recall a fog like this one. When the temperature spiked that morning, the hard, months-old banks of snow hissed an exhalation of heavy steam, a cloak to ward off the warming sun. Mikesh heard the driving advisory on the Waterloo station before he left for work late in the afternoon—stay off the roads. The whole northern half of Iowa would have near zero visibility until late Saturday morning. But he got to work. Eight-and-a-half hours later he had to get home. Driving, he kept the headlights dim, went forward at a crawling speed, and concentrated with what ragged attention he could drag from his bones.

At the road edge to his left, tire tracks cut through the snow bank of the curve, tracks that hadn't been there when he drove to work. Beyond the road shoulder there was nothing but thirty feet of air on that sharp corner. Maybe it would be nothing, but maybe, Mikesh thought, somebody had an accident. He turned at the next field drive, returned to park on the gravel road that intersected the curve, grabbed his flashlight, and walked back. Cold seeped through his clothing. The air had a sweet, half-chewed smell from the silage and cattle of the dairy farm to the south. When the beam of his light caught the scar in the snow bank, he could see that whoever went off that edge made a simple job of it. No other tracks, no footprints, no police or ambulance, just a bent-flat reflector post and the tire marks cutting through the piled-up snow as a vehicle suddenly went airborne. Mikesh's breathing went shallow.

He couldn't see below, but hollered.

He could feel the silence. Damp air nudged back at him. Then Mikesh's nose told what his eyes couldn't. He smelled antifreeze from a damaged radiator. He started down the slope, shoes sliding beneath him.

Even before he was upright, Mikesh's flashlight caught the hazy profile.

Right-side-up a car is designed to be sleek and pretty. Bottom-side-up, a car looks dirty and camouflaged, more like the machine it really is. This one, its wheels pointing up into the fog, had twisted and half buried itself with the impact, like a hulking piece of rusting ordnance that failed to explode. Flashlight trained on the wreck, Mikesh was slow to register what he saw, but then a voice teetered from the smashed car like the echo of Arnie Mikesh's childhood sick-dreams. He felt gripped by a desire to turn around, stroll to the warm cab of the truck, turn the Allmans back on, and drive away. Instead he punched 9–1–1 into his phone and headed toward the broken-out windows of the wreck.

He had training in what to do in an accident scene, but the crack-ups Mikesh investigated in his job at the community college were hardly ever serious enough to trigger the inflation of an airbag. This wreck looked bad. He heard the 9–1–1 operator, a woman's voice. "I'm calling to report an accident, a car headed north," he told her, walking forward. "It left W14 between St. Lucas and Fort Atkinson at 262nd Avenue, and there's a victim."

"A wreck . . . a victim . . . W14" he got in confirmation, and then the phone cut out. He tried redialing, but coverage had gone. When he punched in the numbers again, nothing.

Mikesh circled the upside-down car and noted Bremer County plates. He got down into the snow and shone his light through the exploded windows. That's when he saw my brother. That is, he saw a foot, a leg, the bottom half of my brother's body. My brother's voice was still in the air: reedy enough for Mikesh not to know whether it was a man's or a woman's. When Mikesh shimmied forward and shone the light, the beam caught my brother's head turned toward him underneath the hood. Mikesh, angling to get a better view, saw Josh's badly hurt features, mumbling out a song in something like sleep. Josh quit singing and slowly uncracked his right eye. The left was swollen shut and matted with blood. The right pupil, dilated, stared out at Mikesh. My brother's breathing wasn't good. The facial skin that Mikesh could see was blue. At impact, Josh had been hurled through the windshield like a stone. The weight of the chassis and engine, pressing down into the roof, caught Josh around the waist. He was curled under the center of the car, with his head and shoulders in a red tent of space: burgundy hood above him and blood-stained earth below. From the hips down he was pinched in what remained of the car's passenger area.

Mikesh felt my brother's neck for a pulse. The skin was cold. Mikesh shucked off his cotton jacket and shoved it towards Josh's body. He needed to keep him warm until he got some help. The dispatcher would be in Decorah, at least forty minutes away in this fog, maybe more. If only she had caught the location. He remembered her repeating the highway number to him. That meant the ambulance would come. Mikesh felt more blood. The rearview mirror had caught the edge of my brother's ribcage as the car collapsed, digging its way into his side. As Mikesh stretched to press the soft, insulated fabric where he could, my brother's eye fixed on him.

"The light."

It came as the softest whisper.

"Can you hear me?" Mikesh said.

Josh's eye glinted like a shard of glass in a gravel drive. The stare wasn't fully tracking. Mikesh wished there was more he could do. "I called for help. I can reach you, but I can't get back to you. I can't move you. Do you hear what I'm saying?"

Silence.

"I called for help. You need an ambulance. Are you by yourself?"

There was a pause, the same immobile face.

"Are you by yourself?"

"You. You're here."

Mikesh was puzzled by my brother's answer.

"That's right, I'm here. Is anyone *else* with you?"

"You." My brother's eye focused on him. "I'm thirsty."

Sympathy welled up in Mikesh. No heat coming off the engine, and no ticking, cooling-engine sounds. Mikesh guessed Josh had been there two, maybe three hours. The residual engine heat had probably been keeping him warm, but now the cold alone was enough to kill him. Mikesh, without his jacket, and his face and shoulder up against the snowy ground, was feeling icy himself.

"I'm going to look around the car for a minute. That means I'm going to take the light away and see if there's anyone else I need to help."

"Stay with me. Enter . . . infinity."

Josh's command spooked Mikesh. He stood, and walked around the car once more, swinging the light beam into the fog and giving the scene a careful look. Arcing through the air the car, a Buick, had landed hood-first, slamming onto its top, and ploughed backwards and upside down, to a stop. There was glass and chrome, and a big smear of earth and winter-killed grass, but no other bodies. No one in the passenger seat. Still no phone coverage. Mikesh ran back up to the top of the road bank and tried calling again from that higher elevation. Nothing: rural Iowa invisible even to satellites and towers. He snapped the phone shut. The cold made him shiver. His heart went out to my brother, who now had Mikesh's jacket, who'd been lying there for hours: heat and blood soaking out of him. Mikesh ran to his truck. Pulling open the door he felt the residual warmth spill from the interior along with the yellow glow of the dome light. He cursed not keeping a blanket in the cab. No way he could carry so much as a handful of the precious heat back to my brother. About an inch of coffee remained in the bottom of Mikesh's travel mug. How many days it had been there? It didn't matter; my brother needed liquid. But how would he drink it? He was pinned upside down. Mikesh grabbed the rag he kept on the dash to wipe steam and frost from the Chevy's windshield.

He trotted back to my brother and dipped the cloth into the icy dregs of the coffee. He dropped to his knees, then got down on his belly in the snow.

My brother wasn't making any sound, but the clear eye was not so fixed. The warmth of the coat may have helped him revive. He blinked. Mikesh reached, and pressed the dripping rag against his lips.

"Put this in your mouth."

Like a child, my brother did what he was told, but the taste made him recoil. His good eye widened.

"It's all I have," Mikesh apologized. He pulled back the jacket and traced Josh's arm down to where it was pinned between the roof and his body. He could not reach the wrist or hand. Replacing the jacket, he put his own hand on my brother's neck, index finger searching for a pulse. He pulled away the rag from my brother's mouth and let it drop.

"Can you feel my hand?"

No answer, but the gaze held.

"Can you tell me what happened?"

There was no smell of alcohol in the faint breath. The curve was a bad one, but not the first the car would have encountered heading north from Bremer County in this fog.

"What happened?"

Josh was looking at Mikesh, his eye bright and glinting. "I didn't ask for this," my brother whispered, a terror seeming to grip him. "I've been alone." And then, "Who are you?" The bits of what he said were not connecting, but the question seemed real.

"Arnie. I'm Arnie Mikesh."

"Mikesh," my brother's eye was fixed, his face collected. A long pause, and then a whisper. "Comfort my mother."

Confusion swept over Mikesh. "Is she here?"

My brother, whose jaw and neck remained cool under Mikesh's touch, shook his head. Mikesh could tell he was growing weaker, his breath labored and shallow as he sighed, "It's done."

Josh's lips formed a word that began with a shooshing sound, then whispered, "Take my spirit."

Josh's brow furrowed and he opened his mouth a few times as if to speak, but nothing came out. His eye fluttered shut and his face relaxed. The rigid jaw went softer, and the breathing became labored, then fluttered. Mikesh tried to inch forward, to get at Josh for CPR, but the car had dug its nest tightly, with room for only one. By feel, Mikesh shifted his hand and moved his finger around in my brother's mouth to check that the airway was clear. His hand sensed what was left of the breath: moist heat. But that was all he could do. The labored breaths grew shallow, each one further apart. Mikesh could have comfortably driven his Chevy through the wide spaces in those tiny wheezing breaths. For minute after minute they dragged on without mercy, then quit.

Mikesh gave the face a push, but the eye was closed. After that last breath, the only sound Mikesh could hear was coming from himself: his breathing, his heart, his blood rushing through the tightened vessels of his ears. He touched the neck for a pulse. Mikesh didn't know why, but he rested his left hand on the edge of my brother's jaw. He nudged off the switch on his light, letting everything—including the banging of his heart—go quiet, until, at last, he heard the siren. When it got close, Mikesh pulled back his hand, turned the light on, grabbed his coffee cup, and scrambled up to the road to flag them down. By then he realized he was shivering so much the flashlight jerked in his hand like the hind leg of a dog running crazy in its dreams.

CHAPTER 2

AFTER HE WAS WRAPPED in a blanket and given hot tea, after he talked
to the matter-of-fact deputies, after a tow truck arrived to lift the car,
after the hydraulic spreader pried the crumpled windshield frame apart,
and after two men eased the body out and retrieved the bloody billfold
from the back pocket of the khaki slacks, Mikesh found out the victim
was named Joshua King. Then, his shoulders draped in an ambulance
blanket, Mikesh finished the careful drive home. He tried to sleep, but it
was no good. He had a couple of lagers, staring at a blank window. Over
the hoppy fumes of the emptied second glass he finally nodded off. Sitting in his chair, light coming through the morning fog, he woke from a
bad dream (a face, blood, everything disappearing in a breath of fire) and
found he had a headache. He cleaned himself and changed, took some
aspirin, and drove to Decorah to give the full story to a deputy.

Ten years earlier, a dying great uncle left Arnold Mikesh 120 acres
of pasture, work land, and woods; a farmstead; a modest chunk of operating capital; and a middle-aged Chevy farm truck. Mikesh took it all,
leaving behind a failed marriage and ten years of joyless foot service in
the pork futures trading industry. He found a night security job at the
community college in Calmar, the hometown his parents had abandoned
for the unbroken sunshine of Fort Myers, Florida. Moving to his uncle's
run-down little place near Waucoma, Mikesh used the inheritance to
buy the beginnings of a small herd of Murray Grey cattle from which he
could raise bloodstock. From where he lived, Waucoma was two miles
west, St. Lucas four miles east, Calmar twelve miles northeast. Decorah
was an additional ten miles further in that direction. Mikesh occasionally
hooked a stock trailer to the Chevy and hauled his Murray Greys to buy-
ers interested in a heifer, a bull, or a pair of finishing steers around Iowa
and adjoining states. But Decorah—at eight thousand the biggest town

in a five-county area and the seat of the county north of the one he now called home—had in recent years become the typical furthest limit of his day-in-day-out travel. At forty, Mikesh's world had shrunk to a circle with boundaries rarely more than a fourteen-mile radius of the tiny town where he had attended high school.

Mikesh's visit to the Decorah law enforcement center began badly. He was directed to an inner reception area near the sheriff's office. The sheriff's assistant was on the phone. Mikesh was sure she waved her hand at him, as if to gesture him through the door with *Sheriff* on it. As he got close he heard an agitated voice. He paused and looked back to the woman at the desk. She gave her head a firm nod as if he should go ahead. As he opened the door the voice said, "Listen, I don't know anything about it! What he did, he did on his own!" A dark-bearded man, veins bulging on his neck, turned to Mikesh. The sheriff, on the other side of the desk, looked up, startled by Mikesh's entrance. Mikesh stumbled out an introduction. The sheriff, rising from his chair, eyed him as if he was a housebreaker.

"Who sent you in here?"

Mikesh felt a hand on his shoulder. The woman who had been at the desk was behind him, pulling him back and shutting the door. "Why did you go barging in there?" she said when she had him back in the reception area. Her coffee-brown eyes bored through him. When Mikesh explained that she had gestured for him to walk in, she squinted with mistrust. She led him to a table in a separate room where Jimmy Seegmiller, the deputy on Saturday morning office duty, would take his statement. Mikesh handed her, folded, the blanket sent home with him by the ambulance crew. After that he saw her hover at a desk across the hall, shuffling papers and glancing up occasionally to make sure Mikesh didn't attempt another breaking and entering. Mikesh's Bohemian-American grandmother Clarene used to assure him, "The morning is wiser than the evening," but Mikesh felt like the scant hours of sleep he'd gotten had done nothing to clear his brain of the confusion of last night's fog.

Jimmy Seegmiller, who arrived at the table knowing nothing of Mikesh's blundering into the sheriff's office, sat forward in his seat, savoring the morning's excitement.

"One hell of a foggy night!" Seegmiller was more interested in relaying office news than in getting Mikesh's story. There had been a car/deer accident on the edge of town, where a second car plowed into the first. The police took their cruisers off the streets for fear of another rear-end collision. "I don't need to tell you how long it took the boys to get out to you in that stuff," Seegmiller went on. "I hear you were in bad shape by the time they got there, Arnie."

It gave a deputy like Seegmiller a buzz to remind a security man like Mikesh that he had been in something over his head, preferably *way* over.

"No, Jimmy. You don't need to tell me how long those folks took to get to me last night. I had on my watch. It was cold. And for half the time I was keeping company with a dead man."

"Okay, don't get yourself worked up." Seegmiller sucked in his belly and straightened in his chair: "we got to go through this." Seegmiller was in his thirties but had never lost his baby fat: never had, Mikesh guessed, a decent haircut. Before getting his girlfriend pregnant and marrying her, and before signing on with the county, Seegmiller had at least one under-age possession charge from the bust at a high school beer party, and a DUI while he was doing assembly line work in Howard county. But now Seegmiller was law. He'd put his bad-boy days behind him, and sheriff's business kept excitement in Seegmiller's married life. Since he had never gone out of his way to give Mikesh any trouble, Mikesh wasn't about to stay sore with him.

"What were you doing, anyway, Arnie?"

"I finished my Prairieview shift at one thirty. It was Friday night, and I was tired. I live on Scenic Road over towards Waucoma. County W44 is the most direct route. The fog was so thick, it was tough work just finding my truck in the parking lot, much less seeing the road ahead of me. What was that guy, the driver, doing out there?"

Seegmiller shook his head with knowing self-importance. "Just so happens they knew at state patrol headquarters where King's people were: down in Des Moines. King's been down there these last two weeks for some big come-to-Jesus sort of meeting. Had a run-in with authorities for causing some sort of ruckus, but got released on bail. That gave him a little press the last two days in the capital. Dying on the lam like this ought to keep him in the news another day or two." Seegmiller paused. "It was a church car he was driving. They had another event scheduled for tonight. Sounds like those people also would like to know what he was doing up here.

"His mother and brother and someone from the church are here." Jimmy jerked a thumb toward the sheriff's office. "They've identified the body. I got done with them about a half hour before you came. They're talking to the coroner right now, pretty messed up about this. They want to talk to you, Arnie. They asked for your name."

Seegmiller leaned towards Mikesh and tapped the top of his ball-point against the desk for emphasis. "This little event is going to put that rat's-ass church of theirs out of business."

"So King led a *church*?" Mikesh realized that this explained why he didn't know as much about Joshua King as the people around him. Mikesh and religion, like pickles and cake, were a bad mix.

"That's just it," Seegmiller frowned. "It ain't really a church. It's more like a cult. And what's a cult got without the head guy? A bunch of hippie-crazy-free-love-anti-government nuts living out of their VW microbuses, and not a clue in the world about how to keep a job."

Okay. You, my reading sister, my listening brother, I'm going to stop here, to say that what you just read, just heard, is how *Jimmy Seegmiller* described Josh's lifework to Arnie Mikesh. It's what Seegmiller thought of the group of people I have grown to consider family. Don't hold it against him personally. Seegmiller, like every other law officer from Des Moines to New Albin, was not disposed to think hospitably about Josh.

I'm pausing the story to say that, recording the unconventional way Josh navigated life, I could use the words I place on the page before you like a privacy fence, concealing what isn't nice. Instead, I am working to make these words, this story, if I can, a window, an open one. I'm going to let you hear the trash talk you would get in reply, yourself, if you chatted with the law in the county where my brother died. So you know that Jimmy Seegmiller considered me, your source for this story, a hippie-crazy-free-love-anti-government nut. And you won't be surprised to find that Seegmiller smiled as he pictured the grim future he imagined for my brother's work, my work. I have lived my adult professional life as an archeologist. In that work a projectile point or a fragment of pottery or a piece of charred wood lying in a clean drawer, disconnected from the place of its discovery, can tell me little. But embedded in dirt and grit that I have carefully measured and chronicled and mapped, these objects can begin to speak. I keep Josh in situ. I leave the grit of Josh's environment intact. I leave the window open.

"The cult sucks a few straight, decent folks in now and then, gets their money or their business, and that keeps the whole thing afloat. If they *are* just a church, without their main man, that will all dry up, won't it?"

Jimmy phrased his last question like it wasn't a question. Cops love to talk smack, and Mikesh didn't feel like going down that road. He could still feel the cold, and in his mind still see my brother's eye looking back at him.

"Like I said, I don't know anything about that," he replied.

"In your line of work, Arnie, you don't have to deal with the kind of crap we get from people like that." Seegmiller hadn't put the brakes on yet. "A bunch of gypsies is what they are. And if you have to ask them for an event permit, insurance papers, a vehicle registration, or proof of legal residence, you might as well be talking Bohemian. All you get back is an empty look, a holier-than-thou speech. But they don't fool me. You don't talk that line of crap without needing to hide something. And, if you ask me, that probably was true for the boss as well." Seegmiller focused his anger on my brother. "He was south of the border one too many times for me to believe he didn't have some kind of junk racket going on to keep the whole thing afloat—marijuana, meth, whatever you've got to link up with Mexico to score. The guys from state are checking out his vehicle for drugs, I can tell you that. Maybe as far as that part of the business goes, that church of his won't need him alive to keep the money coming. But if they find drugs, the state might just be able to put an end to their little business."

"Listen Jimmy. You are talking about someone I watched die last night. Take it easy, okay?"

"Right." Having made his speech, Seegmiller needed more oxygen and could start breathing again. "That's what you're here for, isn't it? We need a few more details and a signature. The sheriff wants to speak with you and then you can go."

The sheriff, in his big office, was neither as talkative nor as excited as Seegmiller. Mikesh could see that Paul Fox bore a grudge against him for his earlier entrance. Fox had moved into the county less than five years earlier and spent only two or three years as a deputy before getting elected sheriff. Even though he ran as a Republican, this was no small accomplishment for an outsider in the tight, conservative world of Winneshiek County. Mikesh pegged him for a man who might have his sights on a bigger pond. Fox had the solid, unexceptional look of a guy who might be modeling casual slacks in the men's section of a farm-and-home store catalog, but also wore the confident authority of a man with county voters' mandate to sniff out the criminals that made at least a quarter of them lock their doors at night. Fox sat back in his chair with a wide expanse of desktop between the two of them and studied Mikesh. The accident, Fox said, happened on a county road. It was his jurisdiction to assist in the inquiry, although the state police would take the lead, since it was a fatality. To Mikesh's surprise, Fox announced that he would be taping the interview. Introductory details completed, with a slightly friendlier tone, Fox asked if Mikesh knew the deceased, and reviewed details of what Mikesh reported last night to the deputies. Slowly Mikesh noticed that the questions were getting less friendly. What had Mikesh been doing between nine and ten p.m. the night before? Was there anyone else at the scene who caught his attention? How in all that fog had he happened to notice that a car was in the ditch? Mikesh came to the office thinking of himself as the helpful neighbor. Fox's questions put him on the defensive.

Fox sat straight-backed and wrote down Mikesh's answers. "That car went off the side opposite you on a curve. From every report I got from people out on the road last night, you were lucky to be able to see your own lane," Fox said. "I just want to make sure you didn't meet him on that road, weren't in a place because of all that fog that might have caused him to run off the road like that."

"I was at work from five o'clock on."

"Anybody there to back you up on that?"

"I checked in at the beginning of my shift. After that, though, I was on my own. It was a quiet Friday night. No evening classes. Everyone who could be off the road was home." Mikesh scoured his memory. "I talked to the cleanup guy on the last round of milking at the dairy center, but that would have been before that time, eight thirty, nine at the latest. After that I can't say that I saw or talked to anyone. It's possible one of the kids at the apartments saw me on my rounds there. The last would have been around midnight."

"No one you had to stop, no one you helped, no one else saw you at the school?"

Fox was checking that Mikesh had an alibi that would prove he had not run my brother off the road.

"Listen, I punched in at five o'clock and left work around one thirty. I talked to a guy in the dairy building about nine. On the way home I was watching the road closely and I saw some suspicious tracks in the snow bank. I stopped and found an accident and a victim that no other driver and no sheriff's deputy discovered in what must have been several hours. If you don't feel like thanking me for helping your office do its job, that's fine. But don't try to come up with a story that makes no sense—not to anyone who knows me."

Mikesh was tired and angry.

"I just talked to the family and friends of a dead man," the sheriff told him. "They're distraught. They want some kind of answer about a fatal accident. I'm going to make sure we don't overlook anything."

Fox, in his regulation button-down shirt and his sport coat, talked a good line.

"You can understand why I want to make sure you had nothing to do with this, Arnie. You are telling me you did not pass the scene of the accident any time before you made that 9-1-1 call last night at 1:51?"

Mikesh quit talking. He shook his head.

"Do you have a clearer way of telling me and the recorder that, yes, you were nowhere near the scene before that time?"

Mikesh felt weary. "That's right. I was nowhere near that scene between the time I clocked in and the time I drove that way home after my shift."

"Even though you happened by a long time after the crash, you spoke with King. Remind me again if he told you anything about his accident."

"Not really." Mikesh wished he could find something of help, something that would put him a bit more on Fox's side of that awful desk.

"That car flew a ways before it hit the ground. He was going a good speed when he left the road."

"The tire marks did not indicate the deceased even tried to stop or slow down. And no evidence he had been drinking," Fox said. "Drugs may be another question. We'll let the State Patrol investigation and the coroner answer that. It's a fatal accident. State Patrol is going to go over that car thoroughly. But did you see any sign of drugs? Did you remove anything from the scene?"

"The only thing I touched was the man himself, seeing if I could get a pulse, clear his wind passage, give him a lick of coffee when he asked for something to drink. Beyond that, there was not much I could do. He was wedged in pretty tight. It took a while, even with the hydraulic machinery, for your boys and the EMTs to get his body out. I could see I shouldn't try to move him. I didn't take anything. I just pushed my jacket in around him and waited for the ambulance. Within maybe twenty minutes of the time I got there, he was dead."

"And that left, what? Maybe another twenty or thirty minutes before the emergency response arrived? What were you doing all that time?"

Mikesh tried not to pause, not to sound evasive, but he didn't like his own answer. "I kept my hand against him. . . . . I was talking to him, not sure when it was he really died. I had my hand on his neck, checking for a pulse so I just kept it there. After pushing my jacket in there around him, it seemed like the one other thing I could do."

Fox searched Mikesh's face.

"The jacket you say you pushed around the victim, that is with his effects. We will have to keep it until the investigation is completed. There's a lot of blood on it."

Mikesh was quiet.

"So there's nothing more you can tell me about why you were there, what you saw at the scene, or what you said?"

Mikesh said nothing.

"I see you are a man with a record, and I want to make sure the report for this incident is complete."

Mikesh felt his blood pressure surge. "That *record* is for a high school prank."

"Car theft is more than a prank."

Fox had unearthed the one incident, from Mikesh's careful life, which landed him in court for a criminal offense.

"A buddy and I hid the car of a guy who was just a little too fond of it."

Mikesh was eighteen. The car was a Mustang, the owner Bill White. While his accomplice had gone with White into the house to watch the taped highlights of the 1985 football season where Bill had played fullback and his friend a left tackle, Mikesh drove the Mustang to the parking lot of the hair salon favored by the town's oldest ladies and parked it there, underestimating the frenzy and the wrath of its owner once he found it gone. One night in jail and two levels of reduced charges later Mikesh paid his fine and spent his summer before university on probation, doing community service.

"There aren't a lot of people in this county who have a vehicle theft on their record."

"And not one who was charged for such a stupid reason."

"I wouldn't know anything about that. A record is a record, and I'm just trying to get the report for this death complete and clear. A lot of people are interested in this man."

"I've told you what I know."

"Does your boss over at the community college know about your record, or the state employment people?"

"We're talking about Calmar, Iowa. Anybody who has lived there more than fifteen minutes knows the story, including the color of shirt I was wearing when I walked away from the lot of the Twirl 'n' Curl and probably, for that matter, the brand of my underwear."

"The last time I looked, your boss doesn't live in Calmar."

"What does that have to do with what happened in the fog last night?"

Fox paused. "Maybe nothing. I've got to get the facts, got to be sure I understand my sources."

"Seegmiller said you are still investigating out at the scene."

"We're working with the state. You have to check everything out." Paul Fox picked up a paper clip and tapped it on his blotter. "Make sure in the final report every *t* is crossed, every *i* dotted. That's my plan, so you may need to come in again. You'll probably need to talk to state investigators."

The law enforcement center lot was gray with thinning fog as Mikesh, zipping up his Carhartt, walked across the asphalt. Unhappy that he seemed to be the careless driving suspect in a stranger's death, and surprised at how deeply the sheriff seemed to be invested in proving his guilt, Mikesh hoped he was on his way home, but he was greeted by me, walking toward him from between the cars, offering my hand.

"Are you Arnold Mikesh?" I asked. "I'm Tom King, Joshua's brother."

Okay brother, sister reader. I have already told you I'm the brother of the dying man. What you don't know is that I am not just Josh King's brother, but his twin, the fraternal twin, conceived on the same occasion, only six minutes his junior in entering the cold December air of Northeast Iowa. Ever since Josh left college his main nickname for me has been "Diddy Mouse," which he told me meant "twin." That, at least, is was what it meant to Josh. In the last few months before he died, Josh had some fun with my given name too, sometimes calling me 'Tom-Tom,' saying I would be the Spirit's drum.

If my delay in this information makes you suspicious, excellent. It's smart to be skeptical. Something as basic to your wellbeing as water, administered the wrong way, say in a blinding fog, or the bath into which you pass out from having too much drink—can kill you. It's wise to be suspicious. If you are, you know that I am too close to my brother to tell his story with the detachment you can trust. Better that you get it through the somewhat surprised eyes and ears of one who is just as new to Josh King as you. Hence the tale of Arnold Mikesh. Hence my role as reporter and stage manager. I talked Mikesh into being the star witness of this account. Eventually that meant going over the whole sequence of events that Josh's accident started in motion. This involved some very long talks. The first began outside what most residents in Decorah call "the cop shop."

Surprised by my parking lot introduction, Mikesh was flustered as he returned my shake with the grip of his beefy hand. "I'm sorry . . . sorry about your brother dying."

Mikesh is more at home with empty hallways and feeding cattle than small talk. Not comfortable in this kind of conversation, he was distracted, studying me, trying to imagine what my brother might have looked like when standing and chatting, realizing that even though we were not identical (which we are not) the resemblance was strong.

"Thanks."

I didn't know where to begin, myself. A phone call in the night. A long, slow drive from Des Moines. I sat in the back, next to my mother Maria, with our friend Simon at the wheel. In this strangely formal, but necessary arrangement we drove north, white fog in the headlights. Stumbling around our brains were questions with a hand out for answers that remained short on offer. At our destination was a quiet hospital room where Josh's broken body lay beneath a green sheet, folded back at his groin for the three of us to identify him. Blood had been washed from him, but the crown of rips in his scalp where he broke through the windshield glass were the same raw color as the stew beef in a supermarket meat counter. His abdomen was torn, and ringed round with a purple bruise where the roof and dashboard had clamped him like a vise. And all I could wonder, as I stood and stared at the battered remains of my brother, was what I would next make of *my* life.

"You were there. You know what we had to look at," I told Mikesh.

"It was a bad accident."

"I wanted to thank you for what you did. You probably were not the first person to drive by. No one else stopped."

"It was quiet the whole time I was out there. There weren't a lot of people on the road. I was violating a travel advisory even getting into my truck." Mikesh was thinking about Paul Fox's questions, the sheriff's attempt to place him at the scene at the time of the crash. The quiet of that road *did* make him the only current suspect if you were looking for one. But standing there on the asphalt, looking at Arnold Mikesh's square, vulnerable face, *I* didn't suspect him of anything criminal. Not for a heartbeat.

"I'm sure that's true. My brother wasn't good with directions. He might have been coming to Decorah. We don't know. He rarely drove. I'll have to admit to you that he wasn't very good at keeping his mind on the road. He ended up not watching his speed, making mistakes." Josh's list of mishaps was long: a mailbox knocked sideways, missed turnoffs, driving on the wrong side of the centerline, passengers white-knuckled on a curve. By the time I was working with him, we always arranged to have someone else at the wheel if Josh needed a car. He was not born to drive. With age, his distraction and helplessness behind the wheel got worse instead of better.

"As for this journey last night, we didn't know he was gone. The call from the authorities woke us. Nobody knew Josh was away or why he would have left. All the way here we kept wondering how we let Josh slip away before dinner without any of us knowing he was gone. We each felt part of the blame.

"But I heard from the deputy that my brother was still alive when you got to him, that you talked to him." I hoped Mikesh could dispel the mystery. "If you don't mind, I'd like to hear what he said. Could I get you a cup of coffee?"

Mikesh and I walked to a place just up the hill, on the corner of Decorah's main business street. The college kids with their laptops were away on break, so the coffee shop was nearly empty. Coming in from the damp, the warmth, the strong smell of freshly ground dark roast, and the roar of the espresso steamer felt good. Near the counter four women more Mikesh's age than mine were leaning over their lattes, catching up on the week, their eyes checking us over when we entered. A pair of retirement-aged men sat at one of the booths. I got two filter coffees and we took a table at the far back.

"I'm sure you don't like to think about it, but it would mean a lot to me, and to the people around Josh, to know how he died."

In the last few months before the accident, my brother talked quite a bit about his death. Josh was attuned to a world whose existence I often questioned. He said plenty that I let pass unconsidered. The sudden prospect of a future without him left me clutching for *any* words of his that I had missed.

"I can see that." Mikesh wondered who the "people around Josh" might be: somber Christians, women in trippy flowered dresses, or Latino meth runners. So far, in Arnold Mikesh's short introduction to the world of Joshua King, the reports were contradictory.

Mikesh needed encouragement. "According to the deputy, he was still able to speak. Did he say anything I could relay to his Shekinah followers?"

"Who?"

"Shekinah. That's the name of the group Josh led."

"What's the word again?"

"'Shekinah.' It means 'where the Spirit dwells' or 'Spirit in you.'"

Mikesh squinted in concentration. "I think that was one of the last words your brother said. The word, it started with that "shh" sound. 'Shekinah, take my spirit.' I'll bet those were his last words." Mikesh felt tired, thinking of Josh dying with this antique word, like a well-worn rosary, on his lips.

Mikesh told me what he remembered: Josh's attention to the light, his feeling alone, "join in infinity," "comfort my mother." I had him go through it all. Did he remember the tune Josh was singing, did Josh say anything about where he was going? Did he show any emotion? We were talking about my twin brother, the person to whose body I conformed even before we were born.

"Do you know anything about Shekinah, Arnie?"

Mikesh shook his head. "I didn't know enough about it to recognize your brother when I was trying to help him last night, or the word he was trying to say, if that's any indication. He asked for my name, but he didn't live long enough to tell me his."

"People will tell you that my brother started something that was all about him, that he was the whole show." Mikesh recalled Seegmiller's words: Josh as kingpin in a cult of drug runners. "But I don't believe that. My brother was pointing to something within him but more important, something beyond himself, something that he believed includes *you*."

I sat at a coffee shop table trying to explain my brother, while he lay dead in a hospital room down the road. The image of that fought with others: Josh's face animated with the message he carried, Josh's hands on an old woman's shoulders, Josh helping hold the oven door as someone pulled out a tray of loaves, Josh's voice when he called me "Tom-Tom."

"He was in shock, and only partly conscious, but didn't you feel the way he reached out to you?"

"What do you mean?"

"He asked your name. He asked you to comfort my mom."

"True. That rattled me."

Mikesh's reaction was not unique. People were unsettled by the effect my brother had on them. What he said could jar you. Some got angry and turned that against him. Those people and the media saw my brother as a wolf. They circled the wagons, protecting themselves and their flock against him.

I, your story teller, have to admit that Josh had finally unsettled me, too. I worked as a contract archeologist through fall 2007, but after that digging season ended, I moved in with Mom and Josh. More than moved in. After I'd filed my final reports, I helped Josh with his work and decided that from then forward I would divide my year that way. I wished I had a way to tell Mikesh, over coffee, that stepping back into the long shadow cast by my twin brother after having freed myself of him for ten years was neither automatic nor wholly pleasant. It threatened my pride. Deciding whether I was going to continue that work now that Josh was dead was the next issue to face: once the shock passed and the grim business of my brother's death got completed. That morning in the coffee shop, I had little to offer but questions.

"The people who followed Josh are going to want to know about what you saw and heard. It's going to sound crazy to you, but those people are very definitely going to want to hear from you whether you saw my brother die, whether he quit breathing."

While I pictured the faces of the ones who were not going to believe, would never believe Josh was dead, the thought at the front of Arnie Mikesh's mind was just the opposite: remembering the feeling of his fingers in the airway of my brother's mouth after he quit speaking, and the silence that pounded in Mikesh's brain after that last breath. Josh's dying moment was not an experience Mikesh wanted to speak about to a group of religious fanatics, much less think about himself.

"My mother and I don't care about an autopsy. We want to bury Josh and move forward. But the sheriff says it has to happen. He feels there could be alcohol or drugs involved. In a way I'm relieved that we are going to get a doctor's signature on a report that will detail exactly what killed Josh—that it was nothing illegal."

My phone rang: our friend Simon. I told him where we were, and soon Mikesh, heading back to the parking area, felt my hand—the unfamiliar hand of the dead man's brother—on his back, guiding him toward a pair of people. One was my mother, Maria, and the other was the bearded man who Mikesh saw when he stumbled into the Sheriff's office: Simon Peña, Josh's assistant. Standing outside in the cold, looking into Mom's splotchy face, Mikesh told the story again, thinking about my brother's last request: "Comfort my mother."

"You are sure he didn't say anything else?" Peña pushed. "You are sure he didn't say why he was on that road or why he went off it? Something maybe you forgot?"

Mikesh could taste his dislike for Peña. He thought back to what he saw in the sheriff's office: this man saying he didn't know what Josh was doing on that road. Peña had nerve to press Mikesh on the same question.

"No. I remember it. I wish I *could* put it more out of my head."

Mom placed her hand on Mikesh's arm. "Of course that's how you feel." Mikesh looked into her face: a fifty-one-year-old woman, with the nylon collar of her jacket turned up against the damp, her eyes puffed up from crying, and her sandy hair flat on one side. Her tousled appearance made Mikesh warm to her. She was fingering the zipper of her jacket, where the tab on the slider had broken. And Mikesh heard her give the first sensible judgment he'd heard about the accident: "It was weather, Simon. Bad weather took Josh."

CHAPTER 3

IF MIKESH THOUGHT HE knew what my mother was talking about, he was wrong. As she looked into his face, her hair messed and eyes puffy, she was, for that moment cheerful, thinking of what she told my brother and me many times in the little house she ruled, her story of how she wasn't sure we would make it into the world because of weather. How when she was carrying us she wasn't due until late January. How she was on her own. How she and dad were going to marry. How Dad needed the cash, and went south to work some high-paying construction after hurricane Carmen hit in the fall. But Dad stopped calling or writing. My unmarried mom was left living with her parents on the farm, sleeping in the bedroom in which she had grown up, eating from the same flowered stoneware she had known from childhood. Except that now she was pregnant and the man who was responsible had left with a promise on his lips and then, like the hurricane he had followed, disappeared. It was 1974. Mom said they were not so careful about getting ready for babies in those days. She saw the doctor once, and only knew from that visit that she was pregnant and that the due date would be in the new year. Mom should have gone back, seen Dr. Razavi again, but she was stubborn and angry. She thought that before the end of the year, Dad would come back with enough money to set them up independently. They would marry, and as a new bride she would see the doctor. But Mom promised Grandma that at the end of December she would set up a new appointment, and make arrangements for the hospital stay by the time her due date arrived.

Late December of '74 was cold. No matter the season, my grandfather listened to the farm report and the weather at six o'clock every morning. The day before Josh and I were born, Grandpa announced to Mom and Grandma that a blizzard was forecast. On the morning that Grandpa announced the blizzard, Mom, in the frozen farm country of

Clayton County, craved fresh pie cherries she could pick by hand in mid-summer from the tree in her parents' lawn, just a few yards away from the garden where beans would be ripe for the harvest under velvet leaves. Mom's craving was so powerful that she felt like she would walk to get ripe cherries, even if she had to put one foot ahead of the other all the way to south Florida. But Grandpa was firm. The three of them were going to sit tight, make sure the animals were cared for and everything buttoned down, because heavy snow was coming on a strong wind. True to the forecast, by noon the air was white. While Grandma and Grandpa and Mom listened to the weather bulletins coming in on KOEL and the wind howled in the eaves, Mom daydreamed of biting through the fragile skins of cherries and wiping the juice from her lips. Around bedtime, when the storm was at its worst, her water broke and contractions started.

Mom had not yet turned nineteen, but she knew what was happening. Neither she nor my grandmother anticipated this would be her delivery date. Neither thought ahead to get Mom into town to be near Community Hospital. Grandma called Dr. Razavi. He said with a first baby it might be a long wait before Mom actually needed to get to Elkader. That night with Grandma on the phone, and the winds ready to shake the house off its foundations, the waves of pain knocked Mom sideways. When the contractions grew close, Razavi contacted the sheriff, who said it would be a slow business for the plows to get out to my grandparents' road through the piling drifts. Their best bet for speed was for my grandparents to get Mom to the state highway, meeting the plow and ambulance there.

On its own, Grandpa's tractor might have gotten through, but Mom was in no condition to climb on, and a wagon would get hung up in the snow. Then Grandpa thought about Nels Myhre's sleigh. Nels had the roughest farmland in their neighborhood, steep, all woodland and pasture. Nels kept sheep and was the last farmer in the area to use horses. His place was one farm over. You'd have had to drive twenty miles to find another farmer who still kept work animals or a sleigh. But Nels used a bobsleigh to get hay bales out to the sheep in winter, driving a team of black half-Percherons who weren't put off by snow. About three in the morning, Grandpa called Nels and asked if he thought the team and sleigh could make it. Nels would try. The snow had quit but was still blowing. Grandpa got out with his tractor and blade cleared the drive and their section of road. Grandma stayed with Mom. Around four o'clock Mom and Grandma heard the bells on the harnesses of Nels's team.

Nels, rosy-cheeked and frosted with snow, appeared in the kitchen door. "Elizabeth," he told my grandma, "I'd ask for a cup of coffee, but we better get going." Grandma, two steps ahead of him, handed him the Thermos.

Nels had piled a row of bales around the sleigh and scattered loose hay in between. Over that he piled blankets, with a buffalo robe on top to keep out the snow and weight down the coverlets. He and Grandma got Mom into the sleigh. They could hear Grandpa's tractor out on the road, working away at the drifts, and grandma got down with Mom under Nels's cold pile of blankets. As Nels called out to the horses and the runners crunched down into the hard snow, Mom remembers the smell of alfalfa hay in the close air around her and a weight of blankets pulled up to her chin. Between gusts of snow, she saw stars, one glittering with particular brightness. She nearly lost consciousness during each contraction, but in between she was sharp and lucid. They say the body retains everything, a catalog of every breath, every meal, every fright the organism you inhabit has ever experienced. The library of that cellular memory is one roomy place. But for the average person, we have the call numbers to only a fraction of the holdings. Not so for Mom and that night: everything so clear she can picture, hear, and smell it to this day. She kept praying. It was all she could do: pray the baby would come safe. Seeing that bright star in the clear sky, she felt in her heart that her prayers would be answered.

It was good that Grandpa called Nels because the last three-quarters-mile of road, where it rose to meet the highway, Grandpa parked the tractor and walked ahead of the team holding the bridles to urge on the big black animals. By then Josh was on his way. The harness bells sang as Nels's horses broke through each new drift. "We're almost there, Elizabeth, almost there," Nels told Grandma. He saw the red and yellow flashing of the ambulance and road maintainer on their way up the hill. Nels's sleigh reached the intersection. Grandma told Mom to hold on, but Mom's time had come. Josh was born on the worn wooden bed of that bobsleigh with only my grandmother to help him into the world, born in the rough hay in the blowing snow as Nels Myhre's team stood steaming from the effort of pulling the birthing suite uphill. The eerie thing was, Josh didn't cry. When the sleigh broke through that last drift into the space the maintainer had just cleared, Dr. Razavi and one of the ambulance men climbed into the bobsleigh to help Grandma take care of Josh and hold up a light. Razavi was the one to tell Mom she wasn't done yet, that there was another baby. And that's when I was born. For all the extremity of his birth, Josh, wrapped in one of Nels's blankets, was just fine.

Mom would look at me (one half of her December blizzard surprise, the one assisted into the world by the trained hands of a doctor of medicine under a battery-powered spotlight) when she got to this part of telling her story, and grab my arm. She said Nels Myhre and Grandpa were minding the team, the horses so agitated it took the two men to keep them from jerking the sled one way and another, its runners groaning against the snow, bells ringing. When he heard the news of my arrival, Nels said that the birth of two healthy boys in the teeth of that winter blizzard was a miracle, a sign.

"They're meant to do something special in the world, Maria," he said when he came round to the back.

Dr. Razavi looked Mom in the face and said he thought Nels was right. He took a gold ring off the little finger of his right hand and pressed it into her palm. "Take this, Maria. It will be a reminder to you of what Mr. Myhre says."

Mom now, in the parking lot, over thirty years later, twisted the re-sized ring on the index finger of her left hand as she looked at Mikesh. I know she was thinking Nels Myhre, dead a decade back, was right. Josh had accomplished his special calling.

"The weather claimed Joshua at last." She released the ring and took both of Mikesh's hands. "Thank you for helping my son."

"He told me to comfort you if I could. Is there anything else I can do?"

Mom held onto Mikesh's hands, tears watering her eyes, until she found her voice. "Talk to the people who loved him; tell them how he died." And then, checking herself as she turned away, she shook her head as if freeing cobwebs. "Figure out what he was *doing* out there! It'd be a comfort for me to know."

Simon took my mother's elbow as they walked to the car, but I continued with Mikesh to his pickup.

"I'm sure you would like to just put this behind you, Arnie, but it might be that talking to all the people closest to Josh could be the quickest way to put the questions to rest." I put out my hand again. "Can I get your promise?"

Mikesh wasn't eager to commit. But he remembered Josh and my mother's request, and gave me his telephone number.

CHAPTER 4

MIKESH WAS HAPPY TO put the airless rooms of the Winneshiek County Law Enforcement Center and us, the relations of Josh King behind him. On the drive home he avoided the route that brought him to the accident less than twelve hours earlier. The fog had almost burned off and the day was turning out sunny, the sort of afternoon people hunger for at the late-March end of a winter in which the first snow came before Halloween.

Mikesh, a convert to land owning, came to farming with more deliberation and zeal than his neighbors. He was progressive: selecting an Australian breed of cattle that did well from calf through finish on grass, and were preferred for flavor by customers who would pay extra for quality. He used a system of intensive paddock grazing developed in France to keep his cows on fresh grass through the warm months. In other ways, he was conservative. He raised animals instead of renting out his land to be cropped by a neighbor. He avoided chemicals basic to crops on every farm but his on Scenic Road. He nursed along his aging truck, and allowed, indulgently, that to manage his stock moving in and out of paddocks and fenced away from most of the creek, he needed the bay horse he kept. His best friend Dale Murphy said that Mikesh *played at* farming.

It had been a month since he was in the saddle. Once he got home he caught Zisca. The horse's winter coat was rough and dirty. Mikesh curried him down, talking to him, an act that soothed the horse. Mikesh thought it only reasonable that he get familiar and friendly with the animal before seating himself on his back and ordering him around with the pressure of a metal bit against his soft gums. Once Zisca was saddled, they rode out along the road. Mikesh lived in gently rolling country of wide, fenced fields, broken by small woodlands in the few places where the land steepened as it approached a stream or flooded too often to risk plowing. The sun on the remaining snow was blinding, but felt good. Zisca seemed as interested in the ride as Mikesh. The gelding wanted to break from his walk into a trot down the shoulder as they headed away from the farm. On the wrists exposed between his jacket and his deerskin gloves as he held the reins Mikesh could feel the warmth rising off the horse's neck, could see the alert tension in Zisca's ears, and feel the happy release of energy in the quick spring of his gait.

The higher temperature was melting the snow, and water was running off the fields and pastures. The creek, normally a quiet trickle, that ran through his place and past the cemetery on its way to the river, could today be heard from the road. Its water was foaming. The spillway in the middle of Waucoma roared, the riverish smell of water hanging in the air. Cakes of ice bobbed in the channel of the Little Turkey below the falls. Two boys in loose stocking caps were on the park side of the dam, throwing ice chunks from a snow pile into the water. The din drowned out their splash, but the boys shouted as they added rings of spray to the mayhem. Spring yesterday became official, and down along the river bottom, it felt, smelled, and sounded like the season had really arrived.

Once back at the farm, Mikesh rode Zisca to check the fences along the whole perimeter of his domain. In the course of the last four months, the cattle had only gone into the pasture as far as the hay feeders, wearing the ground raw around them, leaving the snow along the far fences unbroken except by deer. With the weather turning, his cows would be out looking for grass again soon enough, so Mikesh needed to check if the fences were damaged by snow or falling trees. Water was rushing through the creek bottom, and out beyond, in the alfalfa field and the band of woods at the back of the acreage, Mikesh could hear the "cheer-up" trills of robins, gone for a whole season, mixing with the whistle of cardinals in the trees. At the edge of the woods, signs that it had been a grim winter were clear. Starving rabbits had gnawed the bark off scrub, saplings, and fallen limbs. An early crusting of winter ice and later layers of snow buried anything else beyond easy reach. Blood and feathers marked the place where a hungry pheasant strayed far enough from safety to become prey for a fox. Back at the stream Mikesh turned Zisca toward the clump of black willows that ringed a bend where the water swirled in its deepest pool. One of the willows grew parallel to the ground: a large limb stretching along the bank, the other projecting out less than two feet above the water, the half-exposed roots of its fallen trunk reaching upward like a hand. Mikesh jumped down from the saddle, dragging the toes of his boots as he walked through the gravelly snow. Just up the slope from this swimming hole, far enough in elevation that the soil was thin, he had found, eight years ago, a stone projectile point in soil he pulled up with a boxelder seedling. The point was early Archaic. Mikesh kept the narrow wedge of chert in his desk drawer, lifting it occasionally against his flattened palm to register its weight, considering the over-two-thousand years it had lain in the soil. Mikesh valued the skill in its symmetry and the sharpness of its two knapped edges. Since he raised beef cattle, it was his reminder that others had culled animals from this patch of ground before him, that he was not the first to draw his living from the place, that he should take care of its soil, assuming that others would need to make use of it after every trace of him was gone.

Mikesh rode back to the barn, unsaddled Zisca, and checked the hay feeder. Since he appeared without feed bucket or new hay, the mass of silver-gray cattle watched him with black eyes as impassive as the Buddha's. One, however, walked toward him, releasing a high but resonant "ooom!" It was Rosie, Mikesh's favorite in the herd, now carrying her first calf. The cattleman inside Mikesh would have said it was the straight line of her back, her classic Murray Gray dun color, the favorable configuration of her pelvis for calving that earned his favor. But congeniality was the quality that most separated Rosie from the rest. Mikesh chose, with Rosie's first breeding, to try something new, a Square Meater bull. He already had a bull, and the frozen semen sent all the way from Australia cost plenty, but the offspring would be shorter at the shoulder and more compact in configuration than the rest of his herd, a look Mikesh guessed would be the future of this breed in the U.S. market. Rosie nosed the sleeve of his coat and pushed her weight gently against him. Mikesh took off his glove and ran a hand over the springy winter hair of Rosie's neck and back, pressing more firmly as he rounded her flank and belly. It was in part the return of a friendly gesture, but also a check of his investment, making sure the calf still configured as it should, and that the temperature thrown off by Rosie's skin did not feel hot. Mikesh grew uneasy with the thaw, knowing that the health of heifers and bred cows near calving time would get touchy when the afternoons were warm, the nights cold, and the weather damp around the clock.

Mikesh felt prickly himself. The raw air, the snow, the damp smell, even the sound of Zisca's or Rosie's breathing—any of it planted the same tension at the base of his neck, the same tingling in the back of his nose he had felt in the fog a few hours before as he directed his flashlight on my brother's battered face. Mikesh still hadn't gotten rid of that headache.

Just a few miles from the place where he was going through his daily chores, my brother's life had ended, but not before Josh asked Mikesh to join him in infinity. As Mikesh finished his chores the thought came into his head of Paul Fox, sitting in his swivel chair, asking if Mikesh might not have edged Josh off the road. Mikesh thought of his coat deposited in a plastic evidence bag. He kicked a dirty hump of ice for the pleasure of watching it spray across the cattle pen. Instead he tripped. The ice didn't move.

The edgy mood made him glad to get to his security guard shift again as the afternoon sun dipped low in the sky on Saturday. On the weekend at the community college where he worked, most of the buildings were locked and quiet by the time he arrived. The only places he was apt to encounter anybody were the dairy center and the three apartment buildings that housed the school's handful of resident students. Mikesh knew that people associated the word *security* with beefy weightlifters who carry a gun or a Taser. Where Mikesh worked, *security* meant making sure everything was locked up, that the lights were turned off, and the heating plant was running as it should. He could hand out violations, call the Calmar cop or Seegmiller's office, but his most common night run-ins with students involved telling them to clear out of a computer lab or keep the noise down in an apartment, lifting them up in the hallway when they passed out, or cleaning after them if they heaved in the stairs. For Mikesh, while calling the police was part of an interesting night, he dreaded calling an ambulance. He drove to work hoping no one was going to miss a curve on the campus, that his watch would, like most others, prove uneventful.

The night was quiet, but foggy. After a few quick words with the janitor whose shift was closing down, there was no one. Checking the buildings, walking down dark corridors whose locks and switches and vents he had memorized, usually calmed Mikesh. Not that night. He turned on more lights than usual, but couldn't turn down the fog. As he drove his rounds, parked cars swam up at him as he passed. In the parking lot of one rental unit a figure stepped out from the last vehicle in a line of cars and pick-ups. The eyes glinted in Mikesh's headlights. He laid on the horn and braked. One terrified kid with a pizza box hurried off to his apartment and Mikesh nosed the security van back to the office. There was an odd pressure in his chest. He told himself to slow down his breathing. Enough patrolling for one night; the campus was secure until half past one.

By the time Mikesh was driving home his head was pounding, though he had taken aspirin steadily over the course of the day. He made sure to take a different route than the night before.

At home he felt restless, his brain like the target of an afternoon's batting practice. He turned on his computer and cruised the Internet. In a room where the only sounds were the fire settling in the woodstove and a clock ticking, the screen shone and blinked as he clicked on each new site: Duke losing in a basketball upset to West Virginia, cattle prices soft, the Australian grain market pegging itself to ethanol prices, the definition of the word *infinity*. That was his word, wasn't it? "Infinity . . . Join in infinity."

"An assumed limit, increasing without end," but before that, a different definition: "within a boundary."

The last words my brother heard were Mikesh telling him he was going to be okay. What had my brother meant with his last requests? To go someplace without end? To join him in that tight crushing space where he was finding it harder and harder to breathe? And what kind of help did Josh think our mother would need? Mikesh remembered the cold of my brother's cheek. He replayed scenarios of the accident where he didn't fail my brother: scenes where he had a blanket in the cab, a flask of warm coffee, scenes where an adrenalin surge helped him lift the hulking car with his shoulders. A scene where he pushed underneath the crushing weight of the hood to administer CPR even if it meant he, too, was crushed in trying. Not one of Mikesh's imagined fantasies was as real as his failure.

He turned off the computer and went to bed.

CHAPTER 5

A FEW RESTLESS HOURS later Mikesh gave up on the prospect of a night's sleep, and instead baked the dinner rolls he was under orders to bring to his neighbors' house for Easter lunch. Smelling the working yeast, punching dough, and working near the oven's heat blunted the toothy edge of his headache enough to allow him to doze off in his chair before waking for chores. As he walked through the barn and pens, hollow and distracted, enveloped by the smell of fresh manure and hay, his consolation was that he was looking at two days off and a Sunday meal with friends.

That noon, setting the fresh rolls in the roomy kitchen of Dale and Barbara Murphy's big four-square farmhouse, Mikesh had women to greet: Barbara, the Murphys' daughter home from university, one of Barbara's aunts, two mothers-in-law helping at the stove and the sink. He responded to the jokes about bringing baking to a gathering where the only other male contribution to the menu was the carved ham provided by Barbara's father. The air jostled with the clatter of silverware and competing conversations, the smell of smoky meat, casserole, and potatoes. Mikesh made his way to the living room, where six men sat, and where the ambience was less than jovial.

That week a neighbor, Ed Doyle, was ordered to make a payment to the biggest agribusiness firm in the country for the offense of reusing seed corn. In Doyle's absence, Dale's father was defending him.

"I didn't know what it was to buy seed corn the first twenty years I farmed. And danged if with the new, fancy seed it's not the same as the old days; for a second or third year you can plant the corn you harvest and get the same quality as if you bought."

"And how would you know that?" Dale asked. "You better not let the seed police boys catch you airing that view or you'll find your butt dragged into court for a copyright infringement that will cost you your farm and every penny you don't already owe to the bank."

"Copyright infringement!" Dale's father snorted. "You pay good money for the stuff when you buy it from them. Why should some pencil pusher in St. Louis be able to say how long you keep planting it on your field in Fayette County?"

Dale's father wasn't the only farmer who chafed uneasily against the new restrictions. He grew up in a farming world where, if you paid money for an animal or a bushel of shelled corn you owned it, no questions asked. In the agro-industrial world of 2008, he had to keep careful records on every animal, and was being told that he only had renter's rights to his designer-priced seed corn. There were hotlines set up for reporting comments like the one he had made about replanting, or for sharing your hunch that a neighbor was planting unpaid-for, copyrighted seed. It gave unfriendly farm folks a big stick, because in courts where such accusations got resolved, it was guilty until proven innocent for farmers who mounted a legal defense against the claim that they had DNA in their crop for which they had not paid. On the dusty farm roads around Waucoma and St. Lucas at planting and harvesting time you were more apt to see the black Suburban of an industrial detective, with his camera and his notebook computer, than you were to see a sheriff's cruiser. Ed Doyle's seed corn rep filed a complaint with his company when Doyle failed to place an order in the spring of 2007. Detectives richly documented the extent and progress of that year's corn crop, and collected, under threat of legal action against the elevator, a sample of the grain he brought in fall 2007 to market. With no receipts to prove that he had bought new seed corn, he paid, on March 15, 2008, an undisclosed cash settlement that probably erased his entire business investment of the last two years. But it was either that or a trial against the most successful law firm in the Midwest, funded by a company with pockets as deep as here to New Orleans. The risk was that in the end Doyle would lose everything. As matters stood, he had at best a tiny chance of keeping the farm.

The conversation shifted to less troubling concerns: how spring was late in coming. When the talk moved to commodity prices, Mikesh, sleep-deprived and dazed, offered that he had heard Australia had the same ethanol issues, now, as Iowa.

"Ethanol issues in Australia!" Dale barked. "You gotta dial back the intellectualism, Arnie! Get back down to earth or you'll die all alone and cold in that bachelor's shack of yours, with only *Australian heifers* for company."

The men chuckled. Mikesh was used to this, so he closed his mouth and just listened.

Twenty minutes later, once everyone was seated, men and women alike, around the long oval table in the big farm kitchen, and the food passed, the conversation meandered to the accident. In a piece on the television news, the reporter speculated what the death would mean for a controversial new Iowa religious movement. There had been talk about the accident after Easter Mass. People in the neighborhood of St. Luke's basilica knew about Josh. They heard he lured a woman from a few miles west to leave her two children and become a follower, living in some kind of commune—and for what purpose? They knew that in the past two or three years my brother held gatherings at a skating rink north of Calmar and at the fairgrounds over in Decorah, but there were smaller meetings in peoples' houses and even in farm pastures, though no one in St. Luke's parish seemed to be able to name one. They said that, like a nineteenth-century doctor or frontier preacher, houses were where the strange religious leader (my brother) moved, doing most of his work. While Mikesh tried to keep track of this, he also kept thinking how his head hurt.

"I was the first person on the scene of that crash," he offered.

"Arnie, you're kidding," Barbara said. "That was a terrible wreck! Did you see it happen? You must feel awful."

She stopped talking long enough to put her hand on his shoulder as she reached in to take the passing dish for potatoes back to the stove for a refill.

"You should have called us."

"I didn't see it happen. I came on the scene about three hours later, at the end of my work shift. The man, King, he was almost dead when I got there." He paused, realizing that a dozen people were listening. "He didn't make it."

The questions that followed kept Mikesh uncomfortable. He didn't talk religion, even to the Jehovah's Witnesses who came to his door. His father's ancestors were buried in the cemetery of the Czech free-thinkers, the *Ceska Svobodna obec*, where no marker bore a cross and the monument at the center was merely inscribed with the words: "work, sacrifice for families and humanity." That statement of purpose was a more-than-tall-enough order for him. He lived his life staying clear of every religious group (Catholic, Holy Roller, Lutheran, Mormon) the assembled table of people could name. The accident, however, associated him with something Dale kept calling a "hippie church."

As people were leaving, Barbara cornered him. "Really Arnie, you aren't looking good at all. Have you felt sick?"

"No. I'm just shaken up. Just tense enough to have trouble getting to sleep, and to give me a headache."

Barbara was a heavy-set freckled woman of mild temperament who did not hesitate to air the gaudy clothesline of her thoughts. She grabbed his arm. "You know, Arnie, you should drive into Decorah. Get yourself a massage."

Barbara's husband Dale, a compact red-haired man, walked in for a cup of coffee and heard this. "Oh . . . my . . . God," he mouthed in disbelief. "Barb, maybe I should come along with Arnie. We can make it a two-fer!"

"Hush, Dale. I'm serious. There's a woman in our office. She was just about ruined by stress for eight weeks. Her doctor was going to medicate her and send her to the medical center for daily physical therapy which would cost her a fortune because it was only half covered by our health plan, and then she went for a session with this lady massage therapist and she came back to work feeling better than she had felt in a year. No meds, no hospital therapy."

"Like I say," Dale quipped. "Sign me up!"

"I'm not saying I don't believe what happened with your woman friend," Mikesh told Barbara, "but that doesn't sound like my kind of thing."

"I know. You're like Dale. Assume that having a couple of beers, throwing around some hay, tightening bolts for a few hours, will work it out." Barbara's eyebrows knit. "But I'll bet you've already tried that. Forgive me for saying it, Arnie, but you look terrible. Listen, if one of your lady Murray Greys developed so much as a sneeze, you'd call out the vet to look at her. Give yourself at least as much respect, and call for an appointment."

From there the talk shifted to Barbara and Dale's daughter and son, and the three of them shifted to the privacy of the mudroom just off the kitchen. The Murphys' son Davy lived in Des Moines, and with the economy in turmoil, his parents were worried about his employment. They wanted him to have health insurance. Times were good for farmers like Dale with corn and beans to sell, but money was getting tight, the economy swirling its way right down the toilet, and it was giving Dale and Barbara the parental jitters.

"Davy's working two half-time jobs as a sales clerk," Barbara said. "We wish he could find an opening in agribusiness."

"That's for sure," Dale affirmed.

"I know it's been years since you've worn a suit, Arnie, but Dale and I thought maybe you knew someone you could call, to put some feelers out to see if there's a spot where Davy could get a start. He knows how to work, and he's got the right education. With the economy the way it's been for the last year it just seems that everyone he talks to is firing instead of hiring."

Mikesh wasn't happy about this request to help someone get a start in a line of work he had been so anxious to leave. It cost Mikesh some effort to put his life in futures trading behind him. He'd let those old business friendships grow cold. But Barbara and Dale Murphy were his closest friends.

"I'll have to give that some thought," he told them.

After chores that evening, Barbara called Mikesh with the telephone number of the therapist and a name. "I think you should do this, Arnie. You rattle around over there on your own, with no one to take care of you and no one to talk to. You've been through something traumatic. I don't like the way you look, and it's got me worried. If you won't call for yourself, then do it for me. Okay?"

Mikesh said he would make the call, and let Barbara know when he thought of something for Davy.

That night, Mikesh's pain was like a bass drum, hammered by a hundred frenetic monkeys. Once asleep, in his dreams he went flying; when he landed he was underground, up against a face that was going soft but talking, and then bursting into flames. Mikesh sat upright. The clock read four. He didn't have the stomach for staying in bed any further.

He had the day free. At eight thirty he called the number Barbara left. An answering machine said the woman was away on personal business, but Mikesh left his name and number. He went out to tinker with a tractor in the shed and when he came back in at noon the old black rotary phone, still on the wall from his uncle's time, was ringing. The woman, her business completed, could see him at three.

CHAPTER 6

"Silent waters wash out banks."

CZECH PROVERB

THE THERAPIST OPENED THE door at the top of the shadowy, closed-up-smelling stair to find a large, solid man with dark, tousled hair, twisting a stocking cap uncomfortably in his hands.

"Arnie?" She held out her hand. "I'm Mary Towers."

"Hi," the man faltered. "Arnie Mikesh. Thanks for finding time to work me into your schedule. That was short notice."

She gestured him into the bright foyer and noticed that he nervously eyed the abstract red painting on the wall as he stood, parked tentatively in his jeans and his tan canvas coat, like an untamed animal sniffing the air for a reason to bolt.

The truth was she had spent most of Saturday and Sunday in bed, cancelling her appointments to stay there again today. The news of Josh's death had hit her system like a narcotic, slowing her reactions, dulling her senses, draining the energy from her so that her feet and hands, even her head, felt heavy. She slept through much of the past two days, and stood at the windows of her apartment, staring mutely at sky and street-lights for half the night. Then came the voice on her answering machine. It worked a kind of enchantment, piquing her interest, quickening her pulse. With men, her policy was to carefully screen them in conversation before she took them on as a client. But given the circumstances, this was a man she didn't want to scare away.

"I cleared out my schedule for the day, because something came up. It didn't take as long as I thought, so there we are. Have you had a massage before, Arnie?"

"Backrubs from friends. Nothing more than that. Come to think of it, that was in my university days."

"University days," she figured, were probably twenty years ago. He was in his early forties, with no gray in his rough black hair or thick eyebrows. His square face had seen plenty of weather and was showing lines. One of his cowboy boots had an elevated sole and heel. The imbalance in his legs showed in the constricted swing of his body when he walked. Mikesh's worn cowboy boots called up a memory of her father's hard hands and strong grip, the chin bristles that abraded skin, the smell of alcohol strong on his meaty breath. Her dad's battered boots by the couch in the television room or the foot of the bed smelled of him, of mold, and of whatever animals he had most recently herded in or out of the trucks he drove. She cleared her head of the thought, and focused on the added lift on Mikesh's left boot. There was nothing hard or abrasive about the man who stood before her. She could tell by the hunched twist of his shoulders that he was carrying a load of pain that went beyond walking through life on a mismatched pair of legs.

She asked the question she'd had on her mind since she received his phone message, "What made you call?" Mary Towers was one of my brother's oldest friends. Mom talked with her and spent time crying with her on the day after the accident. From Mom, Mary heard the name, Arnold Mikesh, the person who found Josh, and my mother asked if she knew him. Nothing else about him. Now two days later the man himself had left a message on her answering machine.

"I've been having some bad headaches, neck pain, trouble sleeping, some difficulty breathing."

Blinking in the stronger illumination of the reception foyer, Arnie was looking into her face with a lost expression. It wasn't coincidence. His experience at the accident scene had left him knotted up, and he was reaching out for help. She again felt the surprising but welcome surge of energy for work she wanted to do.

"Sounds like you made a good call then. I'd recommend ninety minutes of therapy."

For his part, Mikesh was having a hard time taking it all in. This woman with the red painting that made no sense was a study in extremes. Her skin was pale and freckled, but her eyes had the muddy blue cast of a newborn baby's, and her hair, pushed loosely to the top of her head, was black enough to suck the light from the air around her. She was directing him through an entry, talking about "Swedish technique," using phrases he didn't understand, asking him to strip to his underwear. He hoped the name his neighbor Barbara gave him was not somebody's idea of a prank.

A few minutes later Mikesh was sitting with a sheet wrapped around his waist on a low, padded table, feeling even more vulnerable. Taking off his boots and jeans meant the avenue of a hasty escape was gone. Though alone in the room, humiliation settled over him like an iron hat as he stumped unevenly from the chair where he left his clothes and boots to the table at the center of the room. He was relieved that the woman didn't witness that sorry spectacle. He stared at the black hairs on his bright white legs, conscious of them in a way he had not felt since high school, and hoped the long shower he took before leaving home had cleaned away the worst patches of dead winter skin and whatever other visible horrors might be clinging to him. A kettle steamed quietly on a warming plate. He had a quick image of the woman with the mud-colored eyes splashing drips of scalding water on his exposed back. She entered in a technician's coat, pushing up her sleeves. He noticed a trace of citrus in the air, and the sound of a radiator, hammering as it warmed; he hoped the radiator noise would cover the clanking in his chest and the banging fist that pounded harder inside the back of his head.

She had him lie face down. When she touched his back to rearrange the sheet, he twitched. As she began, his eyes were facing down and closed; still, he could see, in his mind, those energetic pale fingers. But there was no scalding water, no comment on his misshapen calves, his papery skin, his blue veins. No question about his uneven legs, the product of a quirk in his genetics that manifested itself at puberty, placing a kink in his adult body. She was telling him to relax, and how to do it, then asking him about pressure, tension, pain, and the way he imagined them: sharp, dull, throbbing, angry. As she spoke, she was leaning into her hands, pushing her entire weight into him with more force than he guessed possible. Kneading skin and muscle, her hands moved in arcs and circles, starting at the edges, but always inward: closer and closer toward his heart.

Through her fingertips Mary read the terrain beneath Arnold Mikesh's skin, a frozen pile-up of muscle, tendon, and bone without capacity to properly shift or flow—a challenge for an hour-and-a-half of work. With so much seized up within him, she marveled that this man had smiled when he first spoke with her, red faced, with hat in hand, at her door. She needed this workout as much as Mikesh: reconnecting with her hands through an art that demanded she practice as regularly as a pianist or a dancer.

The anatomy that comprised the puzzle before her had gotten rearranged. Slowly but forcefully her hands learned the tangle of disorganized pieces, and located the places for which they were made, the ropes of muscle in their slots and the beadwork of bone in his spine—massaging the knots, testing the tension in cables of muscle, coaxing each piece into relaxed alignment. Mikesh was a man who used his back. Though he was neither trim nor defined, the calluses she saw on his hands, the firmness of his arms and shoulders, told her he was used to heavy lifting. She wondered where he came from, and what propelled him in the middle of a night when no one else was on the road to the lonely spot where Josh died.

Mary Towers was close enough to Josh that my mother chose her for consolation and several hours of shelter after we arrived from Des Moines to identify Josh's body. Mary's thoughts as she kneaded Mikesh's muscle and skin were pulled to one of the last two times she had seen Josh. He had been in Decorah, holding a July gathering at the fairgrounds, healing people, laying hands on them, but it had gone on too long. When he tried to leave, there was a disturbance and he was hauled into jail. When she heard about it through a friend she felt troubled. She checked with the police and found Josh had gone to the home of a local minister. When she pulled up in front of the unfamiliar house in her compact Honda she was conscious of the heat and humidity: the kind of weather that made tomatoes swell and split. She heard voices in the back yard, and could smell barbeque. Slinging her workbag over her shoulder she walked around the garage to a deck where Josh was sitting in an aluminum chair. Peña, the minister and his wife, and three or four others, none familiar to Mary, were gathered around him. She could read Josh's face, see that his mind was elsewhere. He needed time to himself. Josh may have been a healer, but who took time to heal *him*? Used to Peña's aggression, she knew to ignore him, lest he order her away directly. She walked to Josh, crouched at his side and took his hand, explaining she'd heard about the day's troubles. She knelt at his feet, and removed his sandals. Josh tensed, but said little. Pouring a sandalwood-scented oil over her hands, she ran them over the knobs of his ankles, cupped his heels, and then massaged the balls of his soles, squeezing, working back and then forward again to his toes. Conversation broke off. A woman joked, uncomfortably, that this might be something that would do the woman good too. More silence. Peña, agitated, his eyes narrowed, said that Mary had not been invited, that she was not "with" them. Mary had heard people describe the minister's worshippers as "holy rollers." She had heard the man's voice on radio advertisements for Sunday worship. Now he was speaking about her.

"Joshua, you should be aware that this woman has a reputation around town."

Mary felt her skin prickle and the blood rise to her head. The man did not deign to speak to her directly or to use her name. But she did not defend herself, did not speak angry words. She focused on moving the oil into Josh's toes.

"Remember what being seen with her will make upright people think about you."

Only then did Josh answer him: "She understood what I needed. You fed me. You welcomed me. But you didn't do this."

Josh having defended her, Mary looked to the minister and read the disgust on his face as he considered the image Josh suggested. She could not suppress a smile. She was burning at the words said about her reputation. She let her hair fall forward, dragging it back and forth across the upper arches of Josh's feet wickedly, as if to confirm that she was the opposite of upright, to suggest that the minister also do this for Josh. Her unspoken taunt shoved the preacher out of his constrained comfort zone. The man rose in outrage, but Josh said, "let her be."

She left soon after. Though she might have called Josh back into himself, she destroyed his welcome in that household. She had seen Josh only once since then, later in the summer. Then nothing. Josh carefully avoided her.

Mary refocused on her work with Mikesh. She sensed the healing inch forward. Spasmed muscles relaxed. The air Mikesh drew into his lungs pushed up more slowly and firmly against her fists. She methodically worked his back, his fingers, his face, his legs, his chest, the muscle of the shoulders that had pressed into the ground to get near to Josh before he died. This man exchanged last words with Josh. The man beneath her eased and quieted in his breathing. She had helped put him back into himself.

It seemed like barely twenty minutes had passed when Mikesh heard the woman saying he could sit up, get dressed when he liked. Mikesh felt like he had wakened from his first night of Christmas vacation sleep. His headache was gone. As Mikesh finished dressing, Mary Towers knocked, then sat on the massage bench, looking distracted.

Her work done, she felt the lethargy creeping back over her, dragging at her, and fought to keep it at bay.

"The one treatment may not do it for you, Arnie. Your back was twisted and balled up in a bad way. Any idea how that happened?"

"I don't know. But it may have something to do with an accident. Did you hear about the car that left the road in the south part of the county on Friday night, the car driven by Joshua King?"

She woodenly bobbed her head. Helplessness broke over her like a gray ocean wave.

"I'm the one that found the car and called the ambulance. The man in the car, King, was still alive when I got there, but he died while we were waiting. It seems the experience messed me up."

Still no response. Her eyes were closed. Mikesh grew uneasy.

She knew intimately the place where the shadowy waters would sink her and she would lose consciousness, and she knew she must fight, struggle to the surface where there was air she could draw into her lungs, air she could use to say something to this person seated before her, familiar with the source of her grief.

The words she found were, "Poor man."

"I'm sorry. Are you talking about Joshua King?"

"Josh? No. No, I was thinking about you." Her eyes opened.

"You called him Josh. Did you *know* him?"

She pulled back from the slope of her bereavement. "Josh was an old friend, someone I could talk to."

She lowered her head, looking away. Mikesh was again struck by her hair's intense blackness, its messy energy. His doubts, his earlier desire to flee, came rushing back.

"I'm sorry . . . about your loss."

Mikesh rose and walked to her, wondering if his being here was a coincidence or whether half the people he met knew my brother. He remembered my mom's request that he find out why her son was driving this direction.

"Was he coming here to see you?"

She had asked herself this question. My mother had asked it too.

"He hasn't done anything like that for years. I haven't heard from him since last summer."

"Any reason he might have decided to see you?"

"Really, I don't think so." Josh carefully maintained his distance for reasons she did not fully understand or want to share with a stranger.

"Did he know lots of people around here?"

"Yes. Josh was here off and on over the years." Her limbs felt heavy. "Jude Bailey down at the co-op," she answered. "He worked closely with Josh just last year." She thought of Peña, his rage on the minister's deck. She thought of Josh, the waters lapping over her again, and kept silent.

"So what drew people to him? What sort of preacher was he?"

"Preacher?" She reminded herself that this man probably needed more than bodywork to resolve his issues. "I wouldn't know about that. You'd have to judge for yourself."

"Myself? That's not going to be easy. Joshua King is dead."

Her breath tightened.

"True. But there are videos."

It was work for her to talk, to concentrate on connecting.

"I've heard that you can watch Josh on the computer." She'd been tempted to go online. She added, "but I don't have a computer."

"Not into technology?"

"Not into *video* technology. Not into computers."

"Is it a religious thing, like the Amish?" Mikesh wondered if Josh required the material life of his followers to stop at the exit doorstep of the nineteenth century.

"No."

"Just something you aren't into?"

This man was pushing her. Her depression see-sawed into anger.

"It bothers me how people stare at another person on a screen in a way they would never do in the flesh. How a grown woman or man gazes longer and closer every day into the face of a news reader than into the eyes of their own life partner."

She could see the man's skepticism. She saw, with relief, that he was drawing back. She pushed.

"Doesn't it bother you how boys spend their nights and weekends in front of a computer, killing . . . "

She was sounding shrill. Her recent temptation to find a computer was making her talk, partly, to herself.

"How boys use them for games where they get points for *deaths*?"

"I can't disagree with you," Mikesh said, "but it's not bad to catch up on the news. A boy doesn't necessarily have to pretend that his keyboard is a gun."

Mikesh's earlier uneasy sense that there might be something unhinged or threatening about this woman was returning. She handed him a business card and a bill. He paid and left, and the door clicked shut behind him.

CHAPTER 7

As the door clicked shut behind Mikesh, Mary closed her eyes. Once again she experienced the end of time. Not that the clocks stopped on their mantles. Not that the glittering second hands on dials strapped to a billion wrists around the world paused their relentless circuit. It was just that the door closed.

And she was back in her lightless bedroom, thirteen years old, and wakened by that sound, and for the long drawn-out moment of first consciousness a silence filled the room that was not quite silence. Something occupied it. Something, some*body* breathing slowly and unsteadily. Somebody who had been drinking. Somebody who soon enough was struggling with his boots. She could hear the drop of his clothes. And then his slow steps as he crossed the room. Him bumping into the bed, and his hand coming down on the headboard to steady himself. His hand hitting the pillow as he felt his way toward her. His hand covering her mouth as she tried to scream. His other hand planting itself on her belly as his face came close to her ear.

"Ma lil filly. Time yer rode."

He told her in slurred speech that if she behaved it would not hurt, that nobody would get hurt.

But he lied. Even then the way he gripped her jaw pained her. What followed was worse.

Most disgusting was that the pain eased only when her body betrayed her. When it began to loosen and cooperate with the thing he did, though her mind remained a wall, hard and frozen. And her eyes gazed blank, streaming tears into the darkness of the room he occupied, asleep and snoring when he had finished, filling her bed as he had filled her, and she frozen, unable to move, unable to speak about the thing that had happened, to which her body had become a wicked, filthy party.

45

And though morning would come, though she would return to school and walk between classes in a stream of other children who chattered about who had a crush on whom, who was angry at her mom for her refusal to let her wear that skirt, who could argue about whether last night's episode of their favorite show was funny or pathetic, she was not really there with them. When she washed her hands after using the toilet, they would not get clean. When the bell rang to say it was fifth hour now, instead of fourth, it lied. It was still the middle of the night, and the door clicked. For time was refusing to move forward.

When other times it happened again, she found herself returned to that first terror, returned to her entrance into the partnership about which she could not speak, the moment when time stopped.

The world was rank as a billy goat in his shit-filled pen. The world was evil. Mary, standing with a check at the top of the stair, wondered if she had strength to withstand another stopped-time day in the prison of that world. She thought of Josh sitting, drained, in that aluminum chair, where his eyes fixed on something that no one around him saw. Why was Josh dead, while she was walking around? Why was Josh, her kind friend, lying cold when a hundred men in Iowa would beat their wife or their girlfriend to make this particular Monday afternoon interesting, and then sit down and calmly eat this evening's dinner? Why would Josh no longer ask her one of his queer questions, when half a million men in the state of Iowa would, in the course of the coming evening, tune in to gunfire and car chases, to ten sweaty men elbowing their way around a basketball court, to a sportsman's show where it was high-powered rifle and hunting scope against nothing more than an acute sense of smell or sight—tune in to all that brutality just to tune out the people around them? The strain of facing that question made her snap with the man whose head was as disordered by Josh's death as her own, made her rage at him for following up on something she said about computers, even though she began their encounter hoping she would not scare him away.

Bad choice. Bad choice once again. Bad, bad, bad, bad girl. Mary focused on her breathing, like a mother working her way through labor. She must open a door that would let time move forward. *Make* it move forward. Tomorrow she would get back to her clients, feel her way toward being unfrozen through muscle, bone, and pulse in people who needed her help, as Arnie Mikesh had needed help. With Mikesh she hoped she would have a chance to try again.

CHAPTER 8

THE BASS OF HUTCH Hutchinson was shaking his windows. Bonnie Raitt was rasping out "Feeling of Falling," its blues lyrics pitched from the musical sweet spot somewhere near her spleen. With a slender paring knife Mikesh cut earthy-smelling peels from parsnips, carrots, potatoes, and turnips. He was hungry, and grass-fed beef was browning in the pan.

Earlier, doing chores he noticed the ground softening. In less than a month he would be checking for the first calves. Through the window the yard light glowed hazy; the night was going to turn into another fog. But the animals were fine, Mikesh was inside, and he was doing the point check Mary Towers taught him on the places where the tension used to be. A used-to-be refrain, running through his own mind, meant that, no matter how unhinged the healer, his therapy session was money well spent.

After his meal, he sat down with a glass of pale ale and turned on his computer, thinking of Mary Towers' scorn, but typing the words he should have tried out two days ago: *Joshua King*. A few news stories, a few discussion forums, a page warning him that Shekinah would send him to hell, then a Joshua King video: my brother had an Internet movie presence.

My brother's presence. A British scientist once said that the universe is not only stranger than we know, it's stranger than we *can* know. That in part explains why, the autumn before the accident, I left my work in contract archeology for the uncertain future of life on a commune, following a brother whose charisma I always, in part, resented. My brother Josh's charm came from his keen sense for where the Spirit is at work—almost everywhere, as it turns out—and of sad corners where people so easily get trapped: the lifeless places where the Spirit has been nearly sucked away and where evil starts to grow and elbow its way around.

I have a life of experience witnessing Josh's success in drawing people to him.

Twins might look like copies of one another. But don't be fooled. None are. Starting in the womb, one fills out the space the other fails to occupy. If Josh was head up, I was head down. If, as my mother informed us, Josh came into icy air above the bed of that sleigh without crying, so much more startling the silence for me to shatter with howls. Josh's quiet gained him more worried attention from Dr. Razavi, the EMT, and my grandmother than my squalling. In school, when no one raised their hand or volunteered a response, the teachers called on Josh. What he said sparked discussion. Girls wondered, secretly and aloud, whether Josh noticed them. Boys repeated, in their banter, the astonishing utterances that darted from my brother's alien-visiting-earth lips. My brother was like a black hole; you couldn't avoid the gravitational attraction of presence, even when he was out of sight and thousands of miles away. Realizing that as an-almost-thirty-three-year-old adult, I decided to join Josh's fold.

Seeking is the pole star of animal urges, the source of all the rest, just as pride, they say, is the source of all evil. Josh sought people out. Then he redirected their seeking impulse toward what mattered to him. My twin brother sought the Spirit, and with his last breath he asked Arnold Mikesh to join him. Josh had a force that drew people to him. Mikesh was my first evidence that, in his death, my brother might not have lost that power. In turning up at Mary's door, Mikesh traded his knotted-up back for a tiny, hot, Josh-King coal in his brain. Why not admit it? At this same time, even with Josh dead, I was finding some heat of his life burning in me too. To my wonder, in spite of Josh's death . . . no, rather *because* of his death, this would be the first spring in years that I would not return as planned to summer fieldwork in contract archeology.

The clip Mikesh pulled up, titled "Root of Power," had been posted by someone whose address was *sunnybob4*. The setting was a social hall: the camera positioned perhaps ten rows back. The video came on with a low-level murmur of white noise and my brother—Mikesh guessed it was him—was walking to the front of the room, his narrow back to the camera. Neither the brightness nor the resolution was good. The camera was hand-held, unsteady. Mikesh was startled when Josh took the low platform and turned to the people seated in chairs. Mikesh was looking at the whole, clean, right-side-up face he had found buried in that wreck, and the zoom was careening in for a close-up. Mikesh wished he could have slapped sunnybob4's finger from the control button and kept the distance. Instead, he could now read the features of the speaker, my brother, a young man with a mop of wavy, sand-colored hair, firm dark eyebrows that almost met, protruding brown eyes, and Roman nose. His shoulders hunched as he raised his arms out wide toward the audience to talk.

"Brother Randy and Sister Maxine called us together tonight, joined us together here in the Spirit," he began, his voice steady. The words tripped Mikesh's recollection: "Mikesh . . . join."

"They asked me to answer a question. Who do I say I am?"

My brother was looking into faces directed toward him. He turned from the camera. The zoom backed out, and Mikesh could see my brother, dressed in loose khaki slacks and black t-shirt, an unbuttoned white oxford shirt open and hanging free at the waist. From the back, with his rumpled clothing and slightly messy hair, my brother would not have caught anyone's attention. His face, however, and the way he measured his words had power Mikesh could feel, even from a blurry video on a low-bandwidth Internet signal.

"Because Brother Randy comes to us from the Christian Action Fellowship, and Sister Maxine is Catholic, they have asked me to speak tonight. They want to know who I am."

Josh gestured to a woman in the front row. "Sister Maxine, tell them what it is you want to know."

The camera focused on a middle-aged, whey-faced woman. She stood with great self-possession. "I just want to know about my old church. Can I still be a Catholic and also be a part of Shekinah?"

Josh called on Brother Randy. The camera panned back and forth before finding the profile of a thin man with close-cropped hair, wearing a red plaid shirt and sweater vest, who stood up uncomfortably. Mikesh could not see his face.

"I'm like Maxine. I want to know, Joshua, if you mean to drive me from my Christian faith." The questioning man looked at Josh, turned to nod at the person seated at his side, and sat back down.

My brother was looking down at them. "Randy, Maxine, thanks for speaking from your hearts. I am not here to come between you and the Spirit. I'm here to point you back to the root where each of us began, back to the root of Action Fellowship and the Catholic Church, back to the root of Christianity and the ministry of Jesus."

He walked closer to the man who asked the question. "Randy, did Jesus put aside his Jewish heritage to bring his message to his fellow Jews?"

The camera could only catch the back of the man's head: "He can't have been too good a Jew," it sounded as if he said. "They killed him."

"But did he forget Jewish teachings? The Jewish scripture?"

"No," the man shook his head emphatically. "He knew his scripture." The fuzzy, muffled sound quality made Mikesh think, at first, he'd said, "He knew his picture."

"I'm here to tell you to read your scripture, too. Read your Christian scripture. Read the Jewish Old Testament. They carry you back to the root that still sustains us, the place, that small infinitude, where we each look face to face with the Spirit, feel her presence, her breath, the force of the Spirit's words on our own hands and lips as she wakes us each morning. You've dedicated your Christian lives to Jesus. Jesus returned again and again to that presence. In fact, he lived every moment of his earthly life in it. That place, our beginning as well as our end, *is also where we are*, Shekinah, though as we sit in this room tonight it is easy to forget that."

Josh told a story he said was familiar to Jesus, about the garden, the place where the Spirit and people walked together. When the people tasted the fruit of false knowledge they turned from the Spirit. He said this act of turning from the Spirit had been replayed throughout time, billions of times each hour around the planet.

"The error is to think that this was once upon a time: as some have said, the *history* of our first father and our first mother. The story is happening this moment . . . and this: the distracting fruit, our hand reaching out, our desire propelling our hand, the knowledge of what has been and, suddenly, the desire ever stronger of *what might be*! That desire, like a drug, makes us forget that *here we are*, in the garden, in this infinitude, made not to waste away, not to suffer or die, but made instead in the likeness of the divine to know Shekinah—the presence of the divine in this instant, the eternal moment that is without limit, and without death."

My brother's hand extended out as if holding the apple. He brought the hand to his mouth, poised as if to taste. His strongly colored, full lips, loomed in the close view to which the person with the camera zoomed. But the camera backed out. Josh dropped his arms and stood with his hands out and open at his sides, like a person on a beach, facing the sun, his body drinking in its heat.

"Desire, fills you with images of what you do not have, what has been, what might be. Desire is a thief, distracting you with his right hand as he picks your pockets clean with the left."

"Brothers, Sisters, we have never left the garden. The old story tells it like a fact that we were cast out, a wall of fire placed behind us. That wall is there only in our imagination. The curse that we must labor and suffer in pain repeats itself over and over like a constitutional law, cancelling out everything else. But why?

"You were made by the Spirit to see the never lost, never absent, true and shining fact—that you are a child of the Spirit, an extension of the breath that gives each of us life, a living emblem of the Spirit before others.

"Jesus himself said there was only one unforgivable sin: to deny the Spirit. It's in the Biblical gospels. Look also at the Coptic gospel, saying 44: 'Whoever blasphemes against the Father will be forgiven, and whoever blasphemes against the Son will be forgiven, but whoever blasphemes against the Holy Spirit will not be forgiven either on earth or in heaven.' That is why I stand before you, affirming her. I am her child. I'm an apostle of the Spirit. I am, and you are, a vessel of the Spirit.

"The Spirit, what Jesus in his own language called the *ruha*, is what was breathed into us at the moment of our creation. She lives in us in this instant, in this infinity."

Here my brother stopped and closed his eyes, inhaling suddenly and loudly, "Spiiii," holding the breath for a still moment before exhaling with equal noise, "riiiit." He repeated this movement, the loud inhalation and exhalation of his breath. Then he opened his eyes again: "the divine breath—Spiii—riiit—Spiii—riiit—the breath in and breath out—from which the living Spirit, the *ruu—haa* takes her name."

Since Mikesh only heard him whisper at the accident scene, he found himself mesmerized by Josh's full voice. Mikesh was thinking about the weak flow of air he felt with his finger in my brother's throat. He felt the last issue of what my brother was calling "the Spirit" as it left him.

"Ignorance distracts you with its idols. The Bible itself, for many of our brothers and sisters, *becomes* an idol to distract us from the message we were made to know, that the Spirit within us speaks with every breath, calling us with her name to remember, even now, breathing out and breathing in, who we *really* are, to remember our true name as it is breathed out to us by the Spirit.

"Brother Randy and Sister Maxine have asked whether I mean to call them away from their Christianity, whether I am the serpent who comes to separate them from God. No, that is not what I mean to do. I am here to do the opposite: to call them to the message . . ."

Mikesh's screen froze and went silent. Over the top of the image a little clock dial appeared, the hand sweeping round and round to show that the signal had been lost, that the machine was working to reconnect. Mikesh explained it in his head as the work of soupy atmosphere between the dish that angled from the exterior siding of his house and the distant satellite that provided him with Internet. Just as he considered rising to bring his empty glass to the sink, the image snapped back into action, and the sound continued, "of Jesus, to perfect the promise he brought in his time by uttering it again in the present, in the here and now.

"Look in your Bible. Read what Jesus says about himself. 'The son of man,' he calls himself, a person just like you and me, but at the same time 'the son of God,' pointing to what you might call a higher kingdom, the kingdom of the Spirit that is ever at hand, ever at the edge of being born. 'The kingdom of God is at hand,' Jesus told his followers. And he would say the same today, if he was in this room, sitting next to Sister Maxine or in the chair behind Brother Randy, leaning forward to whisper in his ear. 'The kingdom of the Spirit is alive between us!'"

Josh held out his hand, thumb pressed against the index and middle fingers as if holding a broken piece of bread, looked at it, and looked back at his audience.

"I stand as Jesus did, at the base of the tree of knowledge, calling you back to the soil of the place from which we find ourselves banished, back to the root of what you have always known but are always forgetting. Once you open yourself to the Spirit, you are never alone."

This statement called up Mikesh's memory of the anguished face and the words "I've been alone!" Distaste for the hypocrisy and ground-lessness of religion welled up like a gag reflex. He wondered, as Josh talked, to what Iowa municipality Josh had driven, or been driven, to stand and say these things? How many miles from where Mikesh sat was it? What were the people—whose heads were so many round shadows at the bottom of the screen's image—doing at this moment on this damp Monday evening? Mikesh felt that my brother talked a good line, took your brain someplace that felt brisk, the air thin and heady, and exciting.

But no matter the fine words, Josh too, ultimately felt alone, and tonight his body lay, its trunk opened with a Y-shaped slash, its skull lifted, its organs extracted, examined, returned, and sewn or stapled in place, cold, in a box that in a few days my family would bury in the earth.

Asking Mikesh to join him in infinity was Josh's last evangelical moment. He was a driven man who couldn't leave off his mission even as the breath—'the divine breath'—left his body for the last time. Mikesh thought it didn't sound then like it did in Josh's sermon. It was so feeble that without a sound it evaporated into nothing at all. And then his flesh went cold and still: the flesh that was in that box.

As the image of my brother continued to speak, Mikesh clicked off the Internet connection. He realized that he was letting his random act of kindness get twisted, blown out of proportion. First it left him with a kicked-hard headache. Now it was pulling him into something that would lead nowhere. Mikesh was a freethinker. Five generations back his people sold the little they had in Bohemia to buy passage to this country where they happily traded their old security for a new freedom from the dictates of the village lord and a twisted, intricate ladder of clerics that stretched right up to the Pope. Mikesh had gotten through forty-some years without listening to the pieties of Brother Randy's Action Fellowship or the palaver of Sister Maxine's Catholic priests. Even though he happened to have a face-to-face encounter with a home-grown prophet who shared his dying words with him, that didn't mean that he should lose himself in this and give Jimmy Seegmiller a laugh. Hearing my brother talk in the way that won him his followers, gave Mikesh a strange buzz. But so did the glass of ale he just finished. Young, he had overdone it with alcohol, but he learned to know better. He had never been an adult drunk, not a steady one, and he wasn't about to become a religious fanatic either.

Mikesh turned off the computer, picked up a book, and went to bed. He felt better, and that meant he could, at last, sleep.

CHAPTER 9

MIKESH HAD VOLUNTEERED TO take his eighty-nine-year-old neighbor, Oscar, to the Decorah clinic the next morning to see a specialist for what Oscar gruffly dismissed as "man problems." After that Mikesh dropped Oscar off at the Vets club while he ran errands.

Mikesh may have been put off by Josh's message, but remembered that my mother wanted to know why my brother was on that road. Arnold Mikesh wasn't about to become a follower, but he had the zeal of a terrier pup when it came to unearthing facts. With a couple of hours to spend, Mikesh thought he might look up the man Mary Towers had mentioned. Maybe he could find a clue about what propelled my brother, the preacher Mikesh had seen on his computer the night before, into the fog on the night of March 21.

The entry to the food co-op was plastered with fliers: a contra dance, shamanic healing sessions, a meeting about the dangers of food irradiation: the kind of stuff he had yet to see in a doorway in Waucoma. There was nothing advertising Shekinah. A young woman in jeans, t-shirt, and blue produce apron arranging a half-circle tower of organic carrots directed Mikesh to an office downstairs in the back. This store, with its smell of bulk spices and coffee beans, was familiar territory, but Mikesh had never stepped into its netherworld. He found Jude Bailey staring at a computer screen in a cramped and unlit office, a thin, hard-faced man with his red hair pulled up under a crocheted hat colored like a black liberation flag.

"Jude Bailey? I'm Arnie Mikesh." Mikesh held out his hand. Bailey half rose from his chair before sitting back down and looking up at him.

"What can I do for you?"

"I was the first person on the scene at the Joshua King wreck last weekend," Mikesh began. "It's been weighing on me. I don't know anything about him, but I was there when he died. I wanted to talk to someone who knew him, see why he was driving this direction."

"And you came to me?"

"I was told you were close."

"Do you mind my asking who told you that?"

The aggressive edge put Mikesh on warning.

"It's been a rough couple of days. Someone in the sheriff's office?" Mikesh improvised.

"It makes sense it would be the sheriff," Bailey snorted. "Did you tell them when you were going to come by?" He looked over Mikesh's shoulder to see if he had come alone.

"No. I was shaken up."

"I might not be able to help you." Bailey pushed his glasses to the top of his hat and leaned back in his chair. "Joshua King and I parted ways. That's why I'm up here in Decorah. He would not have been coming to see me. I'll tell you that! I heard about the accident, though. What a waste!"

"So it seems."

"Go ahead, have a chair." Bailey cleared away two manila folders and gestured for Mikesh to sit. "I've been staring at these orders too long. I ought to take a break."

"I'm sorry to interrupt. You may not feel like talking about Joshua King."

Bailey, seated again, seemed agitated by the subject.

"Joshua ended up making an impact way smaller than he might have," Bailey said. "He frittered his time on the secret for sprouting angel wings."

"I've seen a video of him teaching."

"If you want what you saw explained, you've got the wrong guy. Everybody has to find something that gives them purpose. For Joshua it was that vision of eternity." Bailey tapped a pencil on his knee. "Me, I'm a communist. That's a dirty word to most Americans, somewhere lower on the list than 'child molester.' But it keeps me going."

Mikesh kept quiet, and Bailey explained.

"I believe in equality: equal access to wealth. That's an idea that scares folks."

"It's not going to get you elected president," Mikesh ventured.

Bailey sized Mikesh up. "Doesn't it seem crazy that we *don't* elect communist leaders in a country based on government by the people?"

"One person's liberty might just be the next guy's ball and chain."

"The *next guy* as you politely call him, is usually a very fat cat. Twenty percent of the people in America sit on eighty-five percent of the wealth, leaving eight out of ten to divide up the remaining 15 percent. Those figures are only getting worse."

"I've listened to King. What you just said doesn't sound like him."

"You're wrong." Bailey fixed his eyes on Mikesh. "In what you heard, did Joshua talk about the devil, about how the devil distracts you with one hand while he picks your pocket with the other?"

Mikesh found the words familiar. "Something like that."

"That's where we were on the same page. Joshua saw the devil in the fat cats who own the politicians, feeding people their lies, keeping them smiling while they pick their poor pockets clean."

Bailey offered a Cheshire-Cat smile.

"I wanted to help Joshua, help his organization. I'm good at that. Everybody has strengths. Mine is organizing; not just like I'm doing with these orders today, but people. People clump together; they like to keep each other company, but they resist organizing. It's a kind of art."

Bailey stood up and rummaged through materials on a shelf.

"I had a notebook I used to keep when I was working with Joshua, a notebook of plans for pushing Shekinah, helping it make a national difference."

He pulled out a yellow legal pad and leafed through the pages, realized it was the wrong tablet and tossed it on the shelf. "It's probably not here," he said, sitting down.

"Was King open to that?"

"You should visit the Big House, the old school building some of Joshua's people bought. Fifty, maybe sixty people live there. It's communal, absolutely without private property."

"What about cars, clothing, food?"

"All property, all wages, go to Shekinah, a religious non-profit. They bake their 'Manna Loaves' bread or hold day jobs, but every check gets signed over to the group. *Those* people have liberated themselves from capital!"

Mikesh was skeptical. "So have the parish priest, the nuns. They take their vows of poverty."

"But they don't ask their parishioners to do that. They ask for just a cut from the people in the churches to assuage their guilt: 'the opiate of the masses.'"

"You sound like a believer."

Bailey leaned forward, ready to contradict Mikesh, but sat back again. "In some ways I am. I lived in the Big House for six months. It was sometimes better than ordering unbleached toilet paper and boutique coffees for this place." Bailey swept his hand around his head dismissively.

"Then why are you here?"

"Arnie—do you mind if I call you that?" Bailey took off his hat and looked into its crown, as if the text was in there for his next comments. "Frustration is the condition my condition is in. When I first came in contact with Shekinah I was working out of Des Moines for a farmers' union." Bailey paused, laying a hand on his desk as if to gain balance. "Do you know how hard it is to unionize farmers?"

Mikesh let out a hearty laugh. "Yeah, I can imagine."

"What do you know about agricultural economics?"

"I've got my own place, a 120-acre hobby farm I run as a cow/calf operation. I work security to pay the bills."

"No surprise in that last part. Iowa farmers get just enough federal money to keep them afloat. About seventy percent of their profit in the three years before commodity prices went up last year was government subsidy, making Iowa one of the biggest welfare states in the Union outside of Alaska. Those farmers get that money, *extracted* out of wage earners like you and me, for producing corn, beans, pork at a squeezed-down price that keeps supply steady and profit and stock prices good for big ag. Thin markets pay the guys that work the land so little that they have to spend their few hard-earned dollars at those cheap big box retailers that put up their tent at the edge of what used to be decent towns. The money goes in and goes out with as little involvement in the local economy as the MBAs can engineer it."

Bailey had warmed to his topic. "An Iowa farmer with his big, high-tech machines worth hundreds of thousands gets paid *less per unit of what he produces* than any worker on the planet. I mean it! Any worker on the planet! Less than the Chinese who assemble your laptop. Less than the Cambodians who stitch together your clothes. So farmers go under. They look for work in places that used to be decent towns, where now there's no manufacturing, no local retail, no ag labor. They end up a convenience store clerk or school bus driver, jumping to the orders of some idiot manager, buying their Jockey underwear made by some even sorrier soul in a sweatshop on the far side of the planet. After running their own land, the insult of it makes them feel like a stinking piece of crap squeezed out the ass of the president of Goldman-effing Sachs. The problem is, farmers are so brainwashed, the last thing they think of is joining a union. They'd be more likely to move to Russia or take up a gun for the Taliban than to join the NFO."

Mikesh pictured the twenty-eight miles he would travel between Decorah and home, counting the small number of working farms he would pass, and the fine old abandoned farmhouse with its roof collapsing and its farmyard grown over in trash trees haunting the intersection where Scenic Road met the county blacktop that ran south into Waucoma. Bailey was a hothead, but he wasn't crazy.

"One farmer I worked with in the union, a guy named Gary who farmed outside Jefferson, lost it all. He could have ended up homeless in Waterloo, but he ended up instead at Shekinah's Big House. There he tells me he's part of something set against the whole capitalist system. He starts running their market garden, delivering produce on a big scale through a community-sponsored operation. He comes to me, and says Shekinah is what I'm fighting for."

"Did that bring you in?"

"Come on!" Bailey cast a withering look. "My mantra is 'question authority.' I checked the Shekinah operation out when I visited Gary."

"So you joined?"

"Not so fast. I'm a secular Marxist. I wasn't into joining any damn church."

"What changed you?"

"Gary had worked that whole angle out. His favorite Bible story is about a guy named Ananias who holds back some money in a real estate deal from the early Christian common pot. God strikes him dead on the spot! Gary said that the longest-lived communist organizations on the planet are religious: the Poor Clares, the Hutterites. Put those up against the handful of years the USSR was truly communist, if it *ever* was, or the PRC. I may not believe in religion, but I believe in *realpolitik*. Gary's history got me just about ready."

"Just about?"

Bailey made the first long pause since he had started talking. "Do you know what Shekinah followers feel about sex?"

Mikesh saw there was a lot my brother had not had explained in the few minutes before he died.

"Sorry. Maybe you could tell me."

"Let's just say it's low on their list of priorities. It's only for married people or, if you're going to be like Joshua, you put it out of your mind."

"Like a priest?"

"They don't have priests, but moving in, for me, meant moving into a single men's dorm, treating the sisters like . . . sisters."

"So what convinced you?"

"I'm used to frustration. I became a brother."

"Why didn't you stay?"

"Like I said before, sex. There are some beautiful sisters at the Big House. I challenged the ideas about sex in a few councils. The two women who I thought were with me turned on me. There was also politics. I wanted Gary's message to become more important, move to a bigger system of cooperative distribution. It fit Josh's idea of lifting people up, giving others what you've got."

"Why didn't that work out?"

"It went far enough that we got harassed by the law in some of those places. It went far enough that hecklers with a script showed up at places Joshua appeared, ready to shout him down. And if you want my best guess, it went far enough that one or two people living at the Big House got there as spies, eyes and ears for one of the big ag companies or for the FBI. It all comes down to the same thing."

Mikesh mistrusted conspiracy speculations. "You're talking about a group of people living in an old school building in small-town Iowa. Do you really think that's going to get the attention of executives in St. Louis or bureaucrats in Washington?"

"Shekinah is little, but they've got a big message and they're evangelical about it. Remember, bro, this is the frickin' heyday of Homeland Security. People in Central America have died at the hands of American operatives for doing exactly what we were doing down there—consumers directly partnering with agricultural workers to own production together. Talk to the family of Fred Hampton; see if the men in blue on Chicago's near west side are above taking out an American citizen who has a talent for legally organizing poor people.

"And then there's Peña, Josh's main assistant," Bailey continued. "Simon's a cool enough dude, got a sweet side most people don't see. I very much love shootin' the breeze with that guy. But he doesn't roll with economic politics. I admire that those folks took their message to Des Moines, closer to the seat of the powers that be, but they were delivering the wrong message. So here I am." Bailey gestured at his little office. "To get back to your original question: this place is owned by its members; they buy local or fair trade. It's a good place to cool my heels and regroup till something better comes along."

Mikesh was glad to shift the topic. "You're sure King wasn't driving up here to see you?"

Bailey gave an indignant look. "Hah! No way."

"So what did you think when you heard he was dead?"

"It makes me nervous."

"How so?"

"You were there. Did it seem like he was alone when he died? From what I hear, the accident happened someplace quiet, a place where there weren't likely to be any witnesses. My guess is, he was offed."

Mikesh realized that Bailey's line of thinking was close to that of the sheriff, the very person Bailey had looked over his shoulder to see when Mikesh introduced his mission. Mikesh dismissed them as possible accomplices.

"It looked like an accident to me. He was by himself. It was so foggy you could hardly see the hand in front of your face."

"Did you see it happen?"

"No. As far as I could tell, I came maybe three hours later."

"Like I said: a very quiet and secluded place. But you were there when he died; did he say anything?"

"Yes. He did talk. 'Join infinity,' he said."

"That's Joshua, himself to the last. But you can bet someone was on his tail out there, maybe dogging him, threatening him in another vehicle. A big truck, a squad car, getting him to do something that would maybe kill him, all under the cover of that fog."

"That's serious stuff. Who would have the motive?"

"Lots had a motive: the boys at the top four ag giants; the government; one of the churches whose members were leaving the ranks for Shekinah; a husband whose wife ditched him to join Joshua; maybe a father whose daughter became a convert, signing away her property rights to a guy whose religious group then owned it all, a guy who daddy thought was probably banging his little girl. Man, I can think of *lots* of possibilities. You can bet someone edged Josh off that road."

Mikesh saw it was a case of what his Bohemian grandmother would have described as "many dogs, rabbit's death."

"Have you talked to the sheriff about this?"

"Are you kidding? What makes you think that if something went down they weren't in on it? The law is never fond of revolutionaries. Like I said, just think of Fred Hampton."

"Okay. Listen, are there a lot of people who follow King around here? A group of you?"

"Arnie, as you can see, it went pretty far wrong for me, so I keep my distance from Joshua King and anyone who followed him. He was doing something good enough that a lot of people wanted him dead. But *his* thing isn't *my* thing anymore."

Bailey pushed back his chair and stood up.

"I've got orders to fill. And beyond that I've got to get together a proposal for the pricing structure and a membership profit return/reinvestment mechanism here. This place is filled with well-meaning folks, but organization is not their thing."

"Well, do a good job. When you're looking through those books you may eventually come to my name. I'm a member owner."

"Cool," Bailey swallowed. "Oh, and hey, something else. If it was the cops who gave you my name, take a look around you when you leave this place. See if anyone is keeping an eye on you. Deputies may not be foxes, but every last one of them makes a decent bird dog."

After Mikesh left the food co-op he walked the two blocks to the law enforcement center. When his head cleared last night he had realized he could produce proof of his Friday night activities. Contrary to Jude Bailey's warning, as he entered the office no one seemed to be watching for him, but Seegmiller came out to a conference room.

"Hi, Jimmy. Anything new on the Joshua King investigation?"

"Turning investigator are we now, Arnie?" Seegmiller sized him up.

"No. Nothing like that. It's just that you were still in the middle of looking into things when I was here Saturday. There hadn't been an autopsy yet."

"As for that, the body was clean. No drugs, no alcohol. But if you want the official word, you better talk to the boss." Seegmiller disappeared into the sheriff's office and reappeared pointing with his thumb for Mikesh to do the same. Paul Fox—Mikesh was trying to remember what Bailey had just said about foxes—was standing when Mikesh came in. He gestured for Mikesh to take a seat.

"I stopped by because I remembered that if you still have any doubts about me you can check with the college for the computer log I made on Friday night. Its IP address will be the desktop in my office."

Fox considered this, taking down the name and phone number of Mikesh's immediate supervisor. He then pushed back in his chair and smiled.

"Jimmy tells me you've taken a professional interest in the King accident."

"No. Call it personal. I watched him, you know, King, die the other night. I thought maybe Jimmy could tell me something about the autopsy."

"It was what you would expect. We just faxed this information out to the media, so it's public." Fox opened the folder on his desk and appeared to look it over. "The coroner says he died of loss of blood from external injuries, exposure, shock, internal injuries including severe concussion, broken ribs, a ruptured spleen and a crushed pelvis. You don't get that banged up and stay breathing long."

"That sounds like what I saw. How about the car?"

"The car was clean, too. No drugs, no alcohol, no firearms."

"No sign of anything suspicious?"

"The car belonged to his organization, Shekinah. It was a clean car with quite a few years on it, and it got pretty thoroughly smashed up when it hit the ground. Nothing weird or funny beyond that. Why? Did you see or remember something odd you didn't mention to me?" Fox sounded more his previous self.

"No, I didn't see anything like that. I was pretty shaken up."

"Is there something you've remembered? Something you didn't tell me the other day?" Fox looked ready to write up his confession if Mikesh had one.

"No, it's just that given all the excitement and the confusion, I thought maybe I could have missed something."

"Right." Fox straightened his shoulders, working hard to keep away a smile. "I hear you were a bit rattled."

"Yeah, rattled. How about the scene? Did you guys check the road for any skid marks or tracks? Did you hear from any other witnesses?"

"You're making this sound like television police work now, Arnie. But as it happens, the State Patrol were investigating that even before we talked on Saturday. What they found was no skid marks, and the footprints you'd expect to find at a busy accident scene. Nothing you wouldn't expect at the site of the impact, a car coming down hard on frozen dirt. How about you, have you stopped back at the scene, noticed something new?"

"No, nothing like that. Strange there were no skid marks."

"That curve in the fog surprised him. It comes up out of nowhere."

"So is the accident still under investigation?

"Exactly. Let me know if you have anything more say." Fox stared at Mikesh.

"Nothing else. Thanks, Sheriff."

"Happy to help," Fox said in a voice he might have used with a third grade classroom. Mikesh had made the Sheriff's Tuesday meaningful and satisfying. Still, Mikesh felt like giving Jude Bailey's theories one more try.

"I just had one other question. King was a controversial figure, got a lot of people riled up. You haven't thought about any suspects who might have tried to make this happen?"

"Deliberately make this happen? How? Fog machines? Do you have a theory I don't know about?"

"No. Really I haven't got a clue. Thanks."

Fox shook Mikesh's hand and watched his back as he walked out. Mikesh thought about his bloody jacket, part of the evidence in whatever investigation Fox was piecing together, and was of one mind with Jude Bailey; he knew the law was watching him. He didn't like knowing his slumped shoulders were providing a double helping of smug cop pleasure.

CHAPTER 10

DAY OR NIGHT YOU have to adjust your eyes to the fish-belly-white fluorescents of the Vets Club. Mikesh was early, but the Vets is not a bad place to hunker down when you need to stay out of trouble from any quarter other than booze. After his talk with Paul Fox, Mikesh was happy to hear the Vets Club door suck closed behind him.

Mikesh's neighbor, Oscar, had an army buddy in Decorah. Oscar had come to this club, as he had to the club in Waucoma, to seek occasional refuge and comfortable companionship for years. Oscar was at a table by the front window where some of the overcast late morning sunshine made it through the slats of the blinds. Oscar had known Mikesh's great uncle. They'd been boys on neighboring farms in the days before tractors became affordable. Oscar traded his Second World War infantryman's uniform for a familiar pair of overalls, never married, and refused to leave the farm even after he was physically no longer able to work it and simply rented out the land. These days he didn't drive more than six miles in one direction, and only in daylight and good weather. He still, however, enjoyed his game of cards.

Oscar and three other elderly men were dealing hands of euchre when Mikesh came in, and the glasses in front of them remained half full of beer. Mikesh got a club soda with a slice of lime and joined them, pulling up a chair. Oscar's euchre partner, his army buddy Phil, wore a neat white shirt. The opposition was Ed, a man in plaid, whose partner wore drab olive work clothes. The players nodded at Mikesh, and went on studying their hands. Mikesh knew better than to interrupt. The card game's small drama came from players thinking, pulling a shaking card halfway up from the hand around it, looking at it, and flicking it down like they were striking a wooden match. There was a soothing rhythm to their play, and about two dozen comments from which to draw: "we'll see how she likes this," "where'd you find that one?" or "by God, you're feeling hard-up today!" The four didn't like their game disrupted with serious conversation.

When the last hand was done, and the cards were sliding into the box, the mood eased, and the card players began finishing drinks. "Well, Oscar, you must have been a good boy this week. You brought your luck along with you today," Phil said.

"Nope, these two boys just came here too distracted. Got their minds on something other than cards. Otherwise I couldn't have made some of them bids."

Oscar winked at Mikesh. Ed chimed in, "So Arnie, Oscar tells us you were the one discovered that King fellow when he drove his car off the road out your way this weekend."

"Yeah. I got a nose for trouble."

"Just like my dog," Ed said, "smells a stink from a *long* way off."

"That's for sure," said olive shirt, "not a pretty sight you found there, I'll bet."

"No. It was a bad wreck. He'd been there a few hours before I arrived. He was in tough shape, and buried so far back under the car I couldn't really get to him."

"Oscar says he was still talking when you got to him."

"A bit. He had a concussion, all broken up. He died before the ambulance got there."

"Well that'll surprise a few folks," Ed commented. He had a heavy Norwegian-American accent, and one eye wandered the opposite direction as he fixed his steadier eye on Mikesh.

"Why's that?" said his partner in the drab olive.

"Oh, him being such a famous healer and all."

"Who, Arnie?" Phil said.

"No, the King fellow. He was quite a preacher," Ed continued. "Had a commune or something down south of here, where he was stocking up on girlfriends, I hear. Got quite the power for laying on of hands!"

There was laughter around the table.

"By God," Ed lectured his partner. "You mean to tell me you didn't hear about the brouhaha last year at Nordic Fest?"

"No!"

"Jesus! I'll be half surprised if the Fest survives the mess that fellow caused."

"What mess?"

Because, through Oscar, Mikesh had met Phil and Ed before, he knew the men had well-worn favorite topics of conversation. He now saw that my brother might be one of them.

"Well, to give him his due, it ain't all the dead fellow's fault," Ed continued. "Larry Rasmussen should have his head examined about that deal! He's the fair board secretary. He's the one rented out space to that King bunch on the same Saturday as the Nordic Fest parade.

Ed was now ready to deliver. "You would think Larry would know better. He's been a Sons of Norway his whole life, and he knows we got fifty thousand extra people in town on a Fest Saturday. Those King people must have known it, too, because that's the day they asked for. My God, half of creation is down at that end of town on Fest parade morning. All the parade people park down there, and half the traffic coming into town comes in down there. It's one serious mess on a Fest Saturday, even without some extra screwy church service, I can tell you!"

Ed's unhitched eye was now wandering to his empty glass, which he picked up and gently tapped on the table for emphasis.

"Well, King and his people set up a meeting down at the fairgrounds for eight thirty that morning. He'd quite a reputation as a kind of faith healer, don't you see. So before eight they started dragging in. It was crip-ples, cancer victims, old folks in wheel chairs with oxygen bottles. They were all there, and the King fellow shows up with his string of converts: quite the flea circus, I can tell you."

"You're making this up, Ed." Oscar said. "It's the Alzheimer's at work." His old neighbor gave Mikesh another wink.

"No, it's true," said the man in olive. "I heard about it at the time. Swear to God! The governor was even in the parade."

"The governor!" Ed exclaimed. "That's just the worst part of it. Don't you see the local Democrats got the governor to come up here to drum up a few Leftie voters to come to the caucus we had in January: stand up for Hillary Rotten What's-her-Name, stand up for the black man? So he's here with all his security people—the governor, not that Hussein charac-ter—waiting down by the fairgrounds for the parade to begin.

"Well, along about ten it seems King needs a rest, so he bolts from the outdoor show ring. But there are still lots of folks waiting to get the laying-on of hands or whatever it is he does to cure what ails them.

"These take off after him across the parking lot and into the street where the parade is getting started. Here come the sick folks, stringing out after him, some shouting for him to stop. It's people on crutches and, for all I know, somebody pushing a hospital bed . . ."

"That's true," said the man in olive. "There *was* a hospital bed on wheels, with an IV bag swinging from it and everything. I heard that."

"Well, the trouble was," Ed continued, "King didn't really know where he was going. In the block before the parade turns onto Montgomery, he cuts across the street and, the way I heard it, someone starts waving a crutch or a cane at him."

"A crutch," the olive shirt said, "a crutch, the fellow started swinging his crutch."

Oscar was looking at Mikesh like he needed to call in a witness to have his friends certified, but the old man was enjoying Ed's story.

"That's it, a crutch. That's what got them all in trouble because one of the governor's special goons, a big football-player-sized guy like the man himself—fellow with dark glasses and the wires going into his ears—he sees the person waving the crutch coming toward the governor. This looks fishy to the security man, so he does a special-ops tackle on the guy with the crutch, brings him down, the guy letting out a yell as he goes."

"Yeah, a regular scream," says the olive shirt.

"That gets King's attention," says Ed. "He's been off in dreamland, but he sees the cripple going down with the man in the suit on top of him, and King runs back to help this guy.

"By now the parade has stopped. The band in front of the governor is marching away. The floats and cars behind him have stopped. The guy in charge, that young lawyer from down on Water Street, he's busting a gasket, shouting into his walkie-talkie-deal. There's people running to where the lame fellow has gone down. The governor and his other security man, they've gone into a crouch. Other sick folks have caught up, out there in the street, milling around. Honest-to-God freak show. And King, he's real excited now, pulling at the bodyguard, trying to help up the guy with the crutch. Oh, I'll tell you, it was a fine mess."

"Yeah," says the olive shirt, "they hauled King and the cripple, both of them, off to jail. Delayed that end of the parade for almost ten minutes."

"But were they charged with anything?" Ed continued. "No sir. They didn't charge. The governor was wishing he'd never come to Nordic Fest. He was shitting bricks, by God! worried that somebody might have snapped a picture of one of his statehouse guards beating up a cripple, with him, Iowa's Democratic governor, looking on in a crouch!

The whole table broke up with laughter. Oscar slapped his leg and wiped his eyes.

"I didn't know Joshua King healed people," Mikesh said.

"Well I don't know that he did," said Ed. "He *maybe* healed people and, then again, maybe he didn't."

"Anyway, I'd never heard anything about it."

"Good for you, then. Who pays attention to that kind of stuff?" Ed replied. "Who believes in it? I'm just mad that Larry Rasmussen didn't use his head enough to keep that whole mess clear of here on the biggest day of the year for this little town. It's a damn shame."

On the drive home, out in the flattening country of former prairie, passing fields and farms, on the stretch of State Highway 24 that eventually runs parallel to the Great Northern rail bed, Oscar said, "I hope you don't let my pal's complaining sour you on living around these parts."

"No Oscar. Why should it?"

"He made a big deal of something that, in the city where you used to live, wouldn't have amounted to a hill of beans. That mess with the parade is just the sort of thing people get worked up about around here. Ed could tell that story every week from now until they wheel him out of the Vets on a gurney."

"You don't wave a potential weapon at a governor, wherever you live," Mikesh replied.

"But this King business. It's the sort of stuff that happens out here in the country that would never get started in a city."

"I don't know. Cities manufacture their own special brand of craziness."

Oscar shook his head. "I'm a simple man. Country living suits me. But it allows you to go a bit further your own way, with less there to rein you in. Sometimes that means we turn out some eccentric characters."

Bumping his way up the agribusiness ladder, Mikesh lived and worked in Chicago. He compared the empty highway before him to his memory of the twice-daily commute in heavy traffic down the Eisenhower Expressway, remembering with a flush of embarrassment that he was supposed to be coming up with a name or two to pass on to Davy Murphy.

"Well Oscar, maybe I'm aiming to let myself get crazier with every year I age. But really, even if I wanted to, you aren't going to let me get too far out of line. I know my neighbors and their business better out here than I did when I was putting on a tie and jacket every day and driving into the city. You, Dale, Barbara all keep an eye out. You remember everything that's happened in Eden and Auburn townships for decades. That does a better job than the zoning codes, ordinances, cops, and security cameras they use to try to keep you from hurting somebody or yourself in Chicago."

"I'm glad you feel that way, Arnie. I can tell you; your great uncle Bud would be happy knowing you're on his place, keeping it up and working it like you do."

"Bud's gift allowed me to get sane again, Oscar. As far as I'm concerned, I was stranded and not very happy in my twenty-one-hundred-dollar per month condo when Bud died, and he handed me the deed to a piece of heaven with a note attached that said, 'here—enjoy.'"

"You could have sold the place to one of the neighbors no problem and gotten enough to buy a home right where you were."

"I got the same amount of home I could have bought in Chicago, and over one hundred acres thrown in for free when I moved to Bud's."

"120 acres that you've got to pay property tax on, and work hard to keep up. That's even tougher when you've got your plans for 'prairie' this and 'woodland' that."

"The government's got a few incentives for that. Besides, it keeps me out of trouble."

"Just don't let the business with these religious nuts get you bent sideways."

"I'll try not to, Oscar."

Mikesh could steady Oscar as they walked, so he stopped at the cemetery, where the old man still liked to visit his parents' grave.

The creek wrapped around the graveyard. In summer it often disappeared into the sand and gravel. Today it was rushing through the culvert that carried the water under the drive between the cemetery and the town ball diamond. In another couple of months, there would be games out under the field lights and people watching from portable lawn chairs. The remaining snow was slushy and slick. The continued warm temperature was giving the landscape a patchwork look. With the afternoon temperatures above freezing, there were exposed edges around the snow.

In its graveyard, Mikesh's adopted town aged little and changed slowly. When Oscar was born, Waucoma had twice its current population, a bank, a dozen stores, three hotels, a mill, a railway depot, three churches, a Catholic school, its own public school, newspaper, doctors,

lawyers, a drugstore. The majority of the people that made up that bus-
tling town of long ago reclined now in the cemetery under their neat rows
of stone: Brincks, Bodensteiner, Murray, Ober, Doyle, the families intact
and full, all together at last: mother, father, daughter, sons, "our dear,"
"our darling," "in peace."

The site of the town behind the cemetery, as in Oscar's childhood,
was the prettiest spot you could find for many miles, but the buildings of
Waucoma had the look of a smile when the teeth start to yellow and one
goes missing. A convenience mart, a bar, the grain elevator at the co-op,
a woodworking firm, and a hog-buyer were it for business. Without its
school, and sharing a priest with four other parishes the Catholic church
limped along. The Vets Club was used mainly as an occasional social hall.
The public school was consolidated in a building five miles down the
road where the kids got bussed from everywhere in a twelve-mile radius.
Every year the district grew closer to consolidating again, this time in
Calmar. Mikesh thought back to Bailey's characterization of the gutted
countryside. The cemetery grew while most everything else shrank. In
and out of town, over half the driveways that used to lead to farms, now
led to open fields where a cluster of trees or a shed were the most that
might be left of what was once home to anywhere up to sixteen or twenty
people in the bigger Catholic households. But for all that, oddly, it didn't
feel like the unfolding catastrophe Bailey described. Mikesh's land, his
animals, the people of his daily life were all in place. His mind was like
that cemetery, where little aged or disappeared completely. In the tough
and wrinkled covering of his prefrontal cortex and temporal lobe Mikesh
held the pieces of this quiet world together. That gave him some peace.

The two men walked up to the top of the St. Mary's section of the
cemetery where Oscar's folks were buried beneath a big cedar. Mikesh
could hear Canada geese making a racket by the river. The wind was raw.
A branch in a walnut knocked hollowly against a mate. Oscar kicked at
the snow beneath the brown granite marker. "They made a good living
out of our place. Whatever we needed came from the land. They kept
me out of trouble and they treated me fair." He stood in silence with his
hand resting on the marker. Mikesh considered the service that attached
Oscar to the Vets Club: enlisting instead of taking his farming exemption,
fighting his way on foot behind an automatic rifle, farm by farm, village
and town, from Salerno to Anzio to Bologna and the border of France in
a wall of men whose prime directive was to kill. The Allied cause plucked
up Oscar, used him for that service, and then tossed him back numb from

the violence of which he had been part. The quiet work of farming and the welcome of his parents was the salvation of which Oscar dreamed during his two-year march through Armageddon. Eventually Oscar pulled his hand from the granite and picked his slow way back to Mikesh's Chevy.

"Thanks for bringing me here, Arnie," he said as he closed the pickup door.

Oscar didn't need to worry. The quiet of this town, and the neighborliness of those who peopled the countryside's open expanse, seed police or no, were going to keep Mikesh planted where he was. After he dropped off his neighbor, Mikesh drove over to Dale Murphy's farm. Mikesh knew that the man in Des Moines who hired him out of university was still in business, and Mikesh would give him a call. Davy Murphy had helped Mikesh with fencing, putting up hay, and with his cattle. He owed it to Davy to give what help he could in moving on, even if it propelled him in a direction Mikesh himself was glad to have put behind.

CHAPTER 11

ON THURSDAY WHEN HE arrived at work, Mikesh found a middle-aged woman waiting outside the closet converted into his office. She was bundled into a rigid nylon-shell jacket. With both hands she clutched a purse the size of a shopping bag. Her name was Evelyn Schmidt. Mikesh saw her as little as he saw most who worked in the day world of the school. She was the office assistant for the carpentry, construction, and industrial tech program. Mikesh assumed that there was an issue in her building to deal with. But it was a personal matter, she said. She asked to talk privately. He invited her in and shut the door. Evelyn hefted her purse onto her lap after sitting in the one chair other than Mikesh's in the tiny space.

As Mikesh stared across his desk, Evelyn dug in the purse.

"Would you like a banana?" She held out the fruit, and looked surprised when he asked if she was having one.

"No . . . wait. I'm having an apple," she said, setting a red delicious on the desk next to the banana, "unless you'd prefer this."

"The banana will do."

Mikesh peeled the fruit as Evelyn bit into hers. The juice from its white flesh left a lump of bubbles on her lower lip.

"I hear that you were the one who discovered that accident: the one where Joshua King got killed," she said, between bites.

"That's right." Mikesh dreaded going over that again.

"Funny business." Evelyn shifted in her chair, wiped her mouth, put down the apple, stood up, took off her coat, and put it in her lap, setting the purse on top. "Excuse me. It's hot in here."

"Sorry. Half the heating pipes in this college seem to run through this little room of mine."

Evelyn gave the premises a careful look. Mikesh's cubbyhole made her office look palatial. "Anyway, like I said, it's a funny business." She picked up the apple, bit and chewed furiously.

"The accident?"

"Oh, not that. That church of his. It's funny that the government can't put a stop to an outfit like that." Evelyn Schmidt was looking around Mikesh's office, scrutinizing its pipes. Mikesh wished his quarters made a better showing.

"If it's a religion," Mikesh said, "it's protected by the government." He thought of Jude Bailey's speculation about how Josh died, and qualified himself. "At least government is not supposed to interfere."

Schmidt searched his face. She was trying to make something out and her mouth twitched.

"Your being there; was that an accident?"

Mikesh wondered if this woman had been deputized and sent by Fox.

"I just happened by on the way home from my shift. The first contact I had with Joshua King's church, if that's what you want to call it, was when I met his family the next day."

The woman's eyes narrowed.

"There needs to be an investigation into those people. Now before it all picks up steam again, with the main fellow dead. There needs to be an investigation into what they are up to, and maybe put a stop to the whole thing."

"What *are* they up to?"

"Mind control." Evelyn Schmidt fixed her gaze on Mikesh. "As far as I'm concerned it's mind control, and it's kidnapping!"

"Mind control?"

"They hold them against their normal thinking *through* mind control. That's how they keep them from returning to their homes."

"Who are you talking about?"

Evelyn Schmidt hugged the big purse, and sized Mikesh up. "Arnie," she said, "you don't know this about me, I don't suppose. We don't know each other more than to say hello, but my daughter Linda is in that Spirit church. She joined almost two years ago."

Mikesh had been hearing about families, unhappy about losing someone to Josh's influence. He now had an agitated parent in front of him in the person of Evelyn.

"Linda, she was my second, always a good person. Quick as a wren in her thinking, that girl. She never gave me trouble. Of my three, Linda was the quiet one. She got her bookkeeping certificate right here at this school. A few years later she was working in the office of the grain elevator over in New Hampton and she meets this man who sells his corn and beans there, does other business with them. Hanson his name was, Elias Hanson."

Mikesh tried to picture the office at the New Hampton elevator. He had been there. He draw a blank on all but the calendar on the wall: fall color in Vermont. The route this story was taking to Shekinah looked like it would be wandering. He gave Evelyn a listening look.

"Elias was fifteen years older than my daughter, but they started dating. I didn't like it that she was seeing him, because of the age difference, of course, but also, I didn't know him. I wondered why a farmer his age couldn't already have found somebody before he bumped into my Linda.

"Linda thought my opinion was just empty fretting, so she didn't pay much mind to it. She liked the way Elias made her feel. He can be a real charmer, Elias. In fact, long after they were married and things had gone bad I found out through a friend that he had been a regular playboy. He got at least one girl pregnant: one filed for paternity at least. Quite a ladies' man, and who knows how many others took care of things some different way or kept quiet. Elias Hanson is someone you do *not* want to cross. I've found that out."

Behind Evelyn's placid exterior Mikesh could see there lurked one angry mother.

"But Linda wasn't seeing any of that, not his wicked side. Back then Elias treated her like a queen. And within three months they got engaged, and pretty soon Linda is married, and she has moved to his place out between New Hampton and Cresco and become a farmer's wife. And for a while he stayed charming. Except that he was very strict about their finances. Linda kept her job at the elevator, but now Elias took the check to the bank, and Elias kept the farm account all to himself. He also kept close track of the personal account, always looking over the checkbook, always asking Linda about what she bought, and why the amount was so high, and how not a single expense was near half that amount in his bachelor days. You might say he badgered her until she was afraid to spend so much as a penny on herself, even though she was making good money and needed to look respectable for her job."

She paused. Mikesh filled in the silence by telling her, "it doesn't sound good."

"It certainly does not! That man was meaner than cat water, and Linda still hadn't learned the half of it. In another six months she was pregnant, and once she came close to term Elias told her he would not allow her to stay working once the baby was born. No mother of his child was running off to work and leaving his baby with a woman who took money for what a wife should do herself. Linda quit her job and got things ready for the baby in that pokey old farmhouse."

Mikesh was still trying to recall the grain elevator. He had been there less than a year ago. Though long after Linda Schmidt worked there, he thought he could picture the quiet capable woman who left her job to find herself alone on the farm Evelyn described.

Evelyn went on. "And if she had stayed working, she might have found out about his paying money out for another child, and his treating those other girls badly. Instead she was all by herself in that farmhouse. Once their first son was born, Elias said she shouldn't take their baby out when she got her hair fixed or into a grocery store where she couldn't keep good track of him and that other people would notice.

"You see, he changed his tune. Instead of Linda being the queen, she wasn't good enough. No amount of good behavior on her part could bring out a word of praise. She could cook a meal to perfection and he'd complain about too many onions or too little salt. Once the baby came, the house was never clean enough, the towels weren't hanging as straight as they should, and every time their boy cried it was because Linda failed to do right with his diaper or the way she held him in her arms. And I can tell you, no woman would be a better mother than Linda except she was on her own, no help from me, no other women to talk to."

Mikesh had heard of men like Elias Hanson before. He wondered how this was all leading to Linda Schmidt joining up with Josh.

"Three years later there was a second boy," Evelyn continued. "By then Linda hardly left the house: once a week to go shopping, once to go to church. When she got married, Linda used to have us over, but even with Ralph and me in the room Elias didn't let up on her. When one of us confronted him, it got to be a regular shouting match. Then she wasn't inviting us and had this or that reason they couldn't come when I asked them to Sunday dinner or for a birthday. And, funny thing, while Elias was becoming king of his household, he became a bigger man in the community. He got elected to the Chickasaw County Board of

Supervisors and to the church council. Elias made a respectable family man of himself, but squeezed out every bit of Linda's happiness.

"Linda went along with it even when he started to be hard on those two boys, spanking them for the smallest thing. If she said something to Elias, he got rough with her; not hitting at first, but grabbing and shaking her. That man!" Schmidt glared. "I'd like to shake him myself."

The heat in the room was dry. Mikesh wished he'd made some coffee, but he didn't interrupt.

"Finally he started to push her around, hit her."

Evelyn's voice broke. Crying, she rummaged in her purse and produced a tissue.

"Linda couldn't take it anymore. One night in February she put the boys to bed. Elias was already asleep. And Linda put on her jacket and walked out. She walked four miles to another farm where she knew the wife, and that woman drove her to the apartment of a high school friend in New Hampton. That girl got her connected with a women's shelter, and in a few days they got her connected to a lawyer so she could file for divorce and custody. Her father and I helped, but it was a hard case: Linda's word against Elias. As for custody, it would have gone better if she'd taken those boys with her right away. During that divorce trial, my husband Ralph had a heart attack and died.

"You didn't know my Ralph I suppose."

Mikesh shook his head, bracing for another digression.

"The man was a prince. Not that he was rich. You don't make a fortune delivering LP gas. He didn't talk about it much, but Ralph never liked Elias Hanson. 'Evelyn,' he told me one time. 'Elias has room in that heart of his to love only one thing besides himself in this world, and that's his own shadow.' Wasn't *that* the truth?"

Evelyn seemed like she was leaving off the story of her daughter, but found her way again.

"It was a kind of blessing that Linda was at loose ends when Ralph died, because she could come back home and help me out. In the meantime, Elias found out where she was staying, and he showed up and threatened her. The police came, but that snake didn't make any mistakes except that one. When the hearing ended, he got five-day-per-week custody of those boys because of what his lawyer claimed was Linda's unstable emotional condition and lack of financial means for support and no good proof about him being so rough. Elias's mother was ready to step in and do Linda's mothering work. Linda got a job waitressing and an apartment in New Hampton.

"I gave her Ralph's car, because she had to get around and haul those boys. One of the places she went was to that Norwegian church of Elias's they attended out on the prairie, where the boys started Sunday School. It was a friendly place for Linda as long as she was married to Elias, but those good Christians started singing a different tune once she was, as far as they were concerned, an unfit mother who had abandoned her husband and babies. The pastor told her that they could not turn her away from the door but she was not allowed to take communion. She would watch every other adult go up to the front and get right with God while she, an unclean woman, sat while her boys wondered what was wrong with their momma."

Evelyn's voice broke, and she looked down. Mikesh felt a rush of anger and disgust. *This* was the church as it figured in every history book he'd read.

"Why didn't she just get out of there?"

"Oh, she did eventually. She quit going to that church, took the boys to a different one so Elias couldn't say she was turning them into heathens. But even that new church was cool to her, a divorced woman. Maybe by then it was just her. The damage was done. The divorce was hard, and before that there was Elias's badgering. In her mind Linda no longer trusted herself. That man may have *loved* his own shadow, but Linda became *afraid* of hers. She fretted about the way things set with God. Maybe she had been wrong to abandon her husband and children. She was skipping church altogether, and Elias used that to make her feel like dirt when she brought the boys back to him at the end of the weekend. She grew distant from me, too, even though I offered to take her in. She was in a real state, depressed all the time, scatter-brained. She went through a run of very bad new boyfriends, started seeing lots of men, and had trouble at work.

"Then one day Joshua King walks into the place where she waitressed. It was the middle of the afternoon and Linda was taking a break after the lunch crowd was gone. At first she thought he was just another guy making a pass, but he talks to her like he knows her, and asks to sit down. Linda said it was spooky. She wondered if maybe a no-good ex-boyfriend was playing with her mind or talking loose about her and putting ideas into some other man's head. What he *did* say was that she was not the bad person she thought. She is a true and pure child of the

Spirit, he said, and she already had a home in the Spirit. Through her, he said, other people would find the Spirit because she was chosen to be a messenger. He said, 'you will be the light.' And then he walks out."

Mikesh recognized an echo, in what Evelyn said, of his own stunted conversation with my brother.

"Linda wanted to treat him as if he was not right in his head. That or just getting fresh with her. She meant to put the whole talk with him out of her mind, but she kept thinking about it. She went to what those folks call house gatherings, and made new best friends with the people there. One day she gave total custody of her two boys to Elias and moved down to this ex-school in Bremer County, baking bread for I don't know how many people."

Mikesh remembered someone mentioning this woman last Sunday at the Murphy's table; the housewife lured away was Linda Schmidt. "I've heard they call that 'the Big House.' What happened to your daughter there?"

Evelyn gave Mikesh a look that showed his comment confirmed that he knew more about Shekinah than he let on.

"At the start I felt that it was more of the same: no money and no possessions trusted to Linda, no contact with her family, some man calling the shots and Linda doing as she was told. But I've seen her twice, and she seemed happy, happy about everything except not having those two boys. I've let it go, hoping it might just be a transition to help her get back on her feet until she can move on to something else, maybe get my grandsons back again from their crook of a father."

Bailey said an angry family member might have targeted King, run him off the road. Somehow, though, Mikesh didn't feel Evelyn was leading up to a manslaughter confession.

"I miss my daughter, Arnie. And what kind of danger am I to her? What can she ever do about those two boys as long as she's living at that hippie place and not thinking for herself? They have a phone. But does that mean Linda will talk to me when I call? I haven't gotten through to her for months.

"It's mind control. She's just as good as kidnapped. I don't like to say bad things about the dead, but that man put an evil spell on my daughter's mind. I don't know who put him up to it, though I have my suspicion that it *was* one of those no-account boyfriends. King is gone. Now is the time to get her home."

Evelyn stuffed the tissue back into her purse and brought out two jars with canning lids. "I brought these for you: blackberry and elderberry. A man living alone needs someone to help keep him in jam." Evelyn pulled something else out.

"This scrapbook is about them, King's church. It might help you." She laid the vinyl-covered folder on the desk, but was still rummaging. She pulled out a four-by-six glossy of a woman and two boys standing rigid in front of an arbor vitae hedge.

"Help me with what?"

"I figured you'd be going to his funeral tomorrow, and I thought you'd keep an eye out for Linda. Maybe have a word with her when you see her." Evelyn shifted to Mikesh's side of the desk and held the photo out in front of them. Mikesh smelled the laundry detergent emanating from her clothes. "That's her." Evelyn pointed to the woman in the photo. "That's my Linda." The woman was taller than Mikesh had imagined. She and two pre-school boys stood in an uneasy row.

"I hadn't planned on going," Mikesh apologized. "I don't often go to funerals. I didn't really know him."

"You're young. Young people aren't used to going to funerals. But you were with the man when he died, Arnie. That changes everything. You *have* to go. If you see her, tell her to call," she said, leaving the photo and book with him. "She deserves better than what life is giving her down there."

She told Mikesh where and when the funeral was to be held, and then was gone. Mikesh stared at the photo of Linda Schmidt Hanson, his throat scratchy and parched, his somber week grown heavier. In addition to figuring out why Josh was driving north from St. Lucas in the fog, he was tasked with rescuing a cult member. He sensed this new task might be harder than the first. He got up and made himself some much-needed coffee.

CHAPTER 12

ON THE FRIDAY MORNING following my brother's death, Mikesh, on Evelyn's recommendation, drove the highway running the course of what once was the old French trader road on the high ground across Iowa between the Mississippi River in the east and the Missouri River in the west. Before the French arrived three hundred years ago, this road was an open path between big bluestem and compass plants worn clear by the moccasins of the Ioway, and before them people without horses whose names have been lost, stretching back to those who came with the prairie itself. There is no older thoroughfare in this corner of the state, but for Mikesh it was new territory. He lived on the headwaters of the Turkey, but had never been where the Lower Turkey drops through the deep valleys that rib down from Iowa into the Mississippi River.

Neither had Mikesh been to an outdoor funeral. He wore his warmest respectable clothes. He was troubled. In the six days since the accident he had put distance between himself and the death of my brother, but now he was going to have to confront Josh being buried, surrounded by people who, like Evelyn's daughter, maintained what likely was a fanatical devotion. His mood was not lifted as he surveyed the landscape. He liked to see cattle on the land like the bison before them. What he saw instead were long, bleak sheds housing hogs and dairy herds. The buildings reminded him of photos of Auschwitz or Bergen-Belsen—industrial envelopes for the life sealed up inside, the hundreds of magnificent animals without much more space than it took to stand or lie down. He would be happier this morning to be working in the open air with his own stock, letting my family and me bury Josh without his presence.

A sign warned Mikesh of a steep grade before he entered the shadow of a sharp decline. From the hill edge he saw the town Josh and I called home: a cluster of brick and stone spires, turrets, and cupolas.

Elkader clusters around a milldam, with a pretty line of falls above a stone-arched bridge. On the far edge of town Mikesh passed the stone Catholic church with its school and rectory, a little European village set aside on its own, with a cemetery at its edge. Below the church the river takes a long swipe back toward the bench on which the town perches. Mikesh could see the Turkey was up. Snow melted from his own fields was pushing its way toward the Big Muddy in a muscular brown torrent he hardly recognized. Nothing, however, was melting today. Overnight the weather had changed. A cold front had blown down from the Arctic. The day was bright, the wind sharp.

As Mikesh neared the rural site of the funeral he decided Oscar was right about religious movements taking root outside the spotlight of public attention. To bury my brother's body, my mom was returning to the township from which she came: a quiet draw near the east end of Chicken Ridge, in a wooded valley near the mouth of the Turkey. No church, no rectory by the graveyard, just a weatherworn cemetery shed, the name on the metal arch above a cemetery gate was all that would tell you the few quiet buildings at a road junction were Communia, Iowa. There was no parking lot, just a big new road, a broad cold slab of concrete with wide shoulders, cut into the hill on which the cemetery was sited. The rest of what once had been a village was on its way to disappearing.

Cars were pulled off either side of the highway as it rose around the bend of the hill ahead. Mikesh drove through the confusion of vehicles and people. Across the road from the cemetery, two-dozen or so bundled-up protestors held up signs like "Spirit Church / Devil's Church" and "Burn in Hell King." Between protesters and the cemetery entrance, a state trooper was waving cars through, his patrol vehicle pulled over beside him, lights flashing. Mikesh U-turned and parked pointing back the way he had come. A dim silver travel trailer, every window an inky and vacant hole, sat abandoned in the wooded draw next to his car. "Vote Obama" was scrawled with spray paint on the side facing the highway. Hope? Mikesh wondered, or some local's idea of a racist joke.

Mikesh had passed the confusion on the road with the windows rolled up and the heater roaring, but walking towards the cemetery, he heard pieces of shouts: "Come . . . evil . . . Jesus!" They got clearer: "The apostate is dead, dead, dead!" By the gate a television news crew was filming. Mikesh wondered if he would blend in with my brother's followers. With everybody bundled up against the cold and no one pulling up in a stretch limo, it was hard to tell who was a brother, who was a sister, or who was one of my mother's farm neighbors. The weather and the place made this an unlikely event for the just-plain-curious, save for the presence of the television camera. A large number of the people arriving were Hispanic—not something Mikesh expected. It reminded him of Seegmiller's comment that Josh had been "south of the border too many times."

Mikesh could hear someone testing a portable sound system as he got closer, and as he came through the entry gate he saw a simple wooden coffin held aloft over a grave at the back corner. The cemetery slanted down toward a creek: the grave at its lower edge a long distance from other markers. Mikesh was surprised, now he thought of it, to see the open grave in ground so recently hard with frost. Someone had been determined. Beyond the creek rose a brown tangle of winter woods. Two or three hundred people pressed out along the fence above the grave and stretched up toward the crest of the rise where Mikesh entered. He hung back, heading off to his left, sticking close to the row of tall cedars that lined the entrance. He stopped at the base of one of the trees.

Mikesh looked over the tight knot of mourners standing front and center in the crowd. Beside the coffin a few chairs were lined up, and on a table sat two large baskets filled with loaves of bread.

"Hey," said a voice to Mikesh's left. He turned to find Mary Towers looking at him, less tall than he remembered.

He looked at her winter-pale face and colored as he recalled his hasty retreat from her a few days earlier. He wished he had stood his ground and asked a few more questions. "The other day," he said. "You kept me ignorant about you and Joshua King being friends until I was almost ready to leave."

"You didn't tell me about your turning up at Josh's accident until you left. Besides, you needed help. I attended to that first. That's my job."

"It worked, by the way. I've been feeling great. Today I'm feeling a little uncured."

She noticed that in addition to his slight limp, he carried his shoulders pinched.

"Picture each uncured place in your mind, and watch the pressure emptying away. If that doesn't work, keep handy that business card I gave you."

Mary thought few men with that slightly hurt look in their eyebrows would admit right off that they were feeling "uncured." She resolved to make this encounter end better than their last.

Positioned where they were at the back of the crowd, it was easy to hear the shouts from across the road. "What's with the protesters?" Mikesh nodded back toward the road.

"FP," she said: "Faith Protectors, total dirtbags. They'd be standing at Josh's grave with a bullhorn and spitting on the casket if the law allowed it. Those haters, they still can't let up on him." She was angry, knowing they had protested Josh's gatherings before.

Mikesh had heard of these people, protesting at service burials because of the military's open acceptance of gay recruits. He wondered what Josh did to find his way into their bazooka sights. It must have been plenty to get a crowd of them out in the snow in this corner of the state.

"They don't seem too bothered by the cold."

"I can't say Josh would have wanted different—not them, but the cold," Mary looked in the road's direction. "He preferred the open air." She hunched into her coat. "Funny choice when you live in a climate like this one, but Josh liked weather. He liked fresh air. If it was cold, or if it was hot, Josh liked to be out in the open."

Mikesh heard someone testing the mic and getting the crowd's attention. As the voices around him quieted, Mikesh became more aware of the wind again and realized that by standing near the top of the rise, he was going to be more exposed than if he pushed his way forward in the bulk of mourners down towards the creek. The ceremony hadn't even begun, and his feet were already cold.

A stocky man in an army jacket was speaking.

"That's Simon," Mary said, looking forward, "Simon Peña."

Mikesh recognized him as the man from the sheriff's office, the unpleasant one who grilled him afterward.

"Thanks," Peña's voice echoed, wrapped in a feedback whine. A thin man took the mic, then handed it back. The sound was working, but with the wind and distance Mikesh leaned, straining to hear. Peña was starting again.

"Thanks for coming out in this cold to honor our brother, *mi hermano* Joshua. We're here to bury his body, but we'll remind ourselves of his message, and celebrate Joshua coming into the Spirit. Let's start with the gathering song."

Two musicians stepped out. One sat and lowered a wooden drum, a head of stretched rawhide three feet across, to the ground before him. He lifted a single stick and beat a slow deep rhythm. The woman next to him lifted a wooden flute to her lips and played a faint melody.

Either the law was doing its work, or the drum was drowning out the protests. Mikesh could hear no sound from across the road.

Peña, not very tuneful, sang,

Coming together into the Spirit.

Coming together we are one.

Coming together we are travelers,

travelers, coming to the place where we are one.

As Peña sang, Mikesh recognized the chant. He had heard it in the fog just a week earlier.

Peña repeated the song, and by the first repetition, the bulk of the mourners joined, their voices soft, but growing in volume and strength with each repetition. Many joined hands.

Mary was not singing. Mikesh leaned to her and whispered. "What's this song?"

"Josh called it 'People Know Me Wherever I Go.' The words are his. I think he learned the song out West. He said it was Apache."

Coming together we are travelers,

travelers, coming to the place where we are one, we are one.

Hearing the song sung raised the ghost in Mikesh's mind: my brother's bloody face in the flashlight beam, trailing off with his attempt at music, the glint of the eye, the icy cheek Mikesh found as he reached under the car.

Mikesh leaned against Mary.

"This is the song. Joshua was singing this when I got to him."

She looked at him and felt her mouth twist. Tears welling up, she turned to the music, away from Mikesh. If she could only have been there, given Josh her hand. Somehow she would have crawled into the wreck. Somehow she would have warmed him and sung with him. Somehow, if she could not trade her death for his, if she could not help him live, as he had helped her, then she would have comforted his dying. It was wrong to envy Mikesh, but Mary wished herself into the place he, a stranger, had occupied.

After a dozen repetitions, the song was loud but flattening. Then the musicians quit and it grew silent. More wind. Mikesh was watching for Peña to say more, but Peña let the wind speak. When he stepped to the mic he looked awkward, as if someone had pushed him on stage without a script. He looked at the crowd: as if taken by surprise by the wide hillside of faces.

"Joshua was taken from us young. Our brother, our *hermano Josue* had just started his work. What Joshua said when people passed is what he said in that song we all just sang, that we're travelers on a journey returning to a place we've forgotten, a place always there, where we are all reunited. That place, that Infinity, that's where the Spirit stands calling us." Peña faltered. "That place stands open to us just like Joshua's grave here stands open to his body. But Shekinah is not a gloomy place, my friends. Shekinah—it is a place of light.

"Joshua saw his body," Peña continued, more comfortable now with the sound system and finding his voice: "and the grave, and life as shadows. We worship them instead of the Spirit: idols of the flesh, of power, of a self that's not our *true* self. When we place the shell that housed Joshua into the grave, our true brother, *nuestro verdadero hermano*, is stepping out of that shadow, stepping into the light where he can be with us always.

"Every person here began somewhere else: in a job, a family, a church, that kept him from stepping into the light. Brother Josh was always in that light. His message turned us around. No person spoke to us as Joshua did. Who else knew our secret fears, or what we could become? No one will speak to us in the same way again. He wasn't the mouthpiece of the Spirit. He *was* the Spirit. That's right, he *was* the Spirit. Not one of us can be what he was. It's up to us now to work together, to remember his words and follow Joshua through the darkness of his grave."

Peña did well in front of the crowd, Mikesh thought, but Peña called out to another person, "Sister Naomi?"

As Peña stepped from the microphone, the flute player, a woman in blue slacks stepped forward, her long hair in a braid wrapped around her head. She held something in her hands. Though Peña called her "Naomi," Mikesh was sure he was looking at Linda Schmidt. Peña stepped between the crowd and the woman, facing her. When he turned aside Mikesh could see that she was holding a small bowl, a large shell perhaps. Smoke or steam was blowing from it almost sideways in the wind.

"You remember what Joshua said as he lit the fire," Sister Naomi said. "'We are cleansed by smoke; it marks the death of your earthly self. Feel the Spirit rise within you like fire.'"

She turned slowly, holding out the smoldering bowl at each stopping point in a circle that included the empty hill and the creek behind her. Peña stepped forward and took the bowl, placed it on top of the casket, then stepped back to his place. In the strong wind whatever fire was in the container burned itself out quickly.

Sister Naomi moved forward to the mic. "I will repeat some of Joshua's most common words." She opened her arms wide.

"Honor the Spirit and honor the Spirit as it burns in those you greet."

"Empty your pocket that you may fill your soul."

"If all you can see is the light captured by your physical eye, cast out your eye or lose the Spirit."

Mikesh felt the satiny shell of Mary's purple coat pressing against his arm. Mary's head was still turned away. Her hair, which was down, rippled out from under her knit cap like a black halo, defying gravity. She was so close that he could smell a citrus scent he remembered.

"The world we see is upside down. What appear riches are poverty. What appears greatness, a hollow balloon.

"Joshua quoted Jesus to remind us that the good seed that is cast ripens to fullness in eternity. Those who feel loss will know comfort. Those who hunger in the body, shall in the Spirit know fullness. Those who thirst for the Spirit will there be satisfied. Those who suffer for the Spirit's sake will be blessed. Those who make peace are children of the Spirit, hope in a threatening world."

Some of the gathered faithful were mouthing the phrases Sister Naomi spoke. Like a blues fest, Mikesh thought, but instead of the worried pitch Robert Johnson exchanged for his soul at a midnight crossroad, the people around Mikesh shared lyrics about the Spirit, sung to an Apache melody. To Mikesh's left, a figure in a fringed leather jacket, dark glasses and wide-brimmed hat stood among mossy tombstones, a few steps back from the main body of mourners. With his right hand he pushed down his big hat as the wind kept trying to lift it away. With his other, more hidden hand, he steadied a digital recorder, the screen of which he checked now and then. He turned occasionally to pan the assembled crowd or to slowly zoom in on a mourner. Sunnybob4? Mikesh wondered. A freelancer hired by one of the groups Bailey claimed had spies?

Sister Naomi was still speaking.

"You remember that when Joshua was asked whether we would still be ourselves in the Spirit, he told the story of the birthmark. A mother had a baby with a birthmark over his heart. She loved him, and sang him to sleep each night, 'dream baby bright.' But one day as the boy was crawling in the grass of his yard, an evil man threw him into his truck, and drove him away. That man abused the boy, gave him a new name. He told him he was his own child. When the boy grew he saw the evil man beat another little child with a rod. He took the rod and killed the man. He ran away and, without knowing it, returned to the city from which he had come. One day on the street the mother saw her son, now a man. She knew him at once and embraced him. The man was surprised. 'Who are you?' he asked. 'Why did you hug me?' She said, 'Do you have a birthmark over your heart?' When he said, 'Yes,' the mother sang, 'dream baby bright.' The man recognized the song and wept. 'You are my lost child,' the mother said. 'You were taken from me but I claim you again as my own.' The man embraced his mother. This is how the Spirit rejoices to claim us from our exile."

Naomi, finished, stepped away. Peña was back at the mic. "Brother Tom, the first brother Joshua ever knew, wants to say a few things." Peña seemed to hesitate. "Brother Tom."

I'll tell you, my reading friend, it took no small degree of persuasion to get my place before that mic. Simon did not what it to happen. He and I come at the world from crossed angles. Up against what Simon said— 'He *was* that Spirit'—I wanted to put my view of the very *earthly* brother I lost, a brother who revered the Spirit without wearing it like a mantle, without claiming property rights to it. The message I learned from my brother was that we each carry the Spirit. Still, I acknowledged Simon.

"Brother Simon had something in mind he was too polite to say," I started. "My brother Josh said he felt called to give each of us a new family, to cut us from the family into which we were born, and to call us to a new brotherhood, a new sisterhood of the Spirit, *la familia* that our Brother Simon loves, as I do.

"So in one important way I have no special reason to stand up here today, no special claim to speak. My being here is a challenge to what my brother said. In fact, like a lot of biological brothers and sisters, I got a special kind of pleasure arguing with my brother."

I didn't say it, but Josh really liked joking. My brother loved puns, always seeing the other or the *three* other meanings in what the average person took at face value. There I was, sharing Josh's message, being the Tom-Tom. Peña, to Josh was always Rocky, because that's what Peña means in Spanish: the rock. And Big House. Josh gave our ex-school building that name because it *was* big but sometimes it felt to my wandering outdoor brother Josh like a prison. Since this was a funeral, I didn't go into that

"Josh and I felt pushed in different directions. I went to university to study history, and soil, eventually graduate school in archeology, while Josh went off to college in search of something he wasn't sure of, but which he eventually called the Spirit. He left formal study to seek where the Spirit was more abundant than in the hallways of academe.

"Josh and I never knew our father. Dad didn't stay around long. He went off with a building contractor to do work in the South after a hurricane the fall before we were born, and he never came back. He never married my mom. That meant our family was small. Though my mother made a great home for us, not everyone approved. My brother was driven to find something bigger and more whole than what he knew growing up.

"Josh uncovered a message that even the stones would reveal to us if he hadn't given us his voice. Josh pointed to the power within each of us, a power that hums within every rock, holding loose whirring atoms bonded together in a single body. It makes the sun burn. It makes the rain turn a hard dry kernel of corn into a tall green plant that can reproduce itself a hundredfold and give us all nourishment.

"He called that power the Spirit. He reminded us of how many stupid and how many evil distractions keep us from living fully in that Spirit.

"Because I'm his brother, I connect what Josh said to our growing up. My mother supported the three of us. When we were small we went to our grandparents' house until Mom was done with her work. When the bigger boys on the bus harassed us, it was easy to resent Mom not being there to make it better. When she brought us home it was easy to keep nursing that resentment. But our mother is a remarkable woman. She could sense when there was something troubling us, and she wouldn't let us go to sleep without getting it out in the open.

"I can picture Mom in the lamplight, sitting on Josh's bed, with her hand on his hair, saying, 'Josh, let me in. I don't care what caused it, but I have to know what's on your heart.'

"Josh seemed to know how isolated each one of us is, how trapped we can get in our head or in our heart. That's a place even a mother cannot go. But if anyone came close for Josh, it was our mom. Early on he got a glimmer of the idea that the only company that matters is the presence of the Spirit, counseling us, comforting us, calling us to account for ourselves in the intimate recess of our own heart, and that even when we feel most alone, or abandoned, or badly treated by the rest of the world, that company is there, attending to us, insistent on listening."

Reader, in these words about my mom, I was saying something that Josh had never said. It's why, I think, Josh told Mikesh with his dying breath to take care of my mom. But Josh wasn't speaking. I was. I called what I saw.

I looked around the crowd. Mikesh was in the far back. Mary had shifted away from him. Besides missing the distraction of the citrus scent of her hair, Mikesh was minding the cold. He shifted his feet, stamped them, and made a ball of his fists, leaving the cold glove fingers empty.

Because of where he stood at the top of the rise, Mikesh heard indistinct shouts of the protesters, but down in the flat area I wasn't hearing them. A good thing, because I had worked my way around to the message I most needed to deliver.

"What Josh said about separating us even from those we love in one way reflects badly on the family we made for him. And my own training makes me an unlikely partner with all of the rest of you in following my brother. But in the end I cannot help but follow where Josh leads. My brother Josh did not assert special claim as messenger. It was the message that mattered. He knew that each one of us: you, me, Simon, Naomi, carries that message forward now that Josh is gone."

Simon's assertion was not right—that Josh *was* the Spirit herself, her one appearance in a single person. Here, where I so much wanted to put my words up against his, my breath went shallow and the scene grew dim.

"Josh knew that *each of us* carries the Spirit humming in us, not ours, not something we deserve, not at our beck and call, but ours by the tremendous outpouring that fires the stars and hurls a billion galaxies on their course."

I paused. A loud shout from the protesters made its way to where I stood. A roost of crows lifted from the hilltop of the wood behind the grave, getting blown sideways by the wind before they flapped away. I was distracted, convinced no one would be listening to me, but I made my way again.

"Mom and I thank you for the trust you placed in Joshua, for the help you extended in his mission, for the company you gave him in his journey. Josh is dead. The work he started lives on in each of you. That is the mission with which you must go forward each day."

I said what I know Josh would have wanted me to say. When he was still alive, I was not a speaker. I didn't need to be. Now that he was gone, I became what he told me I would become: Tom-Tom, the Spirit's drum. How much my message got through, who knows? Half of the crowd's attention was diverted toward the cries from the road across from the cemetery entrance. People were whispering. Back where he stood, Mikesh noticed that the man with the fringe kept his camera directed before him, undistracted by noise.

"Satan claimed his apostate" a man's voice shouted. "A-poss-tate! A-poss-tate! A-poss-tate!" the gathered protestors repeated in a chant, as if warming up for a football game.

"Murderer! God's Murderer!" They echoed their leader, a man waving his fist in time with the chant.

"God smashed the one who rejected him!"

"Rejected! Rejected! Rejected!!"

Finished with what I had to say, I sat next to my mother. Mikesh tried to turn his attention from the protesters to the service on this side of the road. Simon and Sister Naomi moved behind the table and Simon was talking. Both held up loaves of bread.

"Brother Joshua gave what he had for others. He turned no one away," Simon said. "He taught us to do the same, sharing what we have. He said 'There is no better discipline of the Spirit than to give. No better ministry of the Spirit than to share.'"

Sister Naomi continued, "With that in mind, he taught us to break bread together. Today Joshua's body has been broken. We remember his gift to us with the act in which he led us so many times. And remember the first part of the prayer Joshua taught us: Spirit, Mother, within us and around us, you bless this moment with your presence. The universe is yours. Bless us with justice, and shower us with mercy. Give us the bread we need, and forgive us as we forgive."

Simon broke a piece of bread from a loaf and handed it to Sister Naomi. "With this bread I salute the Spirit in you. Help bring forth the Spirit in me," Simon said. Sister Naomi did the same. They each handed a loaf on to a person near them, and four helpers came forward, a pair taking each basket and passing its loaves into the crowd. People broke bread for each other and repeated Simon Peña's greeting.

Across the road the chanting continued. An occasional word of the man shouting carried clearly: "devil . . . damned . . . hell," but the wind had shifted against them.

Next to Mikesh, Mary was looking towards the road.

"Poor Josh. There was always someone ready to dis him. It's not going to quit. The haters just keep hating."

A loaf of bread was making its way along the row in front of them. Mary stepped toward a round man with a grizzled beard, took off her gloves, and tapped his shoulder. When he turned, she held cupped hands forward. He broke off a piece and spoke. She closed her eyes as received the bread on her palm, and put the bread in her mouth. Taking the loaf, she walked to the man in fringe and held it up to him. He turned the camera at her, to catch her in his digital memory, and waved her off with his right hand. The man recording, Mikesh thought, was not sunnybob4. The bearded man who handed Mary the bread was scowling. Mary returned to the woman accompanying the bearded man, passing a piece of bread and the greeting to her. Before she handed on the loaf, she broke off a piece and walked back towards Mikesh. She planted her feet in front of him and looked him in the face. She held the bread up near his chin. Mikesh opened his mouth. Mary's index finger brushed his upper lip as she pressed the bread to his tongue. The bread was homemade: moist and yeasty. What had Bailey called it: Manna Loaves?

Peña was looking in the direction from which Mikesh could hear the protestors chanting again, "Murr-drer, murr-drer, murr-drer." Peña, Naomi, and the assistants gathered the small remains of the loaves, and headed towards the grave.

Linda Schmidt Hanson, rechristened Naomi, came forward again and led a song, this time singing, with no accompaniment—

River water is chilly and cold.

Chills the body but not the soul.

Every time I feel the Spirit, moving in my heart, I'll pray.

O every time I feel the Spirit, moving in my heart, I'll pray.

After several verses, the song ended. A funeral director and assistant in charcoal dress coats walked to grave's edge. Peña removed the bowl from the top of the casket. Mikesh noticed there was no vault, just a plain wooden box which they lowered into the ground with a winding crank. That completed, the men in suits efficiently pulled out the cable and pieces of the metal stand, lifted away the metal architecture of burial, and when they stepped back, there was nothing but the pit.

Peña lifted a shovel, dug a scoop of earth, and tossed it into the grave. Returning to the mic, he said, "Earth returns to earth. Spirit flies to Spirit." Mikesh watched Mom and I follow Simon in carrying out this last goodbye, as a single high voice sang "Oh freedom" and the crowd responded "over me, over me." Voices united in singing

before I'd be a slave,

I'll be buried in my grave,

and go home to the Spirit and be free.

Mikesh recognized the mournful tune. Those, like him, who didn't seem to know the words walked toward the sound of the protesters, because the service was over. But those who sang moved toward the front where they each cast their spade of earth, singing the verses,

no more moaning, there'll be singing,

there'll be shouting, there'll be praying

several times until the solo leader was silent and there was again only the sound of wind. By then, many had cast their shovel of earth.

Mikesh was conscious of Mary standing next to him, and remembered to work on making a better impression. "I'm glad I came," he told her. "Those bozos gathered across the road; I can see what your friend was up against."

The chants had broken off and the shouts grew ragged as the assembled protestors yelled out taunts.

"What do you think is going to happen with them?" he nodded at the crowd shuffling forward to the grave. "Is this it?"

"For some of them. But you heard Peña and Thomas. As far as they're concerned, this is the beginning."

Mikesh saw Peña hugging mourners as they walked away from the grave, taking some by both hands, speaking face to face.

"I'm going down. I want to talk to Maria King and that woman named Naomi," Mikesh told her. "How about you?"

"Gotta go."

"Are you sure?" Mikesh would have liked her company.

"Positive." She looked him in the face, gave his hand a squeeze, and walked away, hands in her pockets and head bent, her purple coat disappearing into the stream of people funneled through the cemetery gate. Mikesh filed forward toward the core circle of mourners.

I said "Arnie!" when Mikesh neared the head of the line to toss his shovel of dirt. "I'm glad you came." I grabbed Mikesh's elbow and pulled him towards my mother. Up close Mikesh noticed Mom more clearly than the week before: her even features, the olive cast of her weathered skin.

"Arnie, sitting here today, I've been comforted knowing Josh didn't die alone in the cold, but I wish I could have spoken with him myself. You neglect to say what you should, and then it's too late. I understand what mothers used to tell me when I was younger: 'pray you don't outlive your children.'"

She looked over Mikesh's shoulder, expression clouding.

"Simon, you remember Arnold Mikesh, the man who found Joshua?" she said as Mikesh turned to see Peña stepping up behind him.

"Murr-drers! Murr-drers! Murrdrers!" The wind must have shifted. The protesters were at the cemetery gate.

Peña's brow twisted. A breathless man ran up. "Simon, we got to move. The cop's doing nothing to stop the FP folks. They're at the road edge, upsetting the sisters."

The skinny man waited. "Should we try something?" Mikesh recognized him from the video as Brother Randy.

"All right. I'll face them. Come on!"

Peña was built like a left tackle. You could sense the power in him as he strode off. Peña may not have leverage with the law, but with him standing on their side, the departing faithful were going to have a tactical advantage.

"Satan! Satan! Satan!" came toward them in the air.

Mom frowned. "That's what my son was up against. I don't understand. He made a good mark on the world. He was a quiet boy, helping people. I'm happy to hear from Tom that you'll help us out by speaking Sunday at the Big House." She looked at Mikesh.

"I didn't get a promise of that," I said to Mom by way of apology. "I'm still hoping you might do Josh the honor of saying something, Arnie. Sunday will be a big gathering, indoors, not like this. We'll have a proper meal. It would mean a lot if you could be there, share Joshua's last moments."

Mikesh saw that Linda Hanson was gone. He knew Evelyn was not going to be happy until he talked to her daughter. It would have to be at the Big House. So too, the presence of the protesters whetted his sympathy for my mother, reminding him of Josh's request.

"Okay. I'll be there."

I gave Mikesh directions and handed him the shovel. All those people, and there was still dirt in the pile, still a partial hole to fill. Mikesh tossed his shovelful into the just-larger-than-man-sized depression and heard it sigh as it hit, scattered, and settled, earth returning to earth.

CHAPTER 13

IN EARLY AFTERNOON THE following Sunday, Mikesh drove to a Bremer County town four streets wide and four streets deep on a gradual rise above a dam on the Wapsipinicon River. In the ragged end of winter, the widely spaced houses had the look of buildings abandoned in the face of catastrophe, but reoccupied by squatters, some using rolls of plastic to keep the raw prairie wind out of the windows and doors. At the top of the rise, on the edge between the town's public park and an expanse of fields, the most startling reoccupation was a two-and-one-half-story brick building with *Public School* impressed in the concrete arch above the entrance doors of what served as the Big House. The streets looked ghost-haunted, but the lot outside the old school building where Mikesh parked his truck, and where other vehicles were turning in, looked like game day or parent-teacher afternoon.

When he identified himself, the woman who welcomed Mikesh at the door buried him in an effusive embrace, her loose-hanging blouse hiding a big build with a strength that surprised him. As Mikesh untangled, he felt a tug at his elbow. Expecting perhaps the sister of his greeter, Mikesh was surprised to see Peña, who took him down a half flight of steps to a lower hallway, toward the sound of voices, and down a hall past the smell of the kitchen. Peña guided Mikesh through the open doorway of an office. A man in a neat plaid shirt and jeans, standing between two open cabinet doors, looked away from the dials and switches before him.

"I'm checking out the public address system, in case we need it, Simon," he said, "but there's a problem with a contact."

Mikesh recognized the man by his cropped hair and narrow build.

"Randy, this is Arnie Mikesh," Peña said.

Randy extended his hand. "Pleased to meet you," he said. "Simon told me about you."

"That you'd be joining us for a meal," Peña added, as he guided Mikesh through another door. Mikesh realized he was now in the office that, in the building's former days, served the principal. He recognized the feel of the place: big enough to seem important, small enough to make your skin crawl. Peña sat down behind the desk.

"What's going on?" Mikesh asked as he took a chair.

"I need to clear my mind about your interest in Shekinah," Peña said.

"I'm not seeking to become your next convert, if that's what you mean."

"That *is* what I mean. You aren't interested in what we are trying to teach here. Last time I saw you, you were with a person who has never tried to do anything but undermine us."

"Who's that?"

"The woman you stood by at the funeral," Peña answered. "It's hard for me to tell who's a friend and who's our enemy. That woman has never pretended to be a friend of Shekinah. She's only been interested in Joshua—which puts her against the rest of us, against what we've worked together to build."

"What, exactly, has she done?"

"Done? She hasn't had to *do* much of anything except look at Joshua with those eyes of hers. Throw doubt into his mind about his mission. Make him want to throw everything out the window and go to her. The woman's a minx. She makes her living . . . she has a physical way with people that allows her to get what she wants from them. That witch cast her spell on Joshua years before I met him."

"A neighbor lady recommended Mary Towers to me last weekend for a massage: very professional, nothing improper, and it helped. Before that, I never heard of Mary Towers. I would hardly call that a friendship."

"She had nothing to do with your being here?"

"No."

"The other person I'm concerned about is that sheriff whose office you and I visited before we were introduced."

"Why is a religious man like you worrying about the law?" Mikesh asked, his tolerance for Peña soured by this trip to the office.

"You didn't have the talk I did with Paul Fox. I just wanted to make sure that your interest isn't something he's encouraged. Have you been back to see him?"

Mikesh admitted that he had.

"Nosing into things. That's what I thought. I heard Maria ask you to look into what Joshua was doing on the road that night, what happened to cause that accident."

"Joshua asked me to take care of his mom before he died. Other than that, I have no idea why she would have done that."

"And why does the sheriff have you working for him?"

"He doesn't. I just stopped in to find out about the autopsy. Nothing else."

"Have you found out anything while you were sniffing around our affairs?"

"Nothing you don't know yourself."

"Tom King tells me you work security. Maybe that will help you understand. I'm like you, a security man: the security man of Shekinah."

"Who is it you are trying to protect?" Mikesh asked.

"I'm trying to watch out for all of us." Peña paused. "When we drove up to Decorah it was to identify Joshua and make arrangements. But the sheriff also wanted to know what Joshua had been doing, seeing if I had something to do with him leaving Des Moines so quickly after posting bond."

"Posting bond?"

Mikesh was interrupted by the sound of Mom's voice as she greeted Randy in the reception room of the office and appeared in the doorway.

"Maria," Peña said, "I've just been telling Arnie here about how, the day before he died, police arrested Joshua."

Mikesh stood, and my mom took his hands before sitting down. Randy continued tapping at the PA system in the next room. The smell of food and muffled sound of people in the dining area was loud enough to make its way to the office.

"That's not much of a welcome for your visit here." My mother wasn't happy to find Mikesh detained in Simon's office.

"I've just been explaining to him that a lot of the interest in us is not friendly," Simon said, trying to smooth my mom's entry into the conversation.

"I'm glad you're here, Arnie." Mom tried to ease the tension she could feel in the room. "I asked you to come, and I haven't forgotten that you said you would look into what Josh was doing in your neighborhood last week." She smiled, wanting Peña to know that Mikesh was here at her request.

"Simon is right," she continued, "Des Moines was not the first time that the law has had it backwards with Josh, and with us. You see, there were protests in Des Moines. Josh would answer a question even if it was shouted at him. He warmed to it." Mom's tone suggested Josh had been wayward and, try as she may, there was nothing she could do to change him.

"In the hall that Friday, Joshua spoke well, with fire in his heart, and people listened with *their* hearts. But when Josh left the hall something bad happened. Protestors, a couple dozen unfriendly ones, were waiting where they felt their strength."

Randy now appeared at the door, looking worn out.

"That PA isn't going to work today, Simon," he said. "And I need to go down to the kitchen and try a different cord on one of the roasters."

He looked at Mikesh and said before he left, "In this old place, there's always something needs fixing."

Mikesh nodded his head, but didn't want my mother to lose track of her story. "What happened with the protesters?"

"They had signs. On cue they came forward, shouting what you heard at the funeral. A woman got right up to Josh and asked how he could sleep, tearing children from their parents. You can't reason with a group like that," my mom explained, "but Joshua answered her back."

"What did he say?"

"He said all are called by the Spirit. He looked right into the woman's face and added, 'including you, Sister. But only a few answer.'"

"Another man said, 'You tear them away from God,' and Joshua told him that the call comes from the Spirit, that those who are deaf to it are the ones who will suffer. That didn't quiet anybody."

Peña broke in, "Then a guy with a sign that read 'Shekinah=un-Christian=un-American' shouts at Joshua, 'what makes you different from any other communist?'"

My mom took up the story, "Joshua said he answered only the Spirit. So the man said, 'So, you have no allegiance to the American government?' and Josh said, 'I give all the government asks of me. But I don't serve the dollar. I don't worship the dollar like you do!" Mom was growing animated, surprised at the strength that came into her as she repeated my brother's story.

Again, Peña broke in. "You didn't know Joshua. You may be thinking he was all peace and good will. But you see, you don't draw people like Joshua did without the backbone of a military commander. That's one of the things I admired in him. He calls that man a worm, shouts it loud, grabs his sign, takes it away, and breaks its wooden handle over his knee."

Mikesh tried to picture this. Peña was right. This was not the man he imagined from what he had seen in the grainy video.

"There were police, three or four of them, who had been standing in the background all afternoon, just standing, seeing nothing got out of hand. And, you explain this to me, those cops, they waited until that moment to do anything, and what they did was arrest *Joshua* for what they first said was disorderly conduct. By evening the charge was also unlawful assembly," Peña said.

"I thought you said the people assembling were protesting *against* Joshua." The scene didn't make sense to Mikesh.

"That's what a normal person would think," Peña answered, "but when the police took testimony from the protesters, one of them testified that Joshua asked him to stand out there."

"What?"

"He said Joshua put out the word that he wanted a noisy crowd outside the hall to get public attention. The guy said that he figured maybe the whole shouting match was staged. But when the police asked the protestor whose sign Josh broke if he was with Shekinah the man grew angry, said he had nothing to do with us, and that he wanted to press charges against Joshua for breaking his sign, his property. That was a third misdemeanor." Peña was angry as he recounted the events of eight days previous. Mom sat silent, her face tight with restraint.

"Joshua was in there overnight," Peña continued. "The police who dealt with him were *cabrones*. Said he was using them for publicity. Said he was using religion as a dodge for paying taxes, as a cover for some kind of crime syndicate. They interrogated him a long time. When they put him in a cell, it was with two puking drunks and a repeat assault case. They definitely wanted Josh to know he was behind bars. We got a lawyer who had him out on bail the next morning. Joshua was going to have to reappear in court. The morning we got to Decorah, that sheriff you saw had already talked to Des Moines. When he brought me into his office for questioning, he was wondering why Joshua was headed north after a night in jail, tried to make me admit I had been helping him dodge the law, break his bail."

Mikesh was familiar with Fox's line of questioning.

"We should go and join the others," my mom broke in, standing.

Peña stayed in his chair. "Josh was not a person you could manage. I worked military security when I did a tour in Desert Storm. I was comfortable with that, good at my work. But Joshua went where the Spirit moved him. Trying to keep track of him was something else."

Peña gave a confident glance at my mom, "Maria, I think you might say I was the doorkeeper. I still am. Recently every inspector in the state of Iowa has paid a call to see if we are in compliance. Reporters call nosing around, trying to dig up dirt, or trap you. Peña means 'rock' in Spanish. Joshua, between him and me it was one brother to another. In English he called me 'Rocky,' said I was the rock he could lean on. But those days, I guess they're over now." Peña stood up. "I interrupted your welcome, but someone has to keep this place together."

In what had once been a combination kitchen, gym, auditorium, and lunchroom Mikesh found a scene not unlike a benefit supper, anniversary, or wake, but he was surprised by the mix of well over a hundred people—white, brown, and black, each calling the other "brother" and "sister."

My mother brought Mikesh to meet me before the meal, to introduce him around, but we got separated. Arnie required no introduction. The assembly pressed in, waiting in line to shake Mikesh's hand or to hug him. A brother who ran the Sumner, Iowa meat locker was speaking of him as "Brother Arnie," or "the brother here," or "Brother Joshua's last friend in the world."

No one asked for a word about his vigil with my brother. They offered thanks, and most told him a story. Josh's words at a street corner in Sumner seized the butcher like no one else's. Charlenae, a well-spoken woman from Waterloo, said Josh put in place a sanctimonious reverend who bullied her. Josh's touch relieved the pain in the shoulder of a sister from Greene. Josh seemed to know their sorrow or worry before they knew it themselves, as if he could see and decipher the secret language written on their hearts.

Talk calmed to silence when the hall boomed with the same drum Mikesh remembered from the funeral, throbbing and full-throated in the enclosed space. The gathering ordered itself in a large circle with the drum at its center. "Coming together, we are travelers," a high male falsetto voice sang, "Coming to the place where we are one." Mikesh felt the butcher grabbing his one hand, and Charlenae, who had just been speaking to him about my brother's singing voice, grabbing the other. "Coming together, we are travelers, travelers, coming to the place where we are one." Everyone around Mikesh sang, faces kindled with serious energy. Booming, the drumbeat shook him like a palpitation, then stopped. Linda Hanson's voice said, "Brothers, Sisters, enter into the Spirit."

People shook hands and hugged. "Bless you Brother." "Spirit fill you Sister." "The light shine in you."

Though he had enjoyed open-air music festivals, where people were as likely to pass a joint or a bottle as say hello, Mikesh felt uneasy. I rescued him as people set up chairs and tables. At the end of the room where my mother was unfolding chairs, I asked him to join us, saying, "Sorry I abandoned you."

At the front of the room, Peña fanned the flames in a sage pot, pulling smoke over himself as if bathing. Then he fanned it outward. "Fire in you!" he said, turning in a slow circle and repeating the ritual once for each direction. "Fire in you!" He faced the group and said in a loud voice, "Flesh becomes Fire. Let's walk in the Spirit's path."

As Mikesh found a chair, Linda/Naomi Schmidt Hanson chose the one beside him. He thought about the scrapbook Evelyn Schmidt had given him a few days earlier, a mixture of printed announcements, news stories, and sheets printed from the Internet. One news story included a picture of Sister Naomi: a *Courier* feature about the Manna Loaves bakery, written in chirpy confidential amazement at the odd customs of queer religious folk living a life set aside as the normal world sped past around them. Naomi was quoted: "It's tasty bread, leavened by the Spirit." In red ballpoint, Evelyn had scrawled "Brainwashed!" next to the clipping.

As the food was passed, and the room was getting noisy again, Linda/Naomi spoke to Mikesh, introducing herself. Mikesh noticed Naomi's hair, wrapped in braids wound in antique fashion around the top of her head. She wore jeans, and a fleece vest. Mikesh responded by saying he had seen the article and her picture, and noticed her at the funeral. He worked the conversation around to how she had gotten involved with Shekinah, hoping to go from there to her life before, and Evelyn's concern.

"People get lost," she told him. "*I* got lost. I was drifting, but that doesn't mean I was standing still. No, I was sucked down. Joshua knew that. He found me and reached out. He brought me into the life I'd been meant to live all along."

Mikesh thought back to the story Evelyn Schmidt had told him: "You say he knew about you being lost. How did he know that?"

"A woman I knew, who attended house meetings, told him about me, and Joshua sought me out, repeated the Spirit's call to my own ears. You know, Arnie, the Spirit is always calling. But she calls different people in different ways. Right now she's calling to you too, calling you to enter in."

Sister Naomi's eyes fixed on Mikesh. "You may think you just happened by the spot where Joshua was dying. I think different. I think that was a moment of call for you. The Spirit opened a window, called you in. Of all the thousands of people who could have been there at that moment, you *were* the one. That tells me your call is a strong one, Arnie, like mine."

Naomi continued, "Tom told me what Joshua said. 'Enter' is what he told you. 'Join me.' Joshua spoke those same words to me when I was a slut in a small-town bar at the moment I needed to quit drifting or sink. Joshua showed me that I was called to something better; I was made with another plan in mind. I have been thinking about how Joshua died. I believe he knew you were coming. He would have sensed you. He was holding on before entering into the Spirit, a joyful thing for him, but holding out, waiting for you. You should look into your own heart and ask if you are going where you're meant to be going, or drifting, or like I was, heading into a dreary place, an evil place."

Naomi had mentioned my name. I broke in, "Naomi, Arnie is here because he accepted my invitation to tell us about his moments with Josh. You could say Arnie answered *my* call."

"That may or may not be the same as the Spirit's call, Tom." Sister Naomi gave me a sharp look. Naomi is not an unkind woman, but she is direct. I decided it might be better to change the subject.

"Sister Naomi is from up in your part of the world, Arnie. She comes from New Hampton."

"Yes," Mikesh replied, "we didn't get the chance to talk about it, but her mother Evelyn works at the same place I do. I know her."

Naomi studied Mikesh. He said, "She told me that if I saw you I should greet you from her. She misses you."

"She misses a person who doesn't exist anymore. You could say I'm her daughter. But what you probably don't understand is that the person I *was* is dead. That life I was living, it wasn't the life I was meant to be living. My mom doesn't understand that."

This set of mind horrified Evelyn. But for Mikesh, Sister Naomi's words about the bar life she was not meant to live triggered a memory from Chicago, years ago. He was married, setting out with the woman he loved, in a world where everything seemed possible. But the memory that came to him was from 1991, of a downtown club below an "L" track by the river, him trapped at the back of a booth. The men around him were talking about real estate, about how their jobs were not offering the money needed to buy the lakeside condos they wanted to own. The man on his left was in banking, angry at how the feds were throwing money around to save the savings and loan industry, but tying down banks with restrictions, and giving nothing back in return. The man on his right, working in insurance, hated everything about his job, his office, his boss. These two were friends of an account executive, who stood talking with Arnie's wife Audra. Animated, she was stroking an earlobe as she looked up at him. Her brunette hair was pulled back, exposing her long neck. Her large round earrings glinted as she shook her head, evidently delighted with their conversation. Later she told Mikesh this was a show. The man could help her get an account she wanted. The account executive loved to dance. Mikesh could see this, and when Audra turned to the dance floor, Mikesh saw that his wife's long jacket with the big padded shoulders was cut away to expose a beautiful oval of her back. He saw the man place his hand there, fingers against her skin, to guide her into the mix of dancers. They disappeared as Mikesh's companions lamented the world, their work, their lives. Their conversation made him think hard about his own work, his lack of joy in processing paper, talking on the phone. Audra dancing with the account executive made him conscious of his uneven legs, his orthopedic shoe. This was his bad moment in a bar. Mikesh thought, when he may have been drifting, but drifting toward what, at the time, he did not know. Sister Naomi wanted him to believe he was drifting toward a car wreck between St. Lucas and Fort Atkinson.

But Naomi was talking about Evelyn. "She does not hear the call She doesn't approve of me. She hasn't for a long time. And she doesn't realize that *this* is my family now. *This* is my life."

Naomi shifted her gaze, directing her comments back to me. "You're lucky to have your whole family be part of this, Tom. It isn't an issue for you. But for me, there's no going back. What used to be my family is thirty miles north, and my new family, my new home is here."

"Your mother says your name is Linda," Mikesh began.

"Naomi is a name she gave me. Except she made it my middle name. When I came here, I reclaimed it. It's my biblical name."

"For what it's worth, your mother told me she loves you. She wants you back. She isn't so different than other mothers, spending lots of time thinking about her children, anxious about her grandchildren."

"If she could join us. If my boys could join us, then we'd have that family back again. But the world conspires against us. Evelyn isn't about to move here. The law of the land is not about to give me full custody of my sons. I've committed everything. There isn't any other way for me to commit. My boys have been taken hostage, but I'm not about to surrender. One day they'll understand. In the eye of eternity, my choice is right. I hope, Arnie, you find a certainty of call, too."

Their conversation was interrupted by a red-haired woman across the table, raising her voice as she talked to Maria about the funeral protestors, why the state patrolman had not done more to stop them. "A woman with a big three-color sign saying 'God is avenged' was spitting at me, saying I was going to burn in hell. Spitting! The law is supposed to protect a person. We could have been market steers passing by to the slaughter for all that man cared."

The Big House was uneasy. Between hecklers, state inspectors, and law enforcement, Josh's followers were getting the message that they were not wanted.

When the tables had been taken down and the dishes washed, the chairs shifted into rings, Peña stood and said, "By the Spirit our bodies have been fed. We are called to enter into the Spirit, to consider the light within. Joshua was often with us in the past. He is no longer here to speak to us. We're blessed today with the company of Brother Mikesh. When he feels moved, he'll tell us about Joshua's last moments." Here there was applause. "Remember Joshua. Let's put ourselves in a place where the Spirit may find a voice. If you feel it, let that voice speak."

In the quiet that followed Mikesh tried to gauge when it would be best to say something. A man who liked the sound of his own voice broke the silence, saying he was thankful that, though Brother Joshua had been taken from them, the people gathered had been protected from harm. It was a sign that the Spirit was watching out for them. The red-haired woman said she was fearful they would be pulled their separate ways, that with so many set against them, this would happen soon. "I've been feeling lost, and crying," she said. Peña stood. Mikesh noted that, bearded and burly, the man made a sizeable dent in the room.

Peña said that Josh's death made it important to remember what he taught them, to tell each other the stories about Josh's work, the Spirit entering their lives. "You may have heard this before, but some of you may not know how I met Joshua back when I was still working as a welder down in Waterloo, living by myself. I was respectable, but without much compass. My main passion, what I lived for, was fishing. It was a Thursday in August, a busy month when you work construction, but my homie Andy and I were bound to get out on the water after work. We picked Brinker Lake, close enough to do a couple hours of fishing in Andy's bass boat.

"When we got there I saw this young guy, he's got four or five kids with him. This was Joshua, just about the time he was starting in Waterloo, a few months in, and he's working with homeless kids. They're unloading picnic supplies and fishing gear from an old van. My first thought was to pity the guy. That lake access is just a parking lot and a ramp, and a good view of the Highway 218 overpass. Kind of a miserable place if all you are going to do is bank fishing. But what I found once Andy and I got out on the water was, it didn't matter that we had a boat. It was a bad evening to fish, sticky and hot. Not so much as a bite. After about an hour we gave up. As we got close to the ramp the sun was low, and we saw a crackling campfire. Joshua was down by the water's edge, coaching one of the boys who was reeling in a decent sunfish. As we cut the motor to glide in, I said to Joshua—voices carry across water—'I should have had you help us out. We got skunked!'

"Joshua looks up and says, 'Yes, you could have done better. There's good fishing out there tonight.' That took me off guard. I was just being friendly, maybe a little envious. I didn't expect that answer. So I asked him. 'Where would you fish?' 'Since you're using lures, I'd say off the far side and south end of the island,' he says, just like that, 'at two or three feet down.'"

Peña had a big voice as he told this story, a story he had told many times. Compared to the din of the place when Mikesh entered two hours before, it was very quiet.

"Andy and I decided, what the heck? Normally I wouldn't have listened to a stranger, bad as our luck had been, but he said it so sure. We roared out around that island, out of sight from where Joshua was fishing. For lures we used pink zappers with a white tail, and BAM! they hit right away. A school of yellow bass were going nuts, which that kind of fish will do. We started to fill the fish basket we put over the side of the boat, but quit keeping them, just throwing them back and catching a new one. Throwing them back, catching another. That can happen with yellow bass. But, and this is where it gets weird, the bass left off and crappies started to hit. And the crappies were bigger than the bass. Fishing was so lively our arms were tired from reeling and we were throwing most of the crappies back. Then I hook into a little one: hardly more drag as I reel than just the lure, except its zigzagging like a fish will do. I joke with Andy about how our luck is taking a turn for the worse. Andy's still reeling in fair-sized crappie, and I'm paying more attention to Andy's fish. I'm just kind of toying with the little one, hardly even bothering to reel, when something else hits my line. What I think happened was that the little fish I hooked saw the big fish coming and jerked free, leaving my lure as consolation prize. Suddenly my line is whining because whatever it is, it's pulling out line, and then breaks the surface: the biggest largemouth bass I've ever seen on that lake. And I've hooked him on bait a largemouth wouldn't normally touch. Reeling took some skill. I gave him plenty of play to wear him out so he wouldn't snap that line. He filled that dip net: thrashing like a monster, his back as big and muscular as a python. It was only after he quieted in the net and I was about to lift him out that I remembered—we're out here because of what the guy had told us back at the ramp. In all our fun, I'd forgotten about him.

"I tell Andy, 'That's enough. Let's not get greedy. They aren't going to get any bigger than this. It's dusk now.' I tell you *hermanos, hermanas,* life was good! So we head on in. As we pull up to the ramp again I see the campfire still burning, nobody fishing, just the fire settling down. As I get out at the landing I hear the sound of voices. The boys, Joshua, they're sitting around the fire. I can smell the smoke—one of the nicer smells in the world, oak almost burned down to coals. While Andy is winching the boat onto the trailer I walk up there. The boys are talking and laughing so they don't notice me, but Joshua is facing my direction, and he's watching. I go over, he stands, and I thank him. 'We were skunked, and now I just had the best luck I've ever had in my life. I want to thank you,' I tell him.

"He nods his head as if he knew, and said, 'If you keep listening to me, you'll pull in people the way, tonight, you pulled in fish.'

"'Pull in?' I said, feeling almost creepy, 'what do you mean, pull in people?' I was picturing dead bodies, accident victims in Brinker Lake.

"But Joshua meant something else. 'I have work for you,' he tells me. 'I am here to call people to the Spirit. One day you'll call in more people than I do.'

"I asked him who he was. He said his name. And I don't mind telling you I was happy to get out of there, but I kept thinking about that night. I had that largemouth bass mounted, and months later, seeing that trophy on the wall above my television. I realized what Joshua's words meant. I could do a great work for him, a big work, something bigger than I ever imagined. And from that moment, that's what I've been trying to do."

Listening to Peña's tale, Mikesh almost felt he could like him. Others in the room, having heard the story about the fish before, watched, curious about Mikesh's reaction. They had not come to hear Peña, but to listen to him, and the looks in his direction signaled it was time. Walking to the front of the cafeteria, turning his back to the compact stage that had allowed the room to serve double duty as a school auditorium, he looked out at half circles of folding chairs, row after row of brown, black, and white people in business casual who searched his face for what he would tell them. He thanked Peña, and then unfolded his whole account of the accident scene, this time naming the melody from Josh's lips as the "Coming Together" song.

Finished, he grew uncomfortable. Every eye was directed at him. A woman raised her voice, "So he didn't have a message for anybody here?" When Mikesh shook his head "no," another woman asked, "And he didn't tell you where he was going?" There it was, the mystery with which my mom had tasked him. He replied that Josh had asked him to "*join* him in infinity. Nothing beyond that." A man said, "That's all we need to know. That's where he told us he was going. It's where he was coming from, we know that." A brief rumble of commentary filled the room. Brother Randy asked if Mikesh had noticed anything he had not mentioned. "I'd like to picture Joshua's last moments, put myself there with him. It'd provide me comfort."

"Well, I would just say again that the fog and the temperature made it very cold out there. The engine was cold. Joshua was not wearing a jacket. His skin was cold to the touch, even though he was still breathing. I felt sorry for him, though at that point I didn't even know who he was."

"Thank you, Brother," Randy said, before the place broke into wild applause. As it was dying, a voice Mikesh could not identify followed with, "So you *did* hear him stop breathing? You were sure, out there, that he was dead?"

I looked steadily at Mikesh. I warned him someone would want to hear this from him. Was my remarkable brother a person who could die?

"Yes," Mikesh answered. "I knew he had stopped breathing and that he was dead." Silence deepened. "Another thing I didn't say before. It was just my personal feeling. I was *hoping* he wasn't dead, wishing he was holding on, even though I couldn't feel any breath, or hear any breathing. That's the reason I kept my hand on his face, even though he had grown still. I hoped there was some spark. But no. In the end, he was dead."

Mikesh broke down. He lost emotional control in a way he had not, until that moment, done. I rose and put my arm around his shoulders, thanking him. A voice somewhere in the group began singing.

Once the assembly broke up, Mom and I toured Mikesh around the Big House: its industrial kitchen, lounges; nursery and schoolroom; men's, women's, and married corridors. Mom explained that some who came married, "lived on that way," but others "gave up their married life for a new life. That's not a choice I had to make," she said. "The father of my boys left me years ago. I sold up and moved here to help Joshua and live on the women's corridor. Joshua believed that solitary life left me open to the Spirit, that me being a single mother was part of his inspiration. I won't say I appreciated being left alone all those years, raising the boys single, but Josh helped me see there could have been a purpose in it."

Tired as he drove from the Big House, Mikesh eased his truck west along the edge of town. The last residences out of sight, he turned north on the lonely access road leading to Highway 63. A pair of headlights appeared in his rearview mirror. Blue and red flashers throbbed. There wasn't much shoulder, but he steered onto what he could find, lowered the driver's window, and cut the engine, wondering what could have attracted the attention of the law.

The flashlight didn't pause at his plates. Mikesh had to shield his eyes; the beam pointed directly into his face.

"What's the problem, officer?" Mikesh peered under his fingers.

"Hands down! There's a smell in this cab I don't like."

Behind the flashlight Mikesh heard sniffing.

"Why did you pull me over?"

"I'm supposed to be asking the questions here." The voice was sharp, tenor.

Mikesh made out a uniform, the gleam of a metallic badge, and the man's features: cropped pale hair, pug nose. Anger constricted Mikesh's throat, his breathing shallow.

"Just wanted to know why you stopped me."

"Public safety for starters, sir. You can't swerve in and out of the opposing lane."

"Was I doing that—swerving?"

"I need to see your driver's license and proof of insurance."

When Mikesh turned the latch, the glove compartment fell open. A small plastic bag glinted in the deputy's flashlight beam. As Mikesh's eyes adjusted, he could tell it held dried green leaves. He turned his head to the lawman.

"Looks like we've got a problem, sir. You're going to need to get out of this truck."

The deputy backed him from the cab, ordered him to lean out from the Chevy and submit to a slow pat-down. Mikesh flinched as the hand lingered against the crotch of his jeans. The officer drew his gun, walked him to the back of the truck, angry about Mikesh "trying something," shouted at him to lie face down, and snapped on handcuffs. Alone beneath the frenzied strobes, left cheek against the icy earth, legs spread in a wide V, Mikesh could do nothing but lie humiliated and helpless, raging at somebody's success at framing him in the cold eyes of the law.

CHAPTER 14

RIDDEN HARD. STABLED WET. That's how Mikesh described to himself his feelings the next morning. It hadn't suited him to ride in a squad car to Waverly or to spend the night on a vinyl-covered mattress in the disinfected half-light of a Bremer County jail cell, eyes boring through the plaster ceiling as he fumed about his fate. His insulated cotton jacket, stained in blood, was in the evidence room of one county; this bag of weed was evidence in another. In nine days' time his life had twisted out of recognition. When Mikesh called Dale Murphy at six a.m. to ask him to look after the animals, he also asked him to find a lawyer who would appear with him at eleven o'clock that day for a bail hearing. Once Mikesh arranged for bail, paid for his impounded truck, and bid goodbye to the lawyer, he was a free man until an arraignment hearing in five days.

In fact, Mikesh was *very* free. By the time he had talked over his situation with Barbara and Dale, and returned to his farm, the phone was ringing. His work supervisor was on the line to say that given the charges, already aired on the evening news, a state community college would not look right leaving security in the hands of a man charged with drug possession. He was formally on leave until further notice.

Disassembled, Mikesh's mood had not bottomed this deeply since his wife divorced him. He was going to be found guilty of pot possession, lose his job. His name, even now, was being talked about over the dinner table in five or six rural counties of Iowa: the state employee with a taste for weed. And it all connected to Josh.

I called Mikesh later that night to say how sorry I was for what had happened. By turns angry and quiet he blamed Shekinah and the law. He downed beers to calm his nerves, and by the time I talked to him, nothing was making clear sense, except that he was not having anything more to do with the residents of the Big House. In the short term, his bottle therapy worked. He passed out on his couch.

Tuesday morning, head throbbing, he decided to see Mary Towers again. When he called, he explained that what she heard via local news wasn't true, that someone was framing him. He couldn't tell whether she was shocked or amused, but she said she could see him at eleven the next day for a massage and told him to leave some time for lunch. For the first time since Sunday, the tiniest shaft of light cracked the unmitigated darkness of Mikesh's situation.

On Wednesday, as Mary's practiced hands pushed and coaxed the knotted-up pieces of Mikesh's back into place, Mikesh wondered whether this would help as much as the last time on her table. Today he was job-less and an accused criminal. His gut clenched. After she massaged his back, Mary asked him, gently, about the feeling in his arms, his neck, his hands, as her hands worked those places. She directed him to extend his fingers, turn his head. She focused on his right leg, directing him to extend his toes, wondered about tightness in his calf. She moved to the left leg, the short one. With the arrest on his mind, he had not thought about the leg that gave him the gait of a penguin when he walked without a corrective sole and heel. He spoke about that as her grip ran down the stressed left calf, as she pressed her thumbs into the bottom center of that mismatched foot, took each toe and gently pulled. Mary described the strain that walking on unevenness placed on his legs and back. He listened, recognizing, in her words, symptoms he had experienced since he was thirteen years old. Mary went back to the calf and repeated the process, this time saying nothing. Mikesh's sadness was not gone. Mary's treatment opened up the floodgate of a deeper, and long-held-back grief over the peculiar twisting of his frame. Tears came to his eyes, but behind them was relief. With the flats of her hands she pushed against the sole of his left foot, as if to re-set his whole lower leg into the joints of knee and thigh. She gave his foot quick squeezes, as if to awaken it from sleep. With her last touch of that foot, the session over, even more than the first time, each cell of Mikesh's body registered a keen sense of energy and release. Peña said Mary knew how to get her way with people. If this was her way, it was all right with Mikesh. Mary had asked him to stay for lunch. She left Mikesh to put on his clothes, and from her direction he heard the clink of pots and plates.

The tall windows of the apartment looked out on the wooded creek that flowed across the back of Decorah. The houses in the distance stacked up a hill steeper than those in the countryside where Mikesh lived. The orange-walled sitting room he entered was piled with books. A large antique wooden dining table with mismatched chairs waited in the center. As he walked in, Mary was slicing bread on a bottle-blue countertop in the alcove of the kitchen that opened to the sitting room, placing the slices on a sunburst yellow plate. A large gray cat stared with golden eyes from the top of a refrigerator old enough to have been called an icebox. Jars of dried spices, grain, beans, and fruit sat in rows on the counter around her.

"Make yourself at home," Mary said. He felt both shy and awkward, and offered to help. She handed him dishes and silverware.

The tall and roomy proportions of the apartment made Mikesh feel small as they sat down to eat. It was an echo of his impulse to run on his previous visit, so he focused on the bread he was chewing. Airy inside, flavored with small dusky rosemary leaves, its crust was solid enough to make him really use his teeth: manna from Sicily.

He decided to start with the last time they had been together.

"You disappeared pretty quickly after the funeral."

"That was a mistake. Maria has always been sweet, and I owed a lot to Josh. I should have said something to her."

Mary had declined to join Mikesh talking to my mom in the graveyard when she saw Mom surrounded by a group that included Peña.

Mikesh, for his part, wanted to hear about Mary's link to Josh. "You haven't told me anything about your history with those people."

"Nothing mysterious about it. Josh and I met when he went to college here. I have a technical degree now, but then, straight out of high school, I'd started working in town. We hit it off, and we've kept in contact off and on ever since."

"What do you mean, 'hit it off?'"

Mary Towers always startled at men's need to size up what they perceive as other men's territory.

"I was a townie. Josh was a college boy a year younger than me, and he helped me through a rough patch. He didn't care that I wasn't college material. He could tell I was a country kid like him. So we *hit it off*. We got along."

She was wary, in part because she didn't want to picture the boy of fourteen years past, with wild curls, the love of walking barefoot, the curve of the eyes beneath his lids so beautiful it hurt. Though Mary's depression was no longer clinical, she fought the heaviness that descended at any time, a door weighted with stone. But memories broke through. She was smelling air charged with alcohol and smoke in the west-side apartment. Two college boys had met her at the downtown bar and urged her to accompany them to the party, where she experienced their heady rush of talk and increasing familiarity, their keen attraction to her, their hands on her shoulders, the longer meetings of her glance as they drank beer pumped from an aluminum keg sweating in a busy corner of the kitchen. She didn't know it, but they slipped GHB into her beer. When she blacked out, Josh, who arrived with a friend and heard the pair discussing their plan once the drug took effect, stepped forward. Josh said he was an EMT and that Mary was having an anaphylactic response to something she'd consumed. He would take her to the emergency room. The two, she found out later, tried to stop him, but lost their nerve, evaporated. Josh loaded her into his roommate's car. When she woke up she was under a blanket, sitting in the passenger seat, on a high hilltop just off the highway at the edge of town. Josh had rescued her only to realize he didn't know where the unfamiliar girl lived. Because she wasn't carrying identification he also wondered whether she was of legal drinking age. He could not take her to his dorm. Instead he found this picnic spot just outside the city limits and parked, turned off the lights, and covered her with a blanket. She awakened and vomited. When she first threw up, Josh, a boy she did not recognize, was standing outside watching for the sun. As she stood in the cold, wrapped in the blanket, with Josh cleaning off the dashboard with a snow scraper and tissues, the red sun rose over the far side of the valley.

In those days Mary didn't care much for herself. She knew how it felt to wake in the morning without memory of the previous night, with a headache, perhaps bruises, in a strange but empty rumpled bed, or next to a head of hair she didn't recognize. She defended her independence, living on her own, but when a man was steely in his insistence, her frontal cortex switched off her power to assert herself, leaving her as numb and limp as a patient on an operating table. Mary's cells craved that too, the familiar oblivion of giving up, giving in, making time stop. The morning after her first encounter with Josh, shivering in a blanket, at the edge of a hilltop wood where a predator could easily dump her body, she was confused, then angry, and then hysterical. But the hectic exertions of the

unfamiliar boy with the ice scraper over her vomit made her realize she
was not in any danger.

The following evening Josh stopped by after her shift at the bolts and
fittings factory and made her dinner. He did the same on two subsequent
evenings. She told him off, showing her rough side, but she did not tell
him to go. Then they would walk.

Sitting at the table with Mikesh, Mary mentioned neither feelings
nor details. "Josh was a wonder! I couldn't help but like him." She broke
some bread and placed it in her mouth.

She pictured the night, maybe ten days after she met Josh, when he
had lots of homework and couldn't come by until after dinner. He wasn't
cooking for her anymore, but they'd grown comfortable with each other.
The temperature was in the mid-eighties during a late-summer spell of
heat. The apartment she shared with two other girls above a downtown
café was two floors up and stuffy, no air conditioning. Mary and Josh
went for a walk beyond the college side of town, out along the river. Under a half moon, the glassy song of crickets pulsed in the night air. Dew
clung to the grass. She heard water rushing over rocks.

Josh told her he wished he could go back in time to when people
lived in villages, often on the move. There were places where people still
lived like that, he told her. Not that long ago bands and tribes of people
lived in temporary villages. Mary and Josh were by the highway then. They
walked up to the concrete pavement and crossed the bridge, stopping to
study the river, then strolled a short stretch of gravel that paralleled the
river at the base of a wooded hill. Before they reached the trees, Josh
grabbed Mary's elbow to have her stop. Unused to his touch, she shivered,
anticipating what he wanted. They were far from the streetlights. Joshua
searched the sky. He helped her find three stars in a line, Orion's belt. He
helped her imagine the hunter who wore the belt, pointing out the other
stars in the constellation.

"Look at the bright star that makes up his shoulder on the left. That's
Betelgeuse," he said. "The light reaching us from that star was thrown out
into space before Columbus. When that light left that star, people here
were sitting in a circle around the fire at night, testing their eyes by stars
they could see. For them, Orion's belt was the backbone of an animal.
Betelgeuse was the edge of the animal's ribs."

Mary wasn't used to talking about stars or thinking about the sky,
but it was as if she could feel the touch of that slim point of old light
hitting her cheek as she looked up to find it. She could not imagine the

long-dead world Josh was talking about any more than she could see the
color of the nighttime trees, but she blindly sensed herself near a place
where people sat nightly around a fire, telling stories about animals made
of stars. Mary and Josh continued down the road through the woods at
the base of the abandoned ski-run hill in the county park where the river
made a deep bend. Josh said, "Mary, let's go for a swim."

He took off his shoes in the parking lot and picked his way ahead of
her down a path. He had grown up on a river, and was excited, hopping
around like a kid. She complained that she didn't want river water on her
clothes.

"Where'd you grow up? You don't need clothes," he said.

He took off his shirt and folded it on a log. She was hesitant, told
him she wasn't sure. He said to wade in further up the bank to their left.
She walked a few steps, but turned to see Josh, white and vapory in the
moonlight. He was a cross country runner, long and wiry. It was too
murky to see his face, but she saw the pale slash his body made against
the shadow of hillside. The body disappeared, like an apparition, with
each step he took into the water, making her afraid.

She was mad at Josh. She didn't want to swim in dirty water, but
didn't want him to think her scared or soft. Where she stood on the sand,
she heard contented splashing mingling with the sound of night insects
and the occasional car thumping in the distance as it climbed the hill
north toward Minnesota. She found the star that made the shoulder of
the hunter. Betelgeuse. The animal's rib. She stepped out of her clothes
and waded in to the cold, startling water. The bottom of mud and sand
shifted out from under her toes. When the water surrounded her waist
she dove to erase the shock. When she came up downstream, she could
see Josh's face ahead of her, maybe thirty feet away, a white moon on the
rippled surface.

He swam backwards downstream and asked her how she liked the
water.

"Josh?" Her voice carried across the riffles. 'How old is that
starlight?'"

"Same age as us," he laughed and splashed the water with his feet as
he kicked back toward her.

The cosmos, in that instant, went inside out. Instead of her being an
insignificant twenty-year-old girl in the world, she contained the world.
She contained the universe and all its stars, planets, and people. She felt
an enormous surge of desire to embrace Josh. But when she swam to him

and touched his shoulder, he said "hey!" and pushed himself away. His rebuff slammed her into her small cold body, but she was charged with riotous fire. She splashed after him, as if he had initiated a game of tag. She grabbed his arm, but Josh was not playful.

"Mary, let's just swim," he said.

She laughed and splashed water in his face. He didn't splash back, but swam toward the highway. He feared her and she knew it. She contained constellations. She knew everything. Happy in this sensation, she swam toward her clothes.

The memory of Josh, swimming from her under the night sky, distracted her, as Mary decided how to explain to Mikesh how she and Josh "hit it off." She recollected how, as she returned to the sand bar, walking in the moonlight, she saw herself moon-colored, just as she had seen Josh. By the light of that ancient star she experienced an unfamiliar feeling of being beautiful and powerful. Josh's defensive push had been unexpected, but affirming. She had a power that scared him. Shivering in the starlight, she slowly pushed the water off her skin. She could still hear Josh swimming, like a fish surfacing in the water. She thought, let him see me. I want that.

As she dressed, she heard a car moving on gravel. Headlights flashed through the trees. Josh splashed his way back to shore to get his things as she untwisted a bra strap and snapped it in place, pulled on her shirt, and stepped into her sandals. When she got to him he was pulling his sleeves over the clinging wetness of his arms. The car stopped in the parking lot; its engine turned off. She joined Josh on the log where he was working to get shoes and socks over wet feet and ankles, and she whispered that somebody, a couple, was probably there to make out. He bolted through the woods to the entrance driveway. By the time they walked down the road towards town she was laughing at him, and he was annoyed and quiet.

Mary told Josh she was glad they'd gone swimming. The swim, she guessed, was a way of seeing if he could control himself around a naked girl. What he hadn't been counting on was not being able to control *her*.

From the perspective of her early thirties, Mary held the opinion that on that night she was reborn. That night she realized her place and power in the world. Had it been her first time out with a boy, she might have felt crushed, but she'd been with plenty of boys and men. For them, she'd been no more than their little machine, with a small-town reputation for being easy. Josh, who came from elsewhere, was clean. Josh was interested in stars, skinny-dipping, talk, but not much touch. Mary was intrigued.

As Josh walked her home she chattered with joy, free to say whatever came to mind. They strolled the sidewalk like a very old couple who'd been together for years. She felt an excited, pleasurable chill. That was ten years before Josh started his religious teaching, but Mary believed he led to her infinity, not through words about the Spirit, but by pointing out the star that made the unknown animal's rib.

"I was Josh's first convert," Mary told Mikesh. "He converted me from a person who didn't believe in myself to someone who did." That's how she explained "hitting it off." Mary told Mikesh how she and Josh stayed friends through that year of college, going to movies, a couple of parties, and more walks. Josh went on a trip that January to Israel, Egypt, and Turkey as part of a religion class, and became more preoccupied and distant. Just when Mary was set to suggest they be more than friends, he was gone. The next fall Josh did not return to school. Through a college contact, he found a position as a summer volunteer in the Indian Health Service clinic at Pine Ridge in South Dakota. In the years his classmates were finishing college, he worked as an orderly, a janitor, an aide and co-director in the Oglala youth center.

"He left for South Dakota," Mary continued. "Have you ever been to Pine Ridge, Arnie? Dry grass prairie and big stone hills, and not much to make a living from, one of the emptiest places on the whole planet." She paused. "Josh went out there after he left Decorah. He said he got his college degree and seminary training there all at once."

"What was he studying?"

She answered by quoting Josh's odd words. "Elementary and advanced beatitude."

"What does *that* mean?"

Mary laughed. "That's what I said, too. He said beatitudes are from the Bible, what Jesus says is beautiful, blessed. Josh said that the Oglala— and these are his exact words—are world masters of poverty, no-account-edness, and patience."

"Did he take some sort of classes?"

Mary and a friend drove out to see him, not the kind of vacation her girlfriend had imagined, but it got Mary to Josh. They found him working in a kitchen, overseeing pick-up basketball. He seemed thinner, drawn, and pulled his curls back in a braid. He regularly ran across the

miles of flat spaces. But he had a rough time—swinging between gener-
ous welcome and hospitality from his hosts to aggression: a couple of
fights, one of which became a pounding, ending with two cracked ribs
and a broken nose, nights where there was no one to talk to until, finally,
one of the families took him in.

Mary could picture how the three of them drove to the home two
miles from the town center. Outside, a refrigerator and a box spring
leaned against the enclosed porch. They were greeted by a small boy and
the smell of wood smoke. Behind the child came the grandmother, Lucille
Walks Out, drying her hands on a towel. Walks Out became a mother to
Josh, her two boys his brothers. They took Josh into the country to visit
friends and to hunt. Through Walks Out's sons, Josh got religious training, learned the rituals of Oglala men, activities that made Mary wince.
But Josh was devoted to Lucille. In a place where few had jobs, every job
political, she backed Josh in being hired at the makeshift youth center
after the health service stint was over, a position for which he got a trailer
and food allowance. Though Josh had no car, he could hike to the Walks
Out place and was always welcome at Lucille's table.

After a few years there Josh went to Arizona, working at a Catholic
Mission. Mary never found the right excuse to visit. After that, Mexico.
While in South Dakota and Arizona Josh came home once or twice each
year, and Mary saw him then. For the two years in Mexico, nothing. He
told her that in Mexico he was going to live on a mountain. A vision
quest, she thought, a rite he described to her in South Dakota. But she
learned later that his place in Mexico had not been rocky and uninhab-
ited, but a village, where he most often worked in the fields. In Denver
for three years Josh worked for the Latino Chamber of Commerce in a
residence program that provided alternatives to drugs and trafficking for
Mexican gang bangers. Then he returned to Iowa, to begin his own work.

What kept Josh moving around? Mary wondered if he was afraid
of attaching to one place, one set of friends or fear of intimacy with the
women he met in travel: a troubled girl; a mother of the children he fed
after school, swept up after, or coached; or a lonely woman ready to cook
for him, who enjoyed hearing him talk and ask questions. These speculations she pondered in her heart, letting Mikesh stick to the bare facts of
Josh's changes of address.

"And it all stopped just outside St. Lucas, Iowa," Mikesh said, running a piece of broken bread across the food leavings on his plate. "Funny

place to end up after all that." Once again he was reminded of how little he knew about my brother.

"I don't know," Mary said, trying to explain. "Josh said he was called to the places he ended up. He said that big or small they were home to people you would not run across in a glossy magazine, places you would not see advertised in the living and travel sections of a newspaper. That would fit St. Lucas as much as Pine Ridge."

Mikesh thought of the silence in that road ditch, and the smell of cattle in the air. Sister Naomi insisted that Mikesh had been "called" to that road ditch too. Mary was using the same language used by Linda Naomi Schmidt Hanson who Josh had called in a New Hampton watering place. My brother and the people whose lives he touched believed in a call. Mikesh thought of the anger he'd bumped up against in Evelyn. Contact with my brother had been delivering electric jolts to people before Josh went off in search of his life mission.

"Why didn't you get closer to him, once he came back?" Mikesh asked Mary. "Why not move to the Big House?"

"I knew Joshua before he became the leader those people follow. He didn't use phrases like 'shadow and desire' to describe the world I can feel through my hands. He saw it as a place touched by stars." She blushed, not wanting to explain to Mikesh how fully that was true. "To move down to that old school in Bremer County would mean giving up my place here, getting up in the morning and going to bed at night with women who spend every day learning not to listen to their muscles and their bones. They wrap their heads inside the blanket of the Spirit. How could I do that? I would be making me disappear."

Mary knew that Josh's call to the Spirit demanded denial: discipline he had been experimenting with when he pushed her away in the river; a discipline he deepened in his course in beatitude at Pine Ridge; a discipline he lived by as he tried to reorient the lives of Hispanic kids whose necks were ringed with tattoos and whose veins had been torn up by poison. Her friendship with Josh shouldn't require that she erase what she knew, that she lose the convictions that had saved her own life, her own recovery, and the education she pursued to become a massage therapist.

"I like and respect Josh, but I also like and respect myself. And, Arnie, before it began with all those other people, Josh taught me I was a person of integrity, that I was worthy of love."

CHAPTER 15

BEING A MAN WITHOUT a job unsettled Mikesh. He found it harder to get up in the morning. He stayed on the farm. Going into Waucoma meant facing people who, whether they said so or not, saw him as a man with a taste for marijuana that he couldn't keep from the law. Mikesh was standing at the counter in his kitchen, eating a cold bowl of cereal late Thursday morning, when the phone rang. An unfamiliar woman's voice sounded nervous, talking fast. She said she heard him speak at the Big House. His manner, what happened to him when he left, made her hope he might be a person she could trust because she might need refuge. After riding into Waterloo with a sister going to work, she hitched her way to the convenience store in Waucoma and was calling from their phone. Would Mikesh mind getting her? She needed to talk.

When Mikesh pulled up, the figure who opened the door of his pickup was tiny. Her pale neck looked fragile between the collar of the puffy down jacket and ribbed stocking cap over her ears. She had an underfed appearance and carried a large cloth shoulder bag that she pushed before her onto the seat.

"Hey, thanks," she said, as she shut the door. "I had a hard time thinking where I could go. I'm glad you were home."

"How old are you?"

"I'm twenty-four. Why?"

"Just wondering if maybe it would be good to check in with your family." Mikesh would have guessed she was seventeen.

With ice-blue eyes she gave him an angry look. "No way. My so-called family got the cops after me before I left home."

"Maybe they had a reason?"

"I had my reasons, too."

"Why the police?"

"Just stuff."

"What kind of stuff?"

Silence. Mikesh knew Shekinah attracted its share of souls dogged by trouble.

"Okay," he relented, "I'll take you to my place." It made him uneasy, but he had a hunch she needed to tell him about the death of my brother.

As he drove the pickup back, the heater steaming the windows, the woman, whose name was Julie, talked without pause. She had been on the street and Shekinah had straightened her out. Her mother had told her that if she wanted to spit in their faces, join what she called 'her new Jesus family' then she had better forget contacting them. People she had known before Shekinah were a group she would rather not get involved with any more, but there was trouble for her at the Big House.

Mikesh asked if she wanted him to call her "Sister Julie."

"I'd like to leave the *sister* part out of it, thanks, at least until I get my head cleared."

"So what went wrong down there?"

"Listen Mr. Mikesh . . ."

"Call me Arnie."

"Arnie, it's an issue with one of the brothers. I need time before I talk about it."

Mikesh reminded her that the Big House had councils where they worked out problems.

"They do. But a council is public, and some things aren't easy to talk about in front of fifty, maybe seventy-five people, especially if the person you are worried about is a man who has loads of friends on his side. Like I said, just give me time. I need to get some distance from that place."

When they got back to Mikesh's house, Julie tossed her bag on the couch. When she pulled off her stocking cap, shoulder-length, wavy blonde hair tumbled out. Looking around, Julie asked him questions, was excited about being on a farm. As he answered, she grew more animated.

"I've got to do some chores. You can stay here or you're welcome to join me, though it's messy work. Then we can have lunch, and you can decide what you want to do."

She wanted to tag along for the chores, and jumped up to get her coat. When he asked if she wanted a coverall, she looked indignant.

Julie hopped along the access alley, watching her step, as Mikesh poured a mash of grain and supplement from a five-gallon pail into the feeder

The cold made cows hungry. From their side of the pen they pressed their weight against the heavy wooden slats of the long feed bunk, making it creak. Mikesh could hear the grinding of the cattle's teeth as they chewed. On his way to refill the bucket, he put a hand on the shiny forehead of each of the feeding cows, listening to her breathing as he spoke to Julie. As the animals got to the bottom of their ration, they scrubbed the wood of the bunk with their long, rough tongues, absorbed in pleasure.

"They really love that." Julie said. "What is it?"

He grabbed a handful of the supplement and held it up for her. "Take a sniff. See what it reminds you of."

She hung back, wrinkling her nose and whiffing from a distance. "It smells kind of sweet."

"Like mother's fresh-baked bread: molasses, cottonseed oil, and grain. These cows and heifers are going to be having calves soon. It's the most important time of the year for good nutrition. All but three of them are eating for two."

"Why are three different?" She looked troubled. "Is something wrong?"

"Nothing wrong. Of these animals three are still open, too young to have been bred for this spring. Three others are springing heifers, which means they are pregnant with their first calves. The rest are older bred cows. Most of these girls have been through all this before."

Mikesh jumped over the fence at the end of the bunk to check out the animals, but Julie hung back.

"Are you sure you're safe? They're so big!"

"They're friendly company."

"They're huge! They could crush you."

Julie watched a cow negotiate her way to Mikesh and give his barn coat an upward push with her soft nose.

"Hey!" he shouted. "This one's named Rosie. She's one of the springing heifers." He stroked the straight hard line of her face, patted the top of her head. "They know where their bread is buttered," he laughed. "It's more likely that if I fell down they'd form a ring to protect me from a stranger like you. Especially with this breed, the only time a cow gets touchy is when she's got a calf to protect. Once they've calved I'll need to be more careful."

Mikesh gestured in the direction of the road. "There's a bull in the pen over there. With him, it's a different story. That old boy's brain is addled by testosterone; his mood shifts like wind."

Walking along the back of the row of feeding cattle, Mikesh laid a hand on the hindquarters of each cow. Some udders were swelling and one or two had showed other signs of being almost ready to calf. Mikesh would have to move their feeding time as far to the end of the day as possible to keep their systems working on food through the night. That way their deliveries, when they came, were likely to be during the day when it would be easiest to keep an eye on them.

His thoughts were broken when Julie let out a cry.

"What's wrong?"

"You've got a horse!"

She had spotted Zisca.

"I always wanted a horse. My parents used to laugh at me. We lived in town. I guess they had a point. But that doesn't mean I wasn't crazy about horses and ponies anyway. I used draw pictures." Shy, she stopped and said, "I wasn't the only girl who felt that way."

"I understand," he told her. "It wasn't until I got on the farm a few years ago that I daydreamed about getting a horse. I understand your parents; having Zisca is a way of proving to myself I'm not in the city anymore."

"Do you ride him?"

"Sure, but not so much in the winter. That's why he looks so rough."

"Could I ride him?"

"Well, that depends. Do you know how to ride?"

She did not, but after Mikesh finished up with the feeding, he put a halter on Zisca, brought him into the barn, and showed Julie how to brush him, how to saddle him, and how to use the stirrup to mount. Mikesh led Julie around for a few minutes, but she wanted to ride on her own. Mikesh knew that was courting trouble, so he had her scootch behind the saddle, and he climbed on. She looked over his right shoulder, keeping her arms tight around Mikesh as he showed her how to use the reins, signal with her knees and use the few words to which Zisca was sure to respond.

"It's your turn. I'll climb behind, and you give it a try."

Mikesh now rode behind the saddle, his arms around Julie's waist. She was abrupt with the reins, tentative with her knees, so Mikesh took the reins and showed her how to ease the pressure for turns, give them a shake to get Zisca's attention, how to squeeze her knees at the same time she gave a clucking noise to have the horse speed up his gait. Julie held on tight to the saddle horn. When he handed the reins back to her, though, she relaxed and talked to Zisca. The horse was spirited, but not contrary, so Mikesh jumped off and told Julie to ride around the pasture on her own. Turning Zisca out toward the white field, Julie gave him a squeeze and away they trotted. By the time Mikesh had finished with the hay and checked the water for his cows, the pair had been around one of the paddocks several times.

When Julie rode into the stock pen Mikesh told her he could go in and get something started for lunch and she could do more riding, but this alarmed her. She gave Zisca a squeeze with her knees and rode over to Mikesh, handing him the reins before she dismounted.

Mikesh showed Julie where to get some oats, and had her brush Zisca down. When Mikesh got back from taking the saddle and blanket into the tack room Julie was fussing with the bottom of her jeans.

"I got into some major shit!" she said, scraping with a short piece of board.

Mikesh thought it couldn't have been easy to find that kind of mess, but then he reminded himself it was a barnyard.

Back in the house Julie was agitated about her jeans. He asked if she'd brought another pair. When she said she hadn't, he got her a pair of his and said he would throw hers in the washer. When Julie reappeared from the bathroom her legs were bare except for white socks. She had put on one of his sweatshirts, which was long and baggy, but she had chosen not to wear his jeans. Startled, Mikesh tried not to notice what was, or was not, underneath the big tent of his shirt.

"I decided I'd wear this sweatshirt rather than those jeans. They'd never stay up!" She raised her eyebrows and laughed.

"Aren't you going to be cold?"

"Not with this fire," she said, standing by the woodstove and rubbing her hands. She jumped into the recliner and pulled her feet up under her. "This place is great!"

"Did you dress like that in the Big House?"

"In the women's wing, sure. In that place you don't have to worry, even if you're not wearing a thing. There are some advantages to keeping separate."

"I don't know if you noticed, but this is not the women's wing."

"I know that. That's why I'm here. Remember?" Julie laughed again, deliberately avoiding his challenge. "I need some time away, *totally* away from all that. I needed a break. Who knows? I may never go back. I just want a vacation. Are you okay with that, Arnie?"

"Fine with me, as long as you're comfortable."

When Mikesh's great uncle left him the place, the modest farmhouse was just as it had been for a hundred years. Closed off from each other, Mikesh felt the rooms press in on him. He knocked out the wall shared by kitchen and dining room, leaving just the counter between, and replaced the door to what his uncle had called the parlor with a large opening so the stove burning in the dining room would heat it all. Mikesh exposed the old brick chimney, which helped with heat. With this arrangement, anybody sitting in the parlor could smell what was cooking and keep up a conversation with whoever was in the kitchen. All this, of course, if Mikesh had guests. Usually it was just him and his dog, Mustard.

As he was making sandwiches he heard Julie in the other room. "Wow, look at all this old vinyl! Do you mind if I play one of these?"

When he asked if she knew how to work a turntable she said that would be no problem because she used to date a guy who was "a real audio freak." If true, Mikesh thought, he doubted the man would have liked the way Julie let the needle thump hard on the grooved surface of the album. Mikesh nearly dropped his knife when the amplifier popped. Then he heard a synthesizer chord and the slap of the drums. It was "Born in the U.S.A." Julie had turned the volume up loud and was studying the album.

"You a Springsteen fan?" he asked when she reappeared at the counter off the kitchen.

"My boyfriend was. He loved this. I haven't heard it in a long time. Talk about sweet! We got messed up listening to this. You have any vodka?" she asked.

"Sorry. Just wine and beer."

She asked for wine.

"At lunch?"

"I told you, it's my little holiday."

Mikesh realized, given his suspension, this was his holiday too, no work shift to stay clear-headed for that evening. He opened a Merlot and poured the glasses. Julie picked up the bottle as he chopped vegetables and read the label.

"Like life before the Big House." She tipped her glass and took long, slow swallows.

Sampling his wine, Mikesh wondered where the afternoon ahead was going.

Once lunch was ready and the table arranged, they sat down. As he started his salad, he listened with alarm to the lyrics of the last song on the side, now playing: "I'm on Fire."

Sitting across from Julie at the round oak table Mikesh was aware of her breasts pushing out the front of his baggy sweatshirt. "Beer," his granny used to say, "makes bodies beautiful," but Mikesh decided it wasn't just the Merlot.

"You liking this song?" Julie asked. "This was my boyfriend George's favorite," she gave him a look that lasted so long he had to swallow hard. He needed to change the subject, get his mind off sex.

"You know the *Nebraska* album that came before this one?" he asked her.

Julie shook her head.

"A lot of people don't. He did five albums, all of them good. Millions of people thought so. But he had gotten to the point where everything was coming at him too easy. It wasn't a life he recognized anymore. If you listen to the lyrics, all Springsteen's best stuff is about struggle, and there wasn't the same kind of struggle in his life. He felt like he'd gone astray, lost his edge."

Mikesh hoped he could keep his attention off the song lyrics. "But with depression, suddenly all the old pain was real for him again," he continued. "So he wrote some new material, and once he really listened to the stuff, he realized he needed to release it solo and acoustic, without the band."

"I'm On Fire" over, the turntable clicked off in the other room, but Mikesh kept talking. "When *Nebraska* came out, Springsteen didn't have a hit album. The music was different; it confused his fans. He'd found the real stuff again, though. My favorite is about a state patrolman whose brother has been messed up by Vietnam. The brother gets in fights, finally steals a car.

Julie, focused on her third glass of wine, said, "It sounds familiar. Hypocrite shit."

Mikesh measured her new turn of mood. "The guy tries to make it farming, but the market squeezes him out. That's when he becomes a patrolman. He's not really a hypocrite. He hasn't seen the military action that screwed up his brother. He never arrests him, just chases him across the line into Canada to get him clear of America."

"Double standards," Julie said.

"It doesn't feel like that. In that album the speaker in every song describes everything by the right name." Without the record, the room was quiet.

"So what does that guy call himself: the patrolman?" Julie asked.

"A guy trying to do honest work."

"But he lets his brother get away when he's guilty?"

"Yeah. He says you can't turn against family."

"I could disagree with that."

"From what you've said, I can see that. But not this guy. Family's the base of it for him. For him that's a higher law than the state that employs him. He's caught: a lawman between two laws. The song describes exactly how that feels—being caught between the pressure of one kind of law and another." Mikesh was thinking about his own messed-up situation, a security man with the law against him, and wondering about the true age of a girl he had guessed to be seventeen.

"Joshua said the laws of the Spirit make more sense than laws of the state."

"The patrolman takes his wage for enforcing the lower law," Mikesh said. "Anyway, on Springsteen's next album, the one you just played, the music was hard-driving R&B, but underneath the big sing-along choruses, he put the truer names to things, like in that song you asked me about. The man talking in that one doesn't try to make his feelings sound pretty."

"I don't know. It may not be pretty, but that song's hot! I'm going to put on the other side!"

As Julie left the table, Mikesh couldn't help seeing that her sweatshirt was the main extent of her afternoon apparel, tapered white ankles that somehow were attached to wide, comfortable thighs; he looked away before she bent to turn over the record, but couldn't suppress the stirrings of attraction.

When she sat down she opened a new topic: asking him about Josh, how it felt to be the one to find him.

"Why do you think Joshua died, Arnie?"

"He was battered up."

"Yes, but why do you think his car crashed like that? Was it really an accident or was there some other shit going on?"

"Why?"

"Strange stuff happens, even at the Big House."

"Do you feel like telling me about your problem?"

"Not everyone is like you, Arnie." She gave Mikesh the fragile look of a person heading for a good cry.

"Who made you so afraid?"

"One of the men."

"It sounds like you've dealt with men before."

"That's true, but now I've got no home besides the Big House, no money, no real friends. With Joshua gone, the power is shifting. People thought Joshua was invincible, maybe immortal. But that's been totally disproven. He's gone, not what some people wanted to think, and it's not the same place. I wondered if you've come across anything that seems peculiar about Joshua's accident."

"The truth is, I haven't found a thing. All I've encountered is pure speculation—like yours."

"You haven't felt like looking into it?"

Mikesh wondered why it was other people kept wanting to make my family's business, his business.

"My one trip to the Big House cost me a drug charge—and, by the way, I'd never seen the marijuana that officer found in my glove compartment before. Any idea who might have planted that in my truck?"

"You think someone has it in for you, huh? I can't help you with that," Julie laughed. She was eating a plain slice of bread, tearing it with her hands, with her elbows on the table and her shoulders drawn together. "Like I said, you don't know what might happen down there with Joshua gone."

"What was he like with you?"

"The girls in the women's wing say his name is 'King' because that fit him. He *did* seem to know things. A sister who found me on the streets brought me to Joshua. He said that when I looked for a fix, I was looking for my high in the wrong places." Mikesh didn't like the new spin to his own story: guy with taste for weed picks up girl with drug record. Julie continued, "Joshua said the rush was inside me; white crunch just unlocked it. But like I said, Joshua is gone. Now I'm just a sister who cleans and who bakes bread."

She took a deep drink of wine and tugged down the bottom of her sweatshirt.

"So who is the man who has made you miserable town there?" Mikesh asked.

She looked at him as she thought. "Now that I've got some distance, put it in perspective, I'm pretty sure I can handle it. And before you change the subject, if you get any clues about what happened to Josh, you would tell me, right?" She finished off the glass and stood. "I'll help you with these things." She stepped behind Mikesh and reached in to clear his dishes. He got up quickly and she looked up to his face. The neck of his sweatshirt cast deep shadows above Julie's pale, freckled collarbones, the blue of her eyes intense in the house light.

"I can take care of those things," he told her.

Julie reached up and put her right hand on his cheek. Mikesh shivered with the surprise of how cold her fingers felt, but she didn't move her hand.

"Arnie, I told you I always dreamed of riding a horse. I think I was meant to come here." She pushed up on her toes to kiss the side of his jaw. Her lips were cold. Mikesh wondered if a meth rush was anything like this and drew away.

"I don't know why you chose to come here, but I'm glad it's helped. Your jeans are in the dryer. They should be ready."

The phone rang. It was the secretary of Mikesh's lawyer, who had news about the hearing, papers for Mikesh to sign. Could Mikesh see the lawyer in New Hampton before the end of the afternoon? When Mikesh reappeared with her clean jeans Julie said, "If it's all right, I'd like to stay." She would clean up the kitchen; she was used to that.

Mikesh nodded toward the steps. "There's an extra room upstairs if you want to rest, the one on the left by the bathroom. You know where the towels are. I don't think I'll be gone more than a couple of hours. If you are hungry, I'll make dinner. Might as well enjoy life while I'm a free man."

It was hard for Mikesh to keep his head on his driving or on the meeting with the lawyer as he headed west to New Hampton. He kept reliving the feeling of Julie's hand on his cheek and her lips pressed against his chin, the way she looked up into his eyes. If she spent the night, would she be in the guest room or his? He hoped she was as old as she said. How long, Mikesh thought to himself, had it been since he'd eased into the welcoming arms of a loving woman? For too long he'd been on the run from love, sidestepping to protect himself.

But the meeting with his lawyer put that out of his head. Jim O'Brien's office was on the main street of New Hampton, a block and a half from the courthouse. The woman at the front desk told Mikesh that O'Brien was still on his way when the lawyer came in, shook Mikesh's hand and said, "You're a free man!" ushering him into his office.

At the bail hearing that Monday O'Brien insisted that by the time of arraignment the weight, quality, and value of the controlled substance in question needed to be established, and fingerprints taken from the bag. Just that morning, in lab analysis, the material had proved to be something other than marijuana.

"What was it?" Mikesh asked.

O'Brien raised his eyebrows and leaned forward. "Now that's something the lab might not normally be able to answer. But this particular chemist happened to have a green thumb. He said what you had in your glove compartment was spider plant, a common garden flower." O'Brien, who until then had kept a poker player's face, roared with laughter. "Common to gardeners, I guess, but I've never heard of it. It looks like someone else is clueless about it too. The lab guy said the two plants can get confused by someone who doesn't know what they're doing."

Mikesh realized that even though he had explained his innocence, O'Brien still had some doubt about his story. "I'd never seen that bag before," Mikesh told him. "It wasn't me who got taken for a ride—except for in a sheriff's cruiser."

"The techs couldn't find any prints. Who do you think put it there?"

"Maybe the deputy himself. The authorities have been harassing the Shekinah people. He could have set me up as part of that. But a man in the force wouldn't mess up on the marijuana. It makes him look bad. If he wanted to really hurt me, he'd have access to the real stuff. They confiscate a lot of it. It was someone who either didn't know better, like you said, or someone who didn't want to get in trouble for possession if they got caught with it themselves: maybe one of the innocent pilgrims attracted to Joshua King, someone who knew it was likely their place would be searched too."

Once Mikesh had made it clear that he did not want to pursue charges for false arrest—his name had been in the news enough—he signed papers to acknowledge that charges were dropped and, officially at least, they would disappear from the records. On his return home, Mikesh had a few questions for Julie, such as who was the gardener at the Big House. When he pulled into his drive at dusk he was surprised to find the windows pitch-black. Only his dog, Mustard, greeted him at the door of the kitchen. When he turned on the light he found a note on the table, saying, "Arnie, I thought about what you said about family. I guess Shekinah is my family. I called for them to get me. Thanks!! XXOO" The kitchen was straightened. So was his work desk. But his computer had up a different file directory screen than the one he had left. Sister Julie must have been looking through his files, doing more than simple housecleaning before she walked out the door.

Love, or at least its promise, had sidestepped him. It left something that smelled suspiciously like betrayal in its place.

CHAPTER 16

MARY LAY IN THE strange bedroom, so dark she could barely separate black shapes of furniture from the lighter walls. The room was cold, but under the comforter she was warm. Unable to get back to sleep, she considered what brought her here. She'd heard that the charges against Arnie had been dropped and wanted to congratulate him. She remembered the shift in his muscles as she worked on his left leg and foot earlier in the week, feeling as no one had save Arnie himself, how much weight the imbalance in his legs added to his step. There had been tears in his eyes as she relaxed the clench of his toes. She thought about him, moving alone through his Saturday routines. Since he enjoyed her bread, she decided she would bake a loaf and bring it to him.

That was yesterday. Mary had questioned her wisdom as she turned south off State Highway 24 into the unfamiliar country nearer his place. She had not called ahead. She followed a map drawn on a napkin by a friend: turning at the school, turning onto Scenic at the edge of town. Her mood sank when she saw his house and barn, the leafless trees, and weathered outbuildings surrounded by rough patches of snow. This desolate farm was not unlike the place she came from herself. She didn't like the blank windows of the house, didn't like thinking of the upstairs rooms, including the one in which she now lay, a room like the one to which her father had come once her mother was too deadened with pain medications to stay awake, and too weakened by cancer to stay at home any longer.

But when her Honda hatchback crunched to a halt on the drive, and Mustard's barking announced her arrival, Mikesh appeared, rosy-cheeked, in his work clothes, wiping his hands, asking her to stay for lunch. Curious, she asked him to show her around. He offered her a coverall; she accepted, touched by his concern. She stepped in and zipped its shell around her, rolling its blue arms and legs to fit her, pulling on the oversize boots, until she looked like the plumber who raced around solving problems in the video game she had played as a girl. When Mikesh told her about another woman, one of Josh's followers who came by for lunch just the day before, Mary wondered why she assumed Mikesh would be alone today. For all she knew, maybe he entertained lots of women.

Mikesh beamed. His supervisor had called to say that, no longer in trouble with the law, he could return to work that night. As the April flurry thinned, he stood with Mary below the trees beyond the house. Mikesh pointed out the wood in the distance where his property ended. The pastures sloped down, at their center, to a stream. The property, he explained, was divided into paddocks for pasture and hay, and he shifted these, in warm weather, to keep the animals always on fresh grass. Mikesh kept his passion in check, trying to gauge Mary's interest.

When she arrived Mikesh had been about to move a large bale of hay from a storage shed to a feeder. Mary helped him throw what was left of the old bale into the pen, tossing broken layers of dried grass and alfalfa toward the cattle that bunched around them. As the ghost-colored cows jostled, eager for the hay, Mary was pleased by their size, the deepness of their abrupt breathing as they nosed around her, the steam coming off them in the cold. Surrounded by big animals, Mikesh seemed smaller. He called some of them by name and pushed back hard when they interfered with his labor, matching his strength with theirs. As Mary and Mikesh retreated, Mary noticed the horse. Finding she knew how to ride, Mikesh encouraged her to saddle up Zisca while he moved in a new bale. They worked together to catch, curry, and saddle the animal.

"Interesting name," she said as she drew the currycomb over the curve of the horse's belly. "It sounds like a girl's."

"Zisca? No, he was a general. The name means 'one-eye' in Bohemian. See how he's got one light blue eye and one brown? The general got that nickname when he was blinded on one side in battle. Later he took an arrow in his good eye in the military campaign he led against the Catholics. When he died of plague he ordered his followers to let his body be eaten by birds, but to make a drum from his hide to beat as the troops marched to fight off the army of the oppressors. Zisca was a badass hero in the history of the Czech working man."

"You ought to be ashamed," she laughed. "It's cruel to name an innocent animal after a man who gets shot in both eyes and then dies of plague."

As Mary took a couple of circles on the horse near the farm buildings, Mikesh started his tractor. At the wheel, lifting and carrying the new bale, and tipping it upright for feeding, he moved with the same steady speed he moved on foot, the machine his extension. Manipulating its wheel, pedals, and levers he was hiding none of his enthusiasm: a man showing off.

Mary guided the bay gelding out beyond the broken snow into the open pasture, turning when she came to a far fence used to limit the cattle's stream access. The air had turned clear and bright; Mary felt a rush of excitement and power. She was right to have come. Her dread about Mikesh's farm was evaporating. Nearing the buildings again, she saw the lone animal in the paddock toward the road. As she got closer she knew it was a bull, a large gray shadow whose neck thickened to a hump that rose behind its massive head, the huge chest that made the legs of its body look short. Zisca moved quickly, his attention focused on the barn. She, however, was watching the muscular animal, saw it lift its head and stamp the ground, turn and trot, then charge in their direction. It halted as it crashed into the barbed wire less than thirty feet away. The horse heard the charge, breaking his gait slightly and prancing, but when the wire of the fence groaned the horse reared. As he did so, Mary saw Mikesh, hand on a post, swinging both legs in a high arc over the pasture fence in an attempt to get to her. As he hit the earth, she saw him go down.

When Mary rode up and looped the reins around a post, Mikesh laid in the snow, quiet as a shooting victim. When she knelt by him, though, he opened unfocused eyes.

"Arnie?" she said.

Mikesh only blinked.

"Arnie?"

Mikesh raised himself to an elbow, staring at the ground.

"Are you okay?" she asked.

He looked up at her strangely.

"Arnie, are you all right?"

He seemed not to recognize her. When he tried to raise himself further, Mary put her arm around him and helped him sit upright. He rubbed the back of his head. Then his look shifted to alarm.

"Are *you* all right?" he asked, his eyes focusing on her.

He did not remember anything except seeing the horse rear. As his feet hit the slick ground on the opposite side of the fence they slid out from under him and he head-thumped an icy knob of earth, losing consciousness.

She told him to lie back down, but he staggered to his feet. She made him stand still as she examined the back of his head where, beneath his warm hair, an unnatural goose egg formed. Back at the house he agreed to sit in his recliner, and grudgingly accepted a blanket and a makeshift ice pack, but he did not want to see a doctor, nor would he stay home from his work, not tonight of all nights. She called a friend who was a nurse. The woman prescribed rest, and that someone should stay with him for at least twenty-four hours, waking him twice in the night to see that he did not have bleeding in his brain. Mikesh said his one option was to call a neighboring family and spend the night with them. Knowing he would not, she insisted on taking care of him herself.

So Mary rummaged in Mikesh's closet and freezer for towels and ice, preparing tea, eventually making soup to eat with the bread she brought. Opening wrong doors, and trying to understand the odd logic of his shelves, she saw by the labels that he and she must sometimes shop at the same stores. Surely she had seen him before they met. He told her about his neighbor, a woman she did not know, recommending her within a day or two of Josh's death. Now, two weeks later, she was playing the role of caregiver: refreshing ice, making soup, checking for signs that his brain was healing, massaging his back and neck. It was suddenly her job to see to his horse, check the fence of his bull's paddock to make certain that the animal stayed penned, feed Mustard. From this perspective she understood that, though he held employment, his daily checklist and annual calendar revolved around cattle and land. It didn't set easily with him to lean back in his chair while someone else attended to his chores and the needs he was reluctant to name. When he objected, she called him "Princess Toadstool," the damsel in distress in the video game that featured the plumber in the coverall. Mary threatened to get him a bedpan. The teasing settled him. Though he seemed only slightly bruised and shaken, she knew from what her friend said that there could be a cloud of blood forming in his brain. She wouldn't accept taking chances, even if he was stubborn. His wound had been in part her responsibility.

Mary insisted on driving him to work in her Honda. She knew it wasn't the sort of Saturday night a self-respecting, attractive woman should look forward to, but there was adventure in following him through his evening: checking doors, turning off lights, the smells of boiler rooms and staffrooms and classrooms, his modest office, his trim security van. He insisted that, by contract, he must drive the campus circuit in the van, but she rode along. As they made his rounds in quiet buildings, she learned that Calmar, where he worked, was also his hometown. He attended the old brick high school just a few blocks away, wrestled there, got into his share of scrapes, including a brief arrest for taking the prized car of a friend and parking it outside a hair salon. From here he enrolled at Iowa State, studying business and, in his last three semesters, as much history as he could manage. His parents moved to Florida while he was living in Chicago, and never looked back. As he comfortably moved through his familiar rounds, he did most of the talking, happy to have an audience.

At nine o'clock, as they were eating the sandwiches she packed, she brought up a piece of history she had been hesitant to discuss, but had been on her mind since enquiring about Mikesh. Among her Decorah friends, she found someone who knew someone, who filled her in about him.

"Arnie, I understand your wife died in a car crash."

His jaw clamped, and he stayed silent, but she continued, "I just wanted to tell you I was sorry. It must have been on your mind these days after coming on Josh like you did: being there when he passed away."

That other accident, present to his imagination, was the emotional equivalent of the bruised lump beneath the hair on the back of his head.

"She was my *ex*-wife," he began. "It happened after the breakup. We weren't together anymore, hadn't lived together for a year. We had only been legally divorced for two weeks. She was the one who wanted the divorce: said we had irreconcilable differences. I hoped she might want to patch up what caused us to drift apart, see if we could make another go of it. But she wanted to move on, and by then, the time of the divorce, she was spending most of her time with someone else. That's who she was with when she died: a realtor named Andrew Kiley."

Mary saw that saying the name of the man Audra Mikesh chose in preference to Arnie, her young husband, exacted its cost from him.

"Audra didn't suffer. That's what I found out later. The car burst into flames on impact. She might have already been dead before it burned.

They went, she and Kiley, for a long weekend in Door County, went out drinking at a roadhouse on the other side of the peninsula, and were driving back to the place they had rented on the lake. She had a new car with a lot of power under the hood, and must have been seeing how fast it would go when they missed a curve. It flew a long ways and then end-over-ended and caught fire."

"That's terrible. I'm sorry, Arnie."

"It wasn't my business anymore. Not legally. She was celebrating making the break final. She was no longer Mrs. Arnie Mikesh, no longer someone's wife. She had her own place, her own life. She had this new man. Then she was gone. She'd been thorough about making the break. The authorities called her parents. Her parents called me. I wasn't in on it until I came to the funeral. I sat with the family, but towards the back. The woman who'd been half of me for close to a decade cut herself away, happy to do it, then went up in flames."

"What were the irreconcilable differences?" Mary remembered his bad boy high school days.

"We married young, just after we graduated from university. Being in a university town, with no house payments, no boss, and lots of parties going on, it was easy for us to have fun together, the way she liked. Moving to Chicago was her idea. She said we had to move there if we were going to stay in the Midwest. In her business, fashion, Audra did well. She knew how to follow the bright lights."

"How about you?"

"That's where she saw the problem. At the end of the work day, I didn't want to burn up the night, hang out, party with people who meant business."

"Meant business?"

"Work hard, party hard. Play with the right people. Party 'til you drop. I managed and got on with my job, but those long commutes, that social life Audra wanted—it just wasn't me. At first she was mad when I wouldn't go out with her, but the day came when she was mad if I said I might want to come along. By the end of eight years . . . irreconcilable differences."

Mary, accompanying Mikesh down the half-lighted hallways of the technical college, was getting a picture of the man who opened doors for her and who pulled off the road in the fog to help the friend whose loss she was mourning. He feared opening himself up to someone who, like Audra, would cast him off like a used tissue. He coped by remaining invisible.

On the drive back to his place from the college, following his directions, Mary realized that they would pass, at the same time Mikesh had passed before, the site where Josh died. Not familiar with the road, she asked him about the spot. He pointed as they approached. She slowed, and on a quick impulse turned her Honda onto the gravel, as Mikesh had done, pulled over, and cut the engine.

"I want to walk down there. I want to see where you found him."

She did not have a flashlight in the car, so they walked by moonlight along the gravel to the highway curve. Adjusting their eyes to the thinnest possible sliver of what tomorrow would be a new moon, listening to the night, Mikesh took Mary's hand. With small, feeling steps they edged down into the ditch. There was still a crusted line of snow running along the base of the embankment where Josh's car landed. The smell in the air, Mikesh told her, was from a dairy farm. From the ditch, not even the twinkle of a distant farm was visible. She felt his grip tighten; a car was approaching. They stood and listened. The lights grew brighter on the trees of the wood ahead of them and disappeared as the car roared past, leaving night and silence.

"It may have been like that for him," Mikesh said, "the sound of cars going by, and then blackness. If he was conscious, it was a long wait."

Thinking about that vigil, Mary said, "Josh prepared himself. When he was out in South Dakota, he learned that if you want to be sent a vision, you have to look for it. 'You have to cry out for it,' he told me. That meant experiencing hunger, thirst, pain, cold: all at the same time. He would go out for days without food or water. He did that again in Denver. He went up into the mountains: sought his vision."

"Did he find it?"

They stood under the bright expanse of stars, the specter of moon, and a road bank rising up behind them.

"He found it."

Mikesh waited. "Did he tell you what he saw?"

"He told me. He said that out there in those high mountains after a week without food and almost no water, and after a cold night where he shivered so much he could not sleep, just before sunrise he had this vision."

Mikesh waited.

"In Denver, Josh could understand the gangbangers he worked with; every one of them had gone through some kind of brutal initiation to keep tight with their group. But Josh was doing it the Oglala way, going to a high place by himself. Seeking his vision. He said at first it began as a very strong feeling, a certainty he hadn't experienced before."

"What was it?"

"He felt the power that was in him: recognized that in one way he'd been running from that power, hiding from it. When it came Joshua was in a dream version of the same high place. He was thirsty, and following a coyote. The coyote led him to a lake and instructed him to look at his reflection. What he saw was not himself, but a large bear. The coyote told Josh the water was his to drink, but Josh refused. The coyote told Josh to keep looking into the lake, but not, this time, to tempt him with its water. In its surface Josh saw his life before him, his life with all that power he now knew he had. He saw men and women giving him money, worshipping him almost like a god."

Mary felt her throat grow tight, her muscles tense. "'All that can be yours,' the coyote told him. 'But you need to give me your heart.' Josh looked at the coyote," Mary said, "and as he stared, the coyote's mouth became my mouth, and curled into a smile. 'Worship,' my mouth said. 'Worship what you see.'" To say those words, Mary took on a raspy voice, far different than her own.

Mary turned sideways, as if away from the temptation she had repeated from Josh. "But Josh ordered it away. He ordered the coyote to go, and it disappeared." Mary swallowed dryly.

"When it was gone, Joshua was at the edge of a high cliff. He felt despair, like he should throw himself down. But he didn't. He decided to leave the mountains and the city and come back to the places around home. That was when he decided to move to Waterloo and work there, to do more than listen, become the teacher. That was Josh's vision. He was hungry, thirsty, and cold."

Mary's impulse to walk into the road ditch where Josh died was as much to bring Mikesh there as to go there herself. Mikesh needed to know that Josh prepared for death, and to see with a witness that Josh King died there, not Audra Mikesh. The man with her, Mikesh, needed to see that he was not responsible for killing—or saving—either one.

Back at his house, Mikesh suggested beer. Mary suggested warm milk, and checked the back of his head. The swelling had decreased, but she checked his memory, whether he was nauseous, that his mind was clear.

As she sat finishing her milk she talked about Josh again.

Mary took up the subject of Josh's vision. "You remember how Josh was a bear in his vision? He believed that was a sign he was meant to heal people. If you met him under normal circumstances—not that anything about Josh ever seemed normal—he would have told you his mission was to heal. That's one thing we had in common. Josh said he was called to make people whole."

Mary thought of Mikesh's twisted back when she first placed her hands on him. And about the people who showed up at her door whose eyes, whose shoulders, carrying pain, told her everything.

"Josh hadn't done any healing before he had that vision, before he decided to come home to Iowa and start his work," she said.

Mikesh asked if Josh really cured people.

"That's another way his stays in South Dakota and Arizona and Mexico changed his view. Josh thought a person who was messed up in their thinking or confused or . . ." she thought about Josh's view of her and their disagreements, "or unspiritual was sick. It was what the Oglala called 'medicine.' Good or bad, he said, 'medicine' is a power that is either for you or against you. Good medicine, to him, was the power that kept you healthy. I align people's bones and tendons. Josh said he aligned people's spirits."

Mary straightened, pushed back her shoulders. "Arnie, the greatest powers in a person are meant naturally to make that person alive and healthy. Josh said if you watched a Oglala healer, that person would start a ceremony by getting right with the powers in the room, like the smoking ceremony performed at Josh's funeral. That was the Indian way of starting out right, but the healer would take the sick person back to the beginning, *remind* her of where they were headed, who her people were. With all that done, laying his hands on the person, that healer could command the healing to take place."

"Did it work?"

"I never went to any healings Josh and his group held. I work at making people feel better a few muscles at a time. It takes work and maintenance, nothing miraculous."

She stopped and gazed at him. Mikesh knew she was thinking about the kinks in his back.

"Plenty of therapists don't touch their client's body. They say they learn to work the force, the *chi*, without physical contact. It may not even be religious, just an extension of the body's electricity. It could have been that for Josh. Three years ago Josh and I were walking in the center of Decorah, and passed a middle-aged woman who turned and caught the sleeve of Josh's shirt. 'Please, I know who you are. I've had pain for five years,' she said. She drew her free hand across the bottom of her face, almost as if she was peeling off her skin to let him see the bones underneath. 'They tell me nothing can be done,' she said."

"Sounds freaky," Mikesh frowned. "What did he do?"

"He looked at her steadily and said, 'I don't know you. I've never seen you before. I owe you nothing.' But the woman said, 'I know you can help me!' Joshua said, 'Then the power is in you.' He laid his hand on her forehead, saying 'Be healed.'"

"Was she healed?" Mikesh asked.

"She closed her eyes, and the tension I'd seen in her face drained. She opened her eyes, smiled, said 'Thank you. I knew you could help,' and we walked away. I turned to look back, and saw her staring at us, not moving, but Josh just walked on."

When Josh first met Mary she had her own troubles. One day she would feel sharp, aching pain in her elbows, wrists, and fingers, the next day numbness. She would stand before the bathroom mirror judging her cold reflection, and draw the serrated edge of a paring knife across the underside of an arm. Searing pain from that thin cut offered her substance, convinced her she was alive. Josh was part of what cured her. He later said he exorcised "her seven demons."

Overnight, Mary insisted that Mikesh remain still as possible. She awakened him twice: speaking from his doorway in the soft glow of the screen on her flip phone. She asked about his head and neck, had him spell his name, tell her his birthdate. Since he seemed fine, it was awkward and silly, and the second time he balked.

"What is Zisca's date of birth?" she said. "His mother's maiden name?"

She had him laughing. She was almost certain he would be all right.

As she tried to get back to sleep that second time the sky was lightening. At breakfast she would bring up the other matter she needed to discuss: that Jude Bailey talked drunk to one of her friends, complaining how religion messes up your brain. Jude said threats to Josh, while he was still alive, were worst from those closest to him, someone religious. Yes, she thought, as the contrast between the furniture and walls sharpened, Mikesh would want to know about this.

CHAPTER 17

GIVEN WHAT MARY TOLD him at breakfast, Mikesh decided that Josh was driving to the northeastern corner of the state for a religious reason: a set of issues about which Mikesh knew nothing. He decided it was time to take a step backward and check out Josh's own religious story. He thought of Communia. The place where my brother had been buried was where he and I grew up. The only church Mikesh found in the online directory was Lutheran. He dialed and, after a few rings, a male voice answered: "Pastor Meyer speaking."

After taking a deep breath, Mikesh said: "This is Arnold Mikesh, from up in Waucoma, Iowa. I'm the person who discovered Joshua King's car accident two weeks ago. I was the last person to talk to him. I called on the off chance you knew King or his family."

Silence, then, "What did you say your name was?"

"Arnold Mikesh."

"And where did you say you were calling from?"

"Waucoma. It's not a very big place, up in the northwest corner of Fayette County."

"And what was it you said your work was?"

"I didn't say. I'm a night security guard at the community college in Calmar. But that isn't why I'm calling. I'm calling because of the crash, because I was there. Since I was there, I've experienced pressure from people who followed Joshua. I don't feel sure I could trust them with my questions. I wondered if you might have known Joshua King, if he went to church in your congregation."

"Pressure from Shekinah?"

"Yes. I'm their only witness."

"If you're being bothered by those people, then you and I have a thing or two in common."

"Why do you say that, pastor?"

"This is a quiet place. I have a two-point parish, and it's not easy to keep two rural congregations going in 2008. Joshua King has taken his toll on our membership."

"I think I can see how that could happen." Mikesh hoped he had gotten lucky with his first try.

"You don't know the half of it. We can't afford to lose members, and, yes, Joshua grew up in these parts. His mother's people were from the area I serve. Maria grew up with good church roots, sensible people. But Josh King polarized feelings here. It drove people away, including his mother. I have nothing to say against Maria, but she has not been part of this church for over three years."

"Did you know Joshua?"

"Joshua was in my first confirmation class when I received a call here almost twenty years ago. He was, in fact, my best student. There isn't a person who was in the pews during catechization, who would forget his performance."

"During what?"

"Catechization. It's when teenagers show they understand the teachings of the church. Joshua was prepared. Confirmands were asked to publicly recite sections from Martin Luther's Small Catechism. Do you know what that is?"

"Sorry."

"Martin Luther wanted a church where all members had access to the Bible and to Christian knowledge, a priesthood of all believers. Luther presented the basic parts of Christianity: the Lord's Prayer, creed, commandments and explained them in terms that gave every person, young and old, the same access to God. That's what's in the catechism."

"And Joshua memorized that?"

"I'm not sure I should be talking about this. Still, it was a public event, and Joshua is dead, so I'll tell you. Joshua memorized it all, something I didn't require of the other children."

"What was the outcome?"

"There was a hitch. In the creed, Joshua modified the words 'I believe in the forgiveness of sins, the resurrection of the body, and the life everlasting' to 'I believe in forgiveness, the resurrection, and the life everlasting. He left out 'forgiveness *of sins*, resurrection *of the body*.'"

"Why did he do that?"

"He said the gospels, the stories of Jesus's life, say not all sins will be forgiven, and there was also not gospel evidence of the idea that all would be raised in the body."

"Is that true?"

"In two gospels Jesus says there is one sin that cannot be forgiven: a sin against the Holy Spirit. It is also true that Jesus did not say that believers would be raised in the body. It is just that *he* returns in the flesh. Paul, who wrote a lot of the New Testament, assured Christians that they would do the same."

"Did you accept what Joshua said?"

"Eventually. In explaining that article of the creed, Luther stresses the primary and essential role of the Holy Spirit in salvation. Joshua stressed that too. In his explanation Luther says nothing about the resurrection of the body, so I decided to allow Joshua's point there to also stand. Another creed we often use, the Nicene Creed, avoids that affirmation anyway."

"How old was Joshua when he went through this test?"

"Fourteen."

"I wasn't losing sleep about questions like that when I was fourteen."

"Joshua was unusual. He liked to call attention to himself. He questioned everything, was obsessed about sin. He asked a lot of questions about the unforgivable sin, and couldn't let it go. He wasn't a regular attender after confirmation. Few teenagers are. But he was Lutheran enough that he went on to a Lutheran college, the one up in Decorah. He went there a couple of years. He even studied religion. But he dropped out of sight. Then three years ago Maria was scheduled to read the Old Testament and epistle texts one Sunday, but Joshua turned up instead. He stood in for her."

"What happened?"

"He didn't just read the texts. He made a comment after each reading. He read the Psalm which said 'The stone which the builders rejected has become the head of the corner,' and when he finished he said, 'even so, in letting me stand here today, the troublemaker bringing forth the message of salvation, this word is once again flesh.' That made people uneasy. The closing he was supposed to read was simply, 'The word of God.' For the epistle he read a passage from Colossians, a passage about setting your mind on higher things, dying to the earth. It ended, 'When Christ who is our life appears, then you also will appear with him in glory,' but Joshua added, 'We see him now, in this place, in this moment.' A lot of people thought that what Joshua said was in the text, a part of

Paul's original epistle, but I knew better. I'd studied that text carefully for my sermon. Joshua was talking about himself: the people in Communia church, seeing Jesus in him: Joshua. As I said before, he had a very magnified sense, *a messianic sense*, of his own importance.

"When I confronted him after the service, there was an argument. Maria and Joshua left, but before they did there was some shouting from other members. That's not common at Lutheran coffee hours. Shortly after that, Joshua wanted to hold a meeting at our church, in our social hall. We said no. The Lutheran Church is a Christian church, but Joshua King is obsessed with 'the Holy Spirit,' not the Father, not the Son. We let lots of public groups use the hall, but when it came to blasphemy, we drew the line."

"That was Joshua's last contact with you?"

"Yes, except for his mother asking for Joshua to be buried in our cemetery. I drew the line there too. They could get a space for him in the communist cemetery."

"Communist?"

"That's right. Communia was founded by German communists. Communia cemetery is not attached to any religion. From what I know about Joshua King's group, I'd say that's where he belonged. Wouldn't you?"

Mikesh didn't answer. "Thanks. I understand better where Joshua King was coming from."

"He was coming from here, in Clayton County. And he took a few people from here with him: his mother, a family, all in all about a dozen members. It's left a hole in our church. The parishioners that remain, though, have drawn together; our stewardship and giving have been good. People know it's up to them, and they know that if we don't set an example, the alternative that's waiting isn't just another Christian church; it's a cult."

"I don't know if I should ask this," Mikesh ventured, "but if it's so much against what you stand for, did the church at large ever ask you to do anything about Joshua? Did they ask you to take any action?"

Meyer snorted. "That's a good one, Mr. Mikesh. I don't know that my bishop knows my first name. And I doubt whether he's had more than two thoughts about Shekinah. If he has, he hasn't shared them. In this day and age, I consider myself lucky the bishop and his headquarters don't sniff out that some of my parishioners are unhappy and come at me from their side. It's a free country, where people can think as they please, and we don't want to scare anyone away, you know. Today's shepherd follows the sheep."

Meyer's voice was bitter. My brother began as something close to a good Lutheran, but veered into depths my childhood pastor considered vile. Even with Josh dead, Pastor Meyer had not gotten over my brother's defection.

CHAPTER 18

When Mikesh went to Jude Bailey's basement workspace at the food co-op to find him, it was empty. A co-worker jerked her thumb in the direction of the back door. Mikesh found Bailey outside.

"Hi Arnie. What's up?" Bailey stood rigidly, puffing from a cigarette, with a cable-knit sweater to cut the April cold.

"I'm still curious about Joshua King. A friend said you were talking at a bar the other night about some conspiracy among his religious friends."

"Didn't see you at the bar. Don't remember seeing any of your cop friends there either, Arnie. Do you think you could have been misinformed?"

"My days seem chock full of reality checks."

Bailey finished his cigarette, and reached for his pack to get another.

"Smoke?" he tipped the pack toward Mikesh, "I hear you might be into that."

As Mikesh began to rear in defense, Bailey loosed a guffaw. "No artificial additives. Not as good as weed for messing you up, but pure tobacco. Suit yourself." Bailey took a few deep, long drags.

"You ever heard of One Nation, Arnie?"

Mikesh shook his head.

"How about the Zadok Circle?"

"What is it? Sci-Fi?"

Bailey smiled. "It's a name from the Bible. The Chief Priest of the Jewish king. Zadok made the bed in which religion and the state could get it on together." Bailey rubbed his hands together obscenely, laughing again. "One Nation is a brotherhood. The Zadoks are its leaders. Not surprising you haven't heard of One Nation. It's more like a lodge or a country club than a church or political organization. The boys in the

Zadok Circle aren't interested in getting the attention of riff-raff like you and me." Bailey blew out a jet of smoke. "The main work happens behind closed doors. They want to cultivate an elite. Their favorite phrase is 'a membership chosen.'" Bailey raised his eyebrows.

"One Nation has opened an office in Des Moines. They've been in Washington since the Thirties: organized to kick the Great Satan Roosevelt out of office."

Mikesh's brows furrowed. He wasn't sure how much of this he wanted to take.

"I'm not kidding. You can go home and look it up. They've even got their own Internet site, if you don't want to take someone else's word for it." Bailey gestured with his cigarette like a signal flag. "But don't let their PR fool you. One Nation is not all brotherhood-of-man-prayer-break-fasts-and-public-service-projects. On the surface, it seems legit, and it may have members who believe that. But the thing runs in what they call 'circles,' small, private operating groups. The Zadoks. Some of those circles, Arnie, they've got an agenda that is nothing short of holy war.

"In the era of trying to stop the Soviet enemy of freedom in the form of Kruschev, we let Joe McCarthy take over the steering wheel of the federal government and throw his political opponents into our own little gulag. In the era of terrorist mullahs, we hand power to the Zadok Circle. Strict fundamentalists. But their membership roster reads like a who's who in D.C.—congress, administration, lobbyists—you can almost count on any general with more than three stars being a regular at their prayer breakfasts. Their enemy is godless socialism. The dirtbags! I hate their self-righteous fricken' Nazi capitalist guts!"

Bailey spat.

"My friend Gary calls it the *prosperity gospel*. In One Nation's view, if you are rich and powerful, that's because God, who made you and controls his universe, intended you to be rich and powerful. It's God's will, and if someone has other ideas, well then, that someone is not right with God. And maybe God's intention is to eliminate that someone, or to have you do it for him. To the old crocodile who founded One Nation, Roosevelt was an enemy of God because he interfered with the hand of God in the marketplace."

Bailey threw down a cigarette butt and ground it out with his shoe, then lit another smoke.

"Anyway, you can look up the address of One Nation's office in the state capital," Bailey said. "Our senator, Mr. Jim-Iowa-Downhome-Cornish, rents—and I'm using that word lightly because he pays chump change—*rents* an apartment from One Nation in D.C. where he can eat his breakfast and say his prayers daily with a whole house full of the Circle faithful.

"They're just down the street from the capitol and a block away from Jim Cornish's Des Moines office. It's cozy for all concerned. But look out if they think you've got the wrong attitude about God, who's who, and capitalism. Don't you try to go shaking up the social order. You go harass One Nation and suddenly the rain gonna stop and a whole state full of GMO corn gonna wither up and die." Bailey puffed dismissively.

Mikesh reminded Bailey that he heard there was new talk about Josh being threatened by religion, maybe people close to him. "Has that got something to do with what you've been telling me about this organization?"

Bailey seemed to be feeling the cold. He threw down his half-smoked cigarette and asked Mikesh to come into his office. After they entered Bailey closed the door.

"Listen, Arnie, I want to put all that Shekinah stuff behind me. But I've got friends at the Big House. They say Joshua knew he was going to die.

"The night before Joshua went to Des Moines, the last dinner at the Big House, he looked tense. If you've been at the Big House you know what the gig is like. You eat, you sing, people talk. On that last night, Joshua talked about his work. He said, 'What we've started is bearing fruit. That's drawn those who wish to destroy us. People in this room have set about to destroy me. Before the month of March is over, some here will turn against me.'"

Bailey gave Mikesh a wide-eyed look. "Arnie, Joshua was trying to set up shop in the same town as a Zadok office." Bailey was warming up, but he talked under his breath: "As long it was just a few angry pastors, no problem. But get close to people who have a big enough economic stake and someone will make trouble for the children of the Spirit, starting with Joshua. So when Simon Peña made arrangements for that Des Moines gig, the warnings began. Simon thinks Joshua realized there was something behind the threats this time."

"But *who* was it that set out to destroy Joshua? Who, in the room with him, was ready to destroy him?"

"That, Arnie, is the sixty-four-thousand-dollar question. And, Brother, I can't answer it either."

CHAPTER 19

ONE MONTH AFTER THE accident, Mikesh wondered what he was doing, using a free weekday in the heart of calving time to drive to Des Moines, and this before the night of a full moon. Mikesh knew from experience the moon would bring on the birth of calves at odd hours. Translated through the vibrating cones of Mikesh's speakers, Derek Truck's guitar riffs twisted and turned between the howls of a wounded animal and don't-you-do-ooh-me-baby crooning. But the blues couldn't soothe Mikesh's uneasy confusion. His appointment for afternoon coffee would stir up new trouble, and on the way to the capital he needed to stop at the Big House to find answers to some questions.

From the Big House parking lot, Mikesh hailed a man in denim work clothes pushing a wheelbarrow loaded with garden tools and fuel. When Mikesh introduced himself, the man offered his hand. "I remember you. You found Joshua at the accident. I'm Gary."

"Friend of Jude Bailey's?"

"That's me," Gary laughed. "Brothers in arms, more like." Mikesh looked at him more closely, a man about his own age, whose ash-colored hair was streaked with gray. "I'm headed back to one of the hoop houses," he pointed ahead. "Want to join me?"

In the raw April air, tools thumped against the bottom of Gary's wheelbarrow. Mikesh noticed the winter-browned remnants of the previous year's cabbages and corn plants behind the Big House.

"Jude and I come at politics from the same angle," Gary said as they wound their way past garden plots.

"Jude says you convinced him to come here with a story about God striking dead a Christian who wasn't communist enough."

"Wicked Ananias!" Gary laughed. "The Bible's wild stories don't get any better than that! I thought Jude might find sympathetic company here."

"Were you right?"

Gary gazed at Mikesh, taking his bearings before he spoke. "It was probably a mistake. Like I said, Jude and I have the same political economics, but this place is about more than that."

Gary tipped his head forward as he gave the wheelbarrow a push.

"Take these, for example." He rested twenty feet shy of two odd sheds. "Part of what was lost on Jude was shifting from an economy based on capital to an economy based on *life*. We *grow* things. This first building is our hen house. That one houses rabbits."

The houses were wrapped in clear plastic tarps that connected them to a large hoop house. Each animal shed was a box on a chassis with wheels. Each faced the other with a door and entrance walkway in between.

"They're portable, so in summer we can move them across the grass each day. This time of year we keep them in one place, at the end of a hoop house so we can capture the body heat of the animals, add their waste to the working compost. While we are working in here we can let the hens run free. In summer those bunnies and hens help convert our garden waste into first-class manure fertilizer. It's biodynamics in action: plant becoming animal becoming living soil. The operation keeps our tables supplied with chicken, rabbit, and eggs."

Gary gestured for Mikesh to go ahead into the outward rush of air laden with the smell of hens, compost, and freshly worked earth. The white chickens, raising a purring morning chorus, were out scratching the ground this end of the hoop house.

"Jude wasn't into shoveling manure."

Manure and compost, overrun by hens, was heaped on either side of the central path up which Gary rolled the wheelbarrow. "If we want to get Iowa farmers out from under the heavy thumb of big ag companies, we have to help them home grow their own crop inputs and liberate their soil from chemical dependency. Living soil brings your cost down, pushes your yield up, and keeps your dirt out of the nearest stream."

Mikesh warmed to this, and described the pasture system he used with his cows as Gary rested his wheelbarrow between the foraging hens.

"You've got it!" Gary said. "It's more than that, though. Jude never appreciated that for Joshua an economy based on life doesn't run on manure. At base it runs on the Spirit. No matter how many months Jude stayed here, he never got that."

Mikesh did not, himself, want the conversation to take a turn into the vocabulary of the Spirit, so he changed the subject. "Were you with Joshua King in Des Moines?"

"Not me. I'm not much of a city boy. *She* was there though." Gary gazed toward others working under the transparent plastic arch of the hoop house. The nearest was my mom, setting out cabbage seedlings, next to a loaded flat of plants. Before her stretched two green rows already planted. She rose to greet Mikesh, stretching out her hand.

"It's thoughtful of you to stop by. Brother Simon and Tom are at a gathering in Mason City, but Sister Naomi is here. She's working in the office. Let's go over there so you can see her too."

Mikesh wasn't sure why my mother would assume he would want to see Linda Naomi Schmidt Hanson, but he realized that Evelyn would consider it a great favor if he spoke with her daughter. "Thanks," he said. "I'm impressed with what Gary's been showing me."

"When Josh's people bought this place they got eight acres of land along with the school building. I'm a farm girl, so I told Josh he should work the land to help put food on the table. It would beat mowing grass."

Gary was listening. "It also put converts like me in the Big House. Where I come from, west of Des Moines, there aren't any CSA's. Direct ownership by consumers is the way to get the wrecked economy of this state promoting life again: lots of hands working soil instead of one in a hundred operating the wheels of quarter-million-dollar tractors." He lifted the handles of his wheelbarrow and gave it a push down the path toward the far end. "Glad to meet you, Arnie."

My mom watched him go. "Brother Gary has high hopes. This will be our third season, so we've barely started. But selling shares or delivering produce keeps the work of the Spirit in front of people. And Gary's got a knack for building up soil. That's a lost art if there ever was one. As for me, there's nothing I enjoy more than getting my hands in the dirt." She stuck her gloves in her back jean pockets and walked toward the door.

"Was the CSA Joshua's idea?" he asked.

"No. It was my idea. When I joined him here it gave me something to contribute. When I worked checkout in Elkader I kept hearing about a CSA there from the produce section manager who complained about the competition through the summer months. I started our first year with subscription from some of Joshua's followers. Last year Gary took over, and it has grown. The Spirit fires him."

Mikesh remembered Josh's admonition that he help Mom.

"How are you doing without Joshua?" My mom shooed a few chickens that were getting too close to the cabbage seedlings, then went out the door of the hoop house.

"We keep moving forward," my mother answered. "We've got seedlings to set, and contracts to meet. As for the basic work Joshua did, Simon is spreading the word. Tom's gone along to help."

My mother was perhaps as startled as I was that, with Josh gone, I spread the word of the Spirit: a new mission for me. In part it was family loyalty and not letting Simon become the only voice. In part it was to find out what would it be like to leave behind my Marshalltown trowel and soil sifting screen for days working face-to-face with people who sought to do the work of the Spirit. My reading friend, the full answer to that question has yet to be determined.

"I appreciate how you came down here for our Sunday meeting, to share how it was for Joshua at the end," Mom said as they stepped into the yard. "Brother Simon told me you were hesitant to speak, but it meant a lot to us. Joshua had a feeling he didn't have much time left. That's the way he talked near the end. It helped us get ready to go on without him."

"What did he know?" Mikesh asked.

"Know? He knew that deputies were stopping our people on the road—just like they stopped you—the inspectors coming by here to check our bakery, our fire exits. Most other places in rural Bremer County never see a state inspector. Also Josh got more unfriendly questions and insults. The world was waking up to him, Arnie."

"I understand that he said someone near him was out to destroy him."

"That's right. But who could that be? When Josh died, he was by himself."

"What happened that last afternoon in Des Moines?"

"Nothing unusual. It was ugly the day before: Josh spending that night in jail. We were glad to have him back. That afternoon was the calm *after* the storm. At the house where we were staying we had a meal, then gathered to talk about expanding Shekinah in Des Moines. As the group broke up Josh walked one of the sisters from Des Moines to the door, but he came back inside. I thought he went to his bedroom to be alone and get some rest."

Mikesh had heard this from me as well: the quiet afternoon, no clue of Josh's plans.

"It's terrible to have him gone," my mother said. "But what makes it easier is what Joshua showed us. We're Shekinah. That's our name. Joshua said it is the same idea as in the Bible, the kingdom of God being at hand. He said being 'at hand' doesn't mean it's coming soon. It means you can reach out and touch it: always there, at your elbow, just waiting for you, waiting *within* you. 'Enter in with me,' Joshua was always saying. He said it to each of us. Not every mother chooses to follow her grown-up son. But I did. He's crossed into the Spirit, leading the way, Arnie. Still, that doesn't stop us from being fearful now and then."

"Fearful of what?"

"Fearful of what the future might bring, that without Joshua there is nothing left. That's what you feel in odd moments, between lying down and falling asleep. In other times, you stay afraid about the usual: not enough money, that two people will fight and you'll be forced to choose a side."

As Mikesh gave her a quizzical look, she laughed. "Oh, we get plenty of that here. We're a family of hundreds. You find me the family that doesn't have its squabbles."

Mikesh thought about his Florida parents, scornful of his choice to hang onto his uncle's farm instead of selling off and buying a condo in Chicago or moving to the Sunshine State. He knew what my mother meant.

"We've always got some disagreement brewing. But don't think life here is exactly like it is outside. In the other life I was a grocery clerk. I had a kitchen garden. I rang up vegetables along with cake mixes and beer. The pieces didn't connect. But Josh was transforming people, making a difference. That's why I joined him, transformed my work. Raising food, putting it directly into the hands of the people who prepare and eat it, that's what farming is meant to do. Josh helped me get back to my roots. He was called to do that."

My mom saying, "In the other life" struck Mikesh as chilling.

Mom saw his look. "Living in the Spirit makes cultivating land, daily life with people around me, feel more roomy, more embracing than my life felt punching buttons on a grocery store cash register."

Walking up the concrete approach to the Big House, Mikesh asked, "Speaking of cultivating, do you ever grow spider plant around here?"

"Spider plant!" My mom laughed. "You mean *cleome*?"

"Beats me," Mikesh answered. "Last time I pulled away from your place my lawyer tells me someone placed a sandwich bag of dried spider plant leaves in my glove compartment, and a deputy sheriff mistook it for marijuana."

"Spider plant is cleome," my mother said. "We have a bed of it that grows along the south side of the house. It re-seeds and does fine in a hot, sunny place. A person doesn't need to pay attention. It grows itself!"

"Ever noticed anyone who *did* pay special attention to it?"

"Only me," my mother replied. "It blooms all through late summer and makes a good cutting plant. I cut heads of cleome and put them in jars of the women's wing all through August and September."

"You didn't make me a present of some before I left?"

My mother enjoyed that one. "Arnie. I *am* sorry that happened. You are not the first to get stopped by a deputy when you left one of our gatherings, but you're the first with contraband in your car. Somebody dislikes you."

They entered the back door of the house. Walking down a passage mother called out, "Morning, Naomi!"

"Morning, Sister," Naomi said, appearing in an inner doorway.

"Brother Arnie here stopped by to see how we've been doing since he saw us last."

"I was on my way to Des Moines, and so I thought I'd stop by. I had a couple of questions. Maybe you could help. I'd appreciate your confidential perspective on something."

Sister Naomi looked as she had before, the same crown of braids, the same jeans. In this office, however, she had the bearing of a woman who could run a mid-sized corporation in her off hours. She swept her hand toward Peña's office.

"We can step in there. It irks Brother Simon when I do that," she and Mom gave each other complicit smiles before my mom decided to go back to the garden, "but he told me I was in charge if anything came up today. I've been working on the bakery accounts."

Seated in Peña's office, Mikesh asked whether Naomi had heard of One Nation or of its interest in the work of the people at the Big House. Sister Naomi shook her head 'no.' She couldn't help him with that.

His first question out of the way, his mind raced, trying to think how to phrase what he next wanted to ask. "What I'd like to know, what I'd like your perspective on, is the sexual politics here."

Sister Naomi looked blankly at him.

"I don't mean anything creepy by that, but I've heard some things. I've had experiences that make me wonder what goes on."

Sister Naomi's posture went straighter.

"What are you talking about?"

Mikesh said, "my curiosity started just after the accident. County law talked about this place as a commune where there might be a lot of open living, free love, drugs, that sort of thing. But then when I first talked to a person who had lived here, Jude Bailey, he said it was the opposite. He said he got thrown out for treating it like open living would be fine."

"Jude Bailey! You started with an interesting take on us." Sister Naomi relaxed. "I had my sexual adventures before I came here. I moved to the Big House to get away from that. I know the roller coaster of sex, Brother Arnie. After my marriage ended, being with men boosted what I felt. It confirmed the hatred I had for my life. I used sex with men like some sisters use a knife on themselves. Each new man gave a sharper edge to that hurt and angry feeling. Each gave added reason to hate the rest, especially my ex-husband." She took a deep breath. "But what did Jude say had happened here?"

"Well, as far as I can tell, he said he got kicked out of here for trying to have a threesome with two women."

Sister Naomi's intense expression broke. She laughed. "That's true! Jude Bailey came here with the idea that if it *wasn't* a free love haven, he could turn it into one."

"He told me that most people at the Big House give up sex."

"People try. Most people either live in the men's wing or the women's wing, and we discourage sexual relationships, except for those who stay with their married partner." She paused, needing to resolve something in her mind.

"Is there something else?" Mikesh asked.

"Did Jude say anything about his interest in men?"

"He only talked about sisters."

"On the public level, that was it. Those women got all tied up with Jude, and he certainly didn't limit his advances."

"Including you?"

Sister Naomi nodded.

"How do you know he was interested in men?"

Sister Naomi blushed. "This isn't really much better than gossip. Is this something you really need to know?"

"It eventually gets around to me."

"Jude spent his leisure time testing the sexual boundaries. Gary works closely with me, and he has admitted that as long as Jude was here, he felt pretty messed up. He's admitted to me, and I think it has only been to me, that on several trips to deliver for the CSA he and Jude got romantically involved. He loves Jude. Jude was happy to let things happen. Here at the Big House I think they always kept their distance. I've thought that given what happened with the marriage laws in Iowa last year, it would have gotten really interesting around here if Gary and Jude had gotten to the point of talking about commitment, a commitment ceremony. As it happens, *commitment* is not the first word on Judy Bailey's lips. Jude got himself into hot water with those two women. Confronted with it, he chose to leave."

"Who confronted him?"

"The final confrontation happened in an assembly where Jude, himself, brought up the idea of a three-person relationship. No one liked that idea. He probably told you that even the two sisters rejected the idea in the end.

"I confronted Jude several times about his lack of respect for me. Though he didn't bring it to a public confrontation, the man who absolutely hated Jude was Brother Randy. Randy is not a flexible person. He was Christian Action Fellowship before he came here, meaning he's pro-life, anti-gay, has strict ideas of right and wrong. Randy came to Shekinah having believed, his whole life, in practicing conservative morals. Randy's just the opposite of Jude."

"Did Jude make some sort of pass at Randy?"

"No." Naomi closed her eyes and laughed at the image this conjured up. "But because of what he saw with Gary, Randy had suspicions, and Jude would get kind of foxy, even flirty with Simon."

"Peña?"

"I'm not saying Simon ever reciprocated. The fact is, it might not matter. Simon has never given any sign of resenting a lack of sex in his life here. So who is to say?" Naomi answered.

"Tell me why you think Jude flirted with him."

"Brother Simon likes the conspiratorial sort of way of Jude has of talking. Those two *did* gossip! In fact, they still do, not here, but on the phone, when Simon is in the office here, at night, he's often on the phone. Brother Randy saw Jude had a way of playing up to Brother Simon that a person *could* see as the way a man plays up to a woman."

"But you're saying nothing happened."

"Not that I know of. But from what he could see of Jude's relationship with Gary, Randy got suspicious. Jude was also always using his chummy relationship to Brother Simon to push his politics. He's way left of center. Randy's way right. If Randy was to have his choice, Shekinah would be protesting abortion clinics, doing what it took to get at those doctors."

Mikesh told Naomi he had a hard time imagining a person following Josh taking that view.

"We get all kinds. And Randy, he's a seeker. He's got fire. I admire that in him. For a while he left the Christian Action Fellowship to join an Adventist church. They believe in a Saturday Sabbath and strict Biblical laws, a second coming near at hand. That's what brought him to Joshua. Someone told him that Joshua might be that: the new Jesus. And so Randy went to hear him. Randy said he felt like the Spirit laid a powerful hand on him, let him know that Joshua was it.

"You would have to ask Randy about this yourself. But that's how he began to follow the Spirit, and he's become very active."

"Simon's right-hand man?"

"You could say that. Randy has a simple, practical way of seeing things, kind of like Simon, and so Randy sticks to him. He got angry with Jude Bailey, who is nothing like that. He and Jude had arguments, but it never became part of a public meeting. Randy wouldn't have wanted that because it might have touched on Simon, who he stays close to."

"Those two women, did either of them have the name of Julie?"

"Julie wasn't one of them. Why?"

"This is why I asked about the sexual situation at the Big House, how it touches me. A woman named Julie came to me a couple of weeks ago and said she needed a safe place to stay after a man started using some sort of coercion with her, using his power over her in the organization to get her to do something she wasn't comfortable about."

Sister Naomi frowned. "Julie worked with me in the bakery. We slept in the same dorm. I saw her a lot."

"Did you notice her avoiding anyone, see her manner change when one of the men's names came up?"

Naomi's look slowly changed to a smile. "Her manner was different with Randy, the man I was just talking about. But if you'd have asked me, I would have said it was just the other way around, Julie chasing after him. Those two shared an idea that Joshua was God. They got heated about that topic when it was just the two of them talking. All that heat seemed to be leading to mutual attraction."

"She's gone?"

"Yes, she moved to Des Moines. We haven't heard from her since."

Mikesh thought back to the note Julie left on his kitchen table. "She turned up at my place on a Thursday, the week of my visit down here, said I was someone she could trust. I left to take care of some business and when I got back home there was a note saying she realized you people were now her family and that she had gone back here."

"That Thursday was the day she left, and she hasn't come back. Besides, what she said doesn't make much sense. Brother Randy wouldn't have had to use any extra coercion with Sister Julie from what I observed!"

Mikesh thought back to the kiss Julie had given him. "I'd have to say, I felt a little bit pursued myself."

Naomi laughed. "That's some magnetism you've got. Drawing a woman all the way up to Waucoma after she'd seen you just that one time!"

"Just remember, once she saw me up close she turned around and ran back the other way before the sun went down. How do you know she's in Des Moines?"

"Gary heard from a friend that a week ago she started a job as a greeter and community contact person in the office of Senator Cornish."

"I'm surprised Cornish would welcome a woman with a drug record as part of his staff."

"I wouldn't know about that."

"But I thought you people rescued from her street life with drugs."

"Julie is a smart woman. She came here on her own. I would say that before she came to us she led a *fast* life, but I don't know anything about a *street* life or a rescue."

Mikesh decided that he would stop at Senator Cornish's office as part of his visit to the capital. Maybe he would find, there, what he had been looking to find out at the Big House.

CHAPTER 20

JUDE BAILEY WAS WRONG about the Des Moines office of One Nation having a listed address. One Nation had a national website with neither number nor address but a "contact us" option for e-mail inquiries. Mikesh wrote, saying he was interested in becoming a member. A reply thanked him, but told him no part of the organization was active in Waucoma, Iowa. He replied saying his interest was working through Des Moines. Two days later he was notified he could appear early Monday afternoon at a coffee shop near the capitol and ask for Frank Garber. Mikesh was set to check out how religion was in bed with politics in the Hawkeye State.

The coffee shop glinted with chrome and white porcelain. Many customers wore suits. Mikesh, in his plaid oxford shirt and slacks, was conscious of being underdressed. Frank Garber, seated near the front window, was immaculately groomed. As he rose to shake Mikesh's hand, the brilliant white of his shirt collar and cuffs stood out against his tanned and freckled skin.

Garber was courteous, but not warm. He asked Mikesh about the drive to Des Moines and the look of the fields. "Farmers get anxious this time of year. A slow thaw, a spell of rain makes it even worse. I'm not in farming myself, but I work for the Corn Council, and that's made me learn to think about farmers' concerns. Their worries become my worries." Garber flashed a smile showing even rows of teeth. "What is it you do, Arnie?"

"I do some farming. I've got a little cow/calf operation." Since Garber worked for the Corn Council, whatever that was, Mikesh did not bother to add that he kept all the land in grass.

"Little? How little are we talking?"

"Very little," Mikesh answered, conscious of the megafarms Garber dealt with through the corn industry. "Around 120 acres. My main business is handling security for a community college."

"What do you mean by 'handle'?" Mikesh noticed that the man's questions didn't give room for being vague.

"What I mean is that I'm a security man. One of only two at the whole place: the night man. My work is humble in the big scheme of things."

Garber gave a tight, practiced smile.

"But you work for the state, then. Maybe that explains some of your interest in One Nation. We are looking for people at all levels of government. We each have a role to play, big and small. And it's important that our work be for the good." Garber paused. "In my own work, I'm a lobbyist for the corn industry here at the capitol. There are plenty of people who look down on the lobbying business. But representatives from places like Des Moines or Cedar Rapids need to be reminded that in Iowa, the interests of corn farmers in Waucoma are the interests of the cities as well, and can't be forgotten. My main work is to stand up for the little guy. You just have to believe that what you do matters." Again the smile.

Mikesh knew that increasingly few of the persons who raised Iowa corn were "little guys." Economics left scant room for that.

"But I may have been jumping ahead. I assumed you were interested in One Nation because of your work for the state. I should let you speak for yourself about that, Arnie."

The door was open to Mikesh, and he didn't have a clue what to say. Why *was* he interested, and what would he tell Frank Garber? He was aided by the arrival of the waiter, who took his order for coffee and disappeared.

"I'm curious. A friend told me about One Nation a couple of weeks ago, and explained how much work they did. I went online and saw that you aim to promote cooperation, help out the people, see that good work gets done where it can," Mikesh improvised.

Garber nodded his head. "Exactly. But there are other organizations that work toward those ends. What was it specifically about One Nation that made you inquire?"

Mikesh needed some sort of secret handshake or code word to allow the whole conversation to go forward. What it could be was beyond him.

"Joshua King." Mikesh decided truth would be the best course. "I'm the man who discovered Joshua King when he had his accident. I haven't made it a habit to think about religion, but since I came upon that accident I've been discovering a lot, and it's made me want to learn even more. You could say I'm interested in the practical side of religion, how it helps everyday people. Isn't that what One Nation is trying to do?"

Garber studied Mikesh, shifting his coffee cup back and forth across the surface of the table between his fingers. Mikesh wished he had worn a sport jacket. He was sweating so much he could feel dampness in his armpits.

"Arnie, One Nation has to be careful. Though we have a public presence, we do our work privately. And that means publicity and the attention of the larger world may be the last thing we need."

Mikesh said he understood this, that he was not a journalist.

"I know you're not a journalist. I checked you out before I came here today. We don't like to take chances."

"My interest is in Joshua King. It seems like he and his organization were doing the kind of thing One Nation promotes. But he's dead now. Would One Nation have been interested in him?"

"Arnie, there is only one thing that brings the people of One Nation together, one thing that unites us: Jesus Christ."

Mikesh nodded, but said nothing.

"Arnie, do you have a personal relationship, a personal commitment to Jesus Christ?"

"No," was all Mikesh could say.

"Do you want to develop a personal commitment to Jesus Christ as the victorious and undisputed king of this world?"

Mikesh shook his head.

"Do you want me to help you develop a personal commitment to Jesus as the center of your life?"

Mikesh swallowed and blinked. "No, I can't say that I do."

Garber rose from the table. "Then Arnie, I thank you for your interest in our organization. You are right about the kind of work we accomplish. I'd like to think we accomplish some amazing things. But it all comes down to what I've just been talking about. That has nothing to do with Joshua King. If you develop the kind of faith I just asked you about, or if you want me to help you develop that faith, faith that helps people move mountains, then we can talk. But until then, I'm going to have to say goodbye." Garber did not offer his hand.

"Are you a Zadok?"

Garber stared hard, then handed the waiter arriving with Mikesh's coffee a folded twenty and walked away. Mikesh's blood pressure throbbed in his neck. He no longer cared about his plaid shirt. No, he liked that he was wearing his plaid shirt in this room of custom-tailored business attire. He sat at his table in his plaid shirt, slowly sipping his drink. When he was finished, he casually paid his bill, tipped generously, and returned to his well-used truck. One Nation took Josh King seriously enough to have sent Frank Garber to size Mikesh up, but there was nothing friendly in the gesture.

From the downtown coffee shop, Mikesh drove east toward the golden dome of the capitol. Bailey said Cornish had his office only a block or two from there, and Mikesh knew that by circling the appropriate streets, he would locate it. Fortunately, he was looking as he drove, because on Grand Avenue, five blocks down from the statehouse, he noticed the Robert Cornish signs. The senator had been representing Iowa in Washington for the whole of Mikesh's adult life. The Cornish profile in the window of the office storefront was hard to miss. His popular appeal drew deeply on his rural background and his unambiguous conservatism. Mikesh didn't have time to scout the office. He simply walked in.

Julie had traded Mikesh's rumpled sweatshirt for a cardinal red business suit and heels. The hair he first saw tumble from a stocking cap was now razor cut and frosted: the picture of control. She was sitting at a table, talking to a constituent. Another woman standing at a greeter's podium asked if she could help Mikesh. He told her he needed to talk to her associate and took a chair. Julie glanced up from her conversation, expression clouding, then regained her composure and turned back to the elderly voter with whom she was speaking. Mikesh took a seat and waited, rising to his feet at the same time the voter rose to leave.

"You're not with Shekinah anymore," was how he greeted Julie. She took him by the elbow and led him into a conference room, closing the door.

"I don't like talking about my recent past around my colleagues," she said.

"Quite a change of residence for you. How did this all come about so fast?"

"My parents. I told you they didn't want anything to do with me when I had all those problems in my past. Once they discovered I'd gotten straightened out, they contacted me and said they could get me a place to live and this job in Des Moines. Joshua is dead. I had issues with the way things were going, so I decided it was a good time to move on."

"So you had old friends who could help you after all."

"Yes. And I've moved on."

"Your parents have some pull with Senator Cornish."

"They're some of his strongest supporters."

"How about the issue that sent you to my place? Did it get resolved?"

"That was a private matter."

"I stopped by the Big House this morning and talked with Sister Naomi. She said that when it when it came to you and a man at the Big House, Simon's helper Randy, the attraction seemed to be more on your side than his. She also doesn't recall connecting you with a street life involving drugs."

Julie stiffened. "I told you, I've decided to move on. I'll be happier when my time in that place has become ancient history."

"I've got less distance on this," Mikesh continued. "I'm still stuck on trying to figure out what was going on in Shekinah when Joshua King died."

"You should move on too, Arnie. From where we sit right now, I can hardly imagine I ever spent more than five minutes talking to a guy like Randy. He swore that Joshua could walk on water: the new Messiah."

Mikesh remembered Julie sitting at his table, talking about Joshua as the king, an idea that put her close to Simon, as Randy was. "Was Peña putting some kind of pressure on you?"

"No."

"Did you come to my place maybe to check out my computer files?"

"Don't insult me. I thought you were someone I could trust. I guess I was wrong."

Julie opened the conference room door. "I've got to get back to my work. Like I said, I've moved on. You should try that too, Arnie. I mean it."

Mikesh's visit in the Cornish office with Julie let him know she could not be trusted. She may have been the person Joshua meant when he said an acquaintance would betray him, but since she was not with Joshua and the rest of us in Des Moines the night of his death, Mikesh had no idea how that betrayal would have worked out in practice. Julie was probably working for Cornish or her dad while she was baking loaves in the Big House kitchen. It didn't seem that Peña's pressure sent her running to his farm. Her visit was probably ordered by someone whose allegiances had nothing to do with Shekinah.

Leaving the capitol district, Mikesh looped north past the meeting center where Josh made his last public appearance before his arrest and his sudden drive into the fog. The marquee advertised a weekend concert by a Seventies band Mikesh thought defunct. The venue was quiet, its expansive parking lot empty. He drove away from the capitol through the central business district of the city. Office towers of the insurance and telecommunications industry rose on either side of the street. The size and shine of the library he passed stirred an envy inside him. It was a far cry from the modest rooms that housed books in Waucoma. Large constructions of metal and stone, facing each across grass and paving bricks in the sculpture park, reminded him of his own urban life. The possibilities back then were big and attractive, but there was so much distance between him and most of the people he knew or met there, including, in the end, between him and his own wife.

The business buildings gave way to a gentrified commercial district, with handsome older houses lining the streets that rose on either side. Here, spring was starting to burst into color: maples budding red or lime green, daffodils and tulips in the beds in front of houses, crab apples and hawthorns in full and showy bloom along walks. Why, when he and Audra lived in Chicago, had they focused on suburbs or high rises instead of looking for a neighborhood like this? Envy rose in him again, for this place and for a life that he did not have now: entertainment and theater, art museums, deep reserves of money. But the thought came to him that he had access to the kind of money that could buy him a place here. It was in his land. It was in his cattle.

The thought of cattle stopped his envy. Making a place where cattle would be happy, living a daily life where those quiet gray animals pushed against him as he delivered their feed or checked their water, calmed him. He remembered that envy was his constant companion in the city—for bigger cars, better apartments, for the dance-loving account executive Audra found more sexy than him. He now had money but it was buried in what gave him peace. People who had not discovered his secret would tell you money cannot buy peace, but Uncle Bud's legacy helped him buy a fair helping of both quiet and contentment after all.

Naomi had given Mikesh the address where Josh and our small party from the Big House stayed during our two weeks in Des Moines, a big square brick and stucco house not far from the freeway. Josh's access to the road north, Mikesh realized, was easy. The tiny sister of retirement age who owned the house appeared at the door when he knocked. She led him through the house, describing the arrangements for the five of us who stayed there with Josh. The sister who owned the house took care of the towels and blankets and room assignments herself: a small basement bedroom for me, and another for Peña and Randy, a room for Maria and Naomi on the second floor, and a small but secluded attic bedroom for Josh. Of the two cars our party drove from the Big House, one was in a gravel parking area, and the other, the Buick, had its own garage space. These arrangements explained why we had not realized Josh was gone on the evening he died. We assumed he went upstairs to be alone, tired from the preceding night's ordeal. That night, I knocked softly on the door at dinner, but thought it better not to disturb Josh when he did not answer, and none of us noticed the absence of the car from the garage until the call came in the early morning from Winneshiek County.

The sister told Mikesh, "Joshua had not been in Des Moines before. We've had house meetings going on two years, so the excitement about his visit was strong. After he got back from the jail I was impressed. You could see he was tired and agitated, but he insisted on having a gathering." The sister pointed from the entrance alcove, where they sat, to a big room beyond the archway which seemed both living and dining room. "Joshua broke bread for us at lunch. You can imagine what a comfort that was, after worrying about him in jail. After we ate, he sat in that wing-backed chair over in the corner by the fireplace. We were talking about buying a building, maybe starting something like the Big House here, a place for gatherings bigger than this house and not so big and expensive as that hall Joshua used the day he was arrested."

The sister reminisced: "Joshua said, 'The brothers and sisters here need to be fed—body and Spirit.' He wanted us to offer food and shelter to women and children who were in trouble. He looked so tired. And then that phone call came in the night. We found out he was gone."

Before Mikesh left he looked around the garage stall where the Buick had been parked. The garage was old, the same age as the house, which looked like it had known grander days. The stall was empty. The dirt floor was stained with years of oil drips and the air smelled still and musty. There was only one bare bulb secured to the rafters. At the front of the garage was a workbench where a few neglected tools were scattered. Along the stall, between the wall studs, sat a few old coffee cans: one filled with rusted bolts and metal, one empty and dry, and another empty but greasy. Mikesh wasn't sure what he expected to find. A note? A security camera? Instead of answers he found empty space and dust.

CHAPTER 21

"it's raining wheelbarrows"

CZECH PROVERB

THE LAST FRIDAY IN the month, the Friday following Mikesh's visit to Des Moines, brought bad weather and it brought trouble. The ringing of the phone woke Mikesh from his sleep. The clock read 7:06.

Jim, who ran the convenience mart, did not wait for a reply or apologize for the early call. "We got a river that's rising fast. They are looking at it cresting at anywhere from twenty-five to thirty feet. I don't need to tell you what damage that same flood stage did four years ago. They're putting up sandbags to protect the low end of town. If you got time, you should get there."

Mikesh thanked Jim for the message and the phone clicked dead. Mikesh lay, remembering the flood of 2004: brown water, carrying trees and debris that churned over the dam in the center of Waucoma. Two villages near the Turkey's confluence with the Volga, half swept away by water, were completely bought out for relocation by the federal government. Out the window Mikesh could hear rain on the eves. He swung his feet out of bed and got ready for a hard day.

Two dozen people were at work when he got to the town center around eight o'clock. Buzz Balk, the coordinator of the volunteer fire department, seemed to be in charge. A small team was filling bags with sand that a county truck dumped on First Avenue, stacking the sandbags in the lift bucket of a yellow end loader driven by Balk. As Mikesh arrived, a farmer drove up with a tractor to provide a second bucket. The bigger group of volunteers in a bucket brigade behind the buildings north of the bridge cheered at the prospect of steady work. Mikesh could hear them shouting to one another as he climbed from his truck. They were working behind the buildings above the bridge, where a line of sandbags, stacked four high, stretched north. The river was well up its bank. The grass, regaining its green, was broken by puddles and patches of mud.

Mikesh was good with a shovel, so he started shoveling to fill bags for the tractor lift. A librarian held open the bags and a carpenter whose boss told his crew to report to the town center for work that day stepped up to secure and stack them. There was a satisfying smack as Mikesh's shovel bit into wet sand, settling into a rhythm of scooping and dumping. Balk drove his loader as he talked on his cell phone or shouted out to workers. Balk hadn't said a word to Mikesh or his helpers. The three settled to their task without comment or conversation. It was cold, in the high-thirties, but the exertion with the shovel warmed Mikesh. As he unzipped his rain-soaked coverall to let in more air, the librarian joked about his lack of modesty. That was the extent of their distraction until they ran out of sand, waiting for another load to arrive. Mikesh saw that the line of persons conveying bags to the growing wall was now to the fifth building north of the bridge and another group was working below the bridge where a new pile of sand had been dumped. The rising water made the workers shout to be heard.

As Mikesh stood waiting for sand, resting and watching the walls grow, the librarian asked him if he wanted water or a sandwich and chips. She had her hands full, so Mikesh took a bottle of water and a barbequed pork sandwich. She told him that the local barbeque company provided sandwiches, the convenience store just up Riverview Drive provided chips, and the women of the Catholic parish provided water and coffee and distributed it all from a minivan near the post office.

"I don't wish our floods on us," she told him as she took a drink, "but weather extremes bring out the best in Northeast Iowa folk. It's good to see." After a bite of potato chips she continued, "I hear you've had a brush with religion, Arnie. No interlibrary loans for European history, no biographies of Howlin' Wolf since you found Joshua King that night."

Mikesh was surprised at her detailed knowledge of his circumstances.

"Not much goes untalked-about in a town of 240 people, Arnie. I get more than the normal share of news, working where I do." She also knew more about Josh than Mikesh would have guessed. "It must have been a shock to that church: Joshua King one day making such a big splash in the state capital, and then turning up dead."

"What kind of splash would you say he made in Des Moines?" Mikesh asked.

"A state library association friend of mine, who goes in for emotional religion, was in the event center where King made his showing the day before he died. She said it was like Bono showing up: everyone clapping, cheering, and lining up just to shake Joshua King's hand or touch his clothing."

"That's funny," Mikesh said, "I heard it was more like a shouting match where King got arrested."

"That's how it ended up," the librarian said. "He held earlier gatherings, smaller ones. My friend was at one of those. In that big event she was inside. She didn't even know about the trouble that started outside until she saw it in the papers later on."

"How did your friend hear about King?" Mikesh asked. "He'd never been to Des Moines before."

"His reputation preceded him."

They were leaning against the empty bucket of the resting end loader. The librarian was a petite, trim woman with salt and pepper hair, who ordered the books Mikesh often requested from the state network: an accomplice in finding materials too exotic to be part of the tiny collection housed in the small brick building just east of the bridge. Her energy always impressed Mikesh. As he sat soddenly on the edge of the machine she seemed less in need of rest than he did.

"Iowa isn't that big. Charismatics go in for rallies like that, 'gatherings of the Spirit,' that throw them together with people from the whole region. They send around video links and DVDs the same way college kids share music or photos. King was a regional rock star."

Mikesh was silent, wondering how the man he had found pinned under the car could have filled a hall of people, just a day earlier, on the strength of reputation.

"I told my friend I knew you. She got excited, said you spoke at one of those Spirit gatherings yourself. She called you a messenger."

Mikesh gave her a look and she apologized: "Her words, not mine."

Mikesh would have liked to ask more, and he guessed that his library friend would have liked to hear about his on-again-off-again drug charge, but the sand truck dumped a new load. Buzz Balk fired up the end loader. Continuing rain meant the river was rising faster. Mikesh zipped his coverall and shoveled.

At two thirty, after finishing the wall to the bridge and smaller barriers between the Turkey River and a handful of houses upstream, they ran out of bags. Buzz Balk sent them home saying that if they didn't get too much new rain, the town should manage. Climbing into his truck Mikesh felt, in his arms and lower back, the weight of the tons of sand he had moved. He needed some milk, and stopped at the convenience mart.

At the checkout, Jim, who had given him his morning wake-up call, talked about the report on the river up and down the stream. Flooding was also bad on the Cedar River, the Volga River, and the Wapsipinicon. With several towns having registered over four inches of rain in the last twenty-four hours, it was hard to know how high the rivers would crest. Jim was a thin man with a permanent unruly cowlick. He often gave the impression of being tired, upset with the world. The weather emergency was animating his indignation.

"You look like you did your bit!" Jim observed. Mikesh could imagine the wet and dirty figure he probably cut. "Did that guy in the fancy suit look you up?"

"Who's that?"

"Didn't know him. He didn't say his name, either. Said he heard you might have some information about that Joshua King deal; said that you'd been investigating it."

"Was he a journalist, a news reporter?"

"I wouldn't think so. Way too nice a suit. He was driving a big pricey black four-wheel drive, too. None of the reporters I ever talked to drove in a car like that. Seemed more like seed police if you ask me."

Mikesh's breath grew shallow.

"I told him where you lived, described your place," Jim said, "and told him if he got to Dale and Barbara's he'd gone too far. But I also said I was almost dead sure you'd be just down the block helping out with the sandbagging."

Another customer was waiting, so Mikesh thanked Jim, took his milk, and drove home. His plan was to take care of the animals, get cleaned up as fast as he could, and get ready for work. He felt tired enough to wish he could take a nap, but the weather was still threatening. He knew he had to take special care with his chores. As he neared his driveway, though, something made him decide to check in with Dale first.

He found Dale in the machine shed, holding a socket wrench.

"How about that. It's my famous neighbor Arnie Mikesh. I was just talking about you."

The same well-dressed man had come to the Murphys' farm, asking about Mikesh. "A black Hummer with Missouri plates pulls in the drive, and out steps a man in a thousand-dollar suit and shiny shoes, asking for you. The friends you keep! I told him where you lived, but he said you weren't home. He said you were working for Shekinah, doing security and investigation, according to him, and he had some questions to ask you."

Dale was looking at Mikesh closely. "If you were a corn and soybean farmer, like me, I might wonder if you had gotten crossways with your dealer. I said as far as I knew you weren't working for that Shekinah outfit, but he said, pretty confident, that you were."

"I'm not working for those people," Mikesh said, wondering if that was as true as he wanted it to be. He asked for a description, thinking it might fit Frank Garber, but the tall blond man Dale described was not him.

"The guy said you were investigating Joshua King, and that he needed to find out if what you knew tallied with the State Patrol investigation." Dale's voice was taking on an edge. "I told him you hadn't said anything about it. And that even if you had, that would be something he should take up with you, not me."

"Thanks, Dale. I appreciate it." Mikesh wished he hadn't taken that trip to Des Moines.

Back at his place Mikesh looked around to see if there was a note or any sign of someone having been there. Nothing on his answering machine. He even looked through the rooms of his house, and checked the computer. If the man had wanted to talk to him, why hadn't he just come to where he was volunteering, or called? It didn't make sense, but it was going to add to the local buzz that connected Arnie Mikesh to my brother.

By the time Mikesh got to his chores it was going on four o'clock. He had to rush them: see to it that the cows and the bull had access to cover, put any cows and heifers that looked ready to calve in special pens, do the feeding, and check the water. The rain made the air cold. The metal bails on the feed buckets were moist with condensation, and the feeding area was mucky. Working to lift his boots from the ground into which they sank, he could feel the long day weighing on him. In his mind he remained distracted. He grabbed food to eat while he drove, changed clothes, and hurried to work.

Sometime after ten rain snarled against the windows. Throughout the first hours of his shift, Mikesh replayed what he knew about the person who had asked after him. The clothes and the car did not sound like either police or the press. Mikesh recalled Jimmy Seegmiller and the sheriff's assumption that Josh was in the drug business. Those people could dress and drive in the style of the man who sought him. Neither Mikesh nor Shekinah had anything to do with seed crop genetics. Most likely it had to do with his visit to Des Moines earlier that week, and his admitting to Frank Garber he was interested in Josh, or his talk with Julie about her past. With the rain, Mikesh worried again about the town, and the sandbags they stacked between Waucoma and the river. Though tall as his thighs, those walls were a thin barrier against the tumult.

When Mikesh went to an entryway to get a better look at the storm, the roof was leaking. He got mop and buckets, tossed water out the door, left empty pails beneath the worst leaks, and logged a maintenance report. When the rain slowed to a whispered hiss against the concrete, Mikesh stood under an awning. He pulled his jacket tighter, glad he was dry, relieved that the torrent had passed, but fretted about his cattle. Which cows and heifers had he examined? There had been three he decided were ready to calve. He moved those to pens with cover, away from the herd. That, however, was not the whole number of bred cows. He wished he hadn't rushed.

At the end of his shift, Mikesh drove through more rain. Out of his truck, he heard the bawling of a cow in the field and the muffled bark of his dog. Somehow, Mustard had gotten shut in the feed room. Mustard put his front paws on Mikesh's belly when Mikesh opened the door. Stroking the dog's head, Mikesh felt a bump, blood in the hair. Blood spattered the floor too. Someone had given Mikesh's friendly companion a cruel thump on the head before locking him in the room. Someone had also opened the gate to the cattle pen. He could see that the cows had been out on his driveway, though he hadn't seen any on the road. He closed the gate and walked to the open shed. He counted two extra head in the herd; a heifer and a cow he had left in calving pens were now with the rest of his agitated stock. Whoever had opened the gate and chased the cows into the drive had also opened the calving pens. In the foul weather, his devoted herd had returned to their home. The only cow not there was Rosie.

Mikesh knew it was her calling from the pasture. He left the tight warm cluster of the herd and walked into the rain, anxiety tightening his chest and shortening his breath. She was five hundred yards down the slope: close enough to the creek bottom that he could hear the churning of heavy water. He found her, hooves splayed wide, her eyes bulging with agitation. She had calved. He tried to scratch her behind her ears and pat her neck, but she jerked her head and ran a few feet, planting her front hooves and calling again, her nose stretched forward as if attached to a tightened cord. She wanted her calf. Mikesh thought of the creek. Surely she wouldn't have crossed or tried to re-cross it with a calf. He did not like to think of the grim possibilities. Instead, he moved in the direction she had paced and trained the flashlight beam out ahead of him.

He walked about fifty feet before he spotted a calf, a heifer, its hind quarters in the water, its nose stiff and half buried in the mud. He crouched by it, feeling blank. As the rain pelted the calf, Rosie continued to call. The dead little Square Meater heifer whose gray coat remained slick, was going to be the future of his beef operation, a future another year and an additional big investment of dollars distant. The person who had hit Mustard and opened the gates must have spooked Rosie into running towards the water, and she had charged as far as she dared go. There she had given birth to her first calf: the animal whose left nostril was plunged in the mud, whose hind quarter and tail rose and fell with the surging of the stream. Mikesh scooped up the stiff body and carried it back up to the yard, Rosie following at a distance, calling in distress.

Mikesh had experienced no real peace since the night, five weeks ago, when he came upon my brother's wreck. Mikesh dropped the calf in the drive, evidence of the toll Josh was taking on his life. Someone wanted him to stop investigating my brother's death. Mikesh returned to Rosie with a pail of feed, hoping to distract her, but she paid no attention. He shut the gate on the calving pen she no longer needed and let her stay with the herd.

Beneath the rain, Mary Towers was sleeping with her cat, Safie, curled in the warming envelope of her quilts. Evelyn Schmidt, after spending the evening cleaning out her kitchen cupboards, rattled the walls of her solitary bedroom with snores. My mother was in the women's floor, the sounds of her breathing mixing with those of the sleepers with whom she shared a room. I was in the men's wing, in a small room of my own, dreaming of a dig where we discovered bones. But Arnie Mikesh, in the stormy small hours, was standing soaked in his driveway.

He resolved to take care good care of his cows for a few weeks, not let himself get careless. He had been delivered a warning. During calving time, he would attend to that warning. But when the time was right, he would find out the answer to my mother's request, and if he could, get back in the face of the thug who had hurt Mustard and Rosie.

CHAPTER 22

MIKESH WAS COMFORTABLE AT his desk on the Saturday before the summer session of classes, signing in, surveying the notes from the previous shift, when he heard a noise in the doorway. Looking up he saw Evelyn Schmidt.

In April Mikesh repeated to Evelyn the conversation he had with Sister Naomi. The distaste Evelyn recognized in him for Sister Naomi's evangelism made Evelyn consider Mikesh an ally. Since then she connived opportunities to see him, working late, dropping by with donuts, advising him on grocery specials in New Hampton. Tonight, however, her presence took Mikesh by surprise and filled him with dread. His wounded dog and dead calf were personal confirmation that his attention to my brother's death came at a cost. This was not a workday for Evelyn, but a mission.

She stood at his door bearing a flat box from which he could smell, no doubt of it, kolaches, yeasty and fresh. The aroma touched Mikesh's deepest wells of memory, drawing him back to his grandmother Clarene's kitchen: a room warmed by a combination electric and wood range, a room where the woman in the smock apron rarely rested or sat down. He had not tasted better cooking than Clarene's. She served up Czech wisdom along with her food. "Arnie, when you go to buy, use your *eyes*, not your ears," she warned, cultivating his skepticism from an early age. And more advice, which the baking smell conjured across the wreckage of the past twelve years: "Do not choose your wife at a dance, Arnie, but in the field among the workers." Had university been a dance? Even though Mikesh was not a dancer, probably so. But whatever his grandmother's opinion of Audra had been, Clarene greeted him with kolaches when he returned home to her after his ex-wife's funeral.

Awkward with her burden of Czech baked goods, Evelyn also looked wet. Mikesh rose and accepted her offering, insisting she join him in sampling the rolls with a cup of coffee. As Evelyn removed her raincoat they talked about the weather. The week had begun with a heat wave, near eighty degrees. For the last three days, there had been rain, and today's was heavy. "Funny times, Arnie. Even the weather is changing from what it was. It all gives me the creeps."

Talk moved on to her Mother's Day with the two daughters who, unlike Sister Naomi, stayed true, and the antics and achievements of her grandchildren. "Speaking of children," Evelyn said, "did you hear about that judge in Texas ordering them children back into that Mormon cult where them girls had all been abused? Said there wasn't enough evidence." Evelyn made it a practice to share gossip about her family and the college, and offer occasional opinion on the American political landscape, which she considered shaky. "I thought, those poor kids! Those girls saw this coming all along. Say just one of them—thirteen, fourteen years old—said what really happened to her in that place, and the door closes in that compound of theirs, where the big man sits in his mansion, and the other men know that if the truth gets out they could get years behind bars. Psst!" Evelyn scowled as if the kolache she had just eaten was filled with a paste half wormwood, half gall.

She continued, "It's just like that outfit of Linda's; the biggest problem is the brainwashing. This Texas bunch teaches them from the time they're babies that the world outside those walls—doctors, nurses, social workers—is the devil. Freedom of religion? It's the big man down in Texas getting his way and slamming the door on children who don't know anything different and never will because there is a law in this country that says religion is free to do what no one could get away with outside a so-called church. It stinks if you ask me."

Evelyn stared into her cup of coffee. Her brow smoothed as she regained her breath. She looked at Mikesh. "You don't want to hear about that spirit church, Arnie. And I don't blame you. But you can understand why I keep it on my mind. And folks tell me things, too. My friends know it is a real conversation starter for me."

They laughed.

"Take for example my neighbor, Louise, was Louise Anderra but she's married to a Wesselman. Louise's cousin lives over in Charles City and knows a banker there who got real interested in that spirit church. This banker was a good Catholic, in fact, very active in the parish and the

Knights of Columbus. But a friend of his from the Rotary starts talking Shekinah this and Shekinah that. The banker ended up at one of those house services where Joshua King was. Kind of how it started for my Linda, too. And the man, this banker, is used to going to mass and doing his Christian duty, but he's never been touched—like—in the way he's touched at this service, so he goes up to Joshua King and thanks him, and tells King he could feel the Spirit's call."

"What happened? Mikesh asked.

"The banker asks King what should he do? King says, 'Do you believe, do you feel the presence of the Spirit?' 'I do,' says the man. 'Do you follow the teachings of the church?' 'Yes,' the man says again. 'Do you help those in need?' King asks him. 'Yes' again.

"But here comes the clincher. King says, 'Give away everything you have, then come back. Join us in our work.' As you can imagine, the man isn't so sure about this. 'Where would I give what I own?' 'That's for you to determine,' King says. 'There's a world of need. Give it to the poor.'"

Evelyn raised her eyebrows and took a deep breath.

"Well, the banker has two kids in high school and two more in college. And he tells my cousin that the more he thought about it, the more he believed he could do more in the world, more *good*, with money and with a good community position, than he could throwing it all away, and leaving his family, too, who needed him to give them a fair start in life. The banker was first sad about this, and shamed. But eventually he got angry, and he's been saying ever since that he can see he almost got trapped into doing something foolish."

Evelyn paused, and said: "I heard from Linda yesterday, for the first time in almost a year."

Mikesh was happy for what Evelyn was bound to consider good news. "What did she say?"

"Oh, she asked had I seen the boys, and she asked about my health. But then she kind of hemmed and hawed, and she asked whether I remembered that she had needed to sign over the papers for her car to the organization when she moved down there. Then it comes out that the car had been in a very bad accident and had been sold as junk."

Evelyn stared at Mikesh to make sure he was listening. "Arnie, you saw that wreck of Joshua King's. Was the car he driving a Buick?"

"Yes, an old red Park Avenue."

"That was my husband's car. That was Ralph's."

Mikesh knew Evelyn was getting to the real business for which everything else, including the kolaches, was a warm-up. "Arnie, my Ralph was a sensible, down-to-earth man. If he said something, you could count on it. And like I said, that car was his. He told me when he bought it that it was more expensive than other cars he could get, but that you could count on that car, that it would be a safe car, and when he was out driving that car I wouldn't have to worry about him."

"He was probably right about that," Mikesh told her, trying to picture Ralph, upon whose wisdom Evelyn depended even as the liquid propane deliveryman rested quiet in his grave.

"That car is a good car," Evelyn quoted her dead husband, "an engine that will last forever, good transmission, good gas mileage, and plenty of vehicle around you if you get into a wreck." She smiled, happy to have received Mikesh's affirmation of Ralph's choice. "Well, I gave Linda the title to that car because my husband passed away, and I didn't need it, didn't even really like to see it, because it had been his. But I wanted Linda to be safe, and I wanted to help her out because she was in a bind and I wanted her and the boys to have good, safe transportation, too. I had no idea she'd use it to drive down to that outfit, and turn the papers over to them. Still, the car was with her. I figured even this way, it would still help keep her safe and out of trouble."

"I see how you felt," Mikesh said.

"Then this!" Evelyn went on. "When Linda told me that her father's car was in the wreck that killed that man, and that it happened when he was driving all by himself up in these parts, I just got this feeling that something was not right, that somebody was covering up something more than what I had heard. So I stopped by, to see if you noticed anything funny about the car when you were at that accident."

"I've wondered about that myself." Mikesh knew it was no good trying to stay out of the conversation. "It's not common to have a fatal one-car crash when there's been no drinking involved. I checked back with the sheriff, talked to a few people, but as far as anyone can tell, it was just caused by Joshua King driving too fast for that kind of fog—that and the curve not having the same warning signs as others that came before it on that road."

"I know the spot. And once I'd talked to Linda, I went by there to look it over last night."

"What did you think?"

"Gave me the heebie-jeebies. There are still marks where the car hit. There was even some metal lying around. I hated to think of it coming from Ralph's car. I just hated to think of Ralph's car in the middle of something as ugly as all that." Evelyn hesitated before what she said next. "I can't forgive King for what he did to my family, but I hate to think of that poor man dying out there."

"It was ugly, all right," Mikesh said.

"I don't care what they say. I've got a bad feeling about it. I think, at the very least, that those people, the ones in that church, weren't taking the proper care of that car. Ralph said that if you took proper care of the car, it would take care of you, simple as that."

Evelyn gave this a long thought, set her mouth in an almost frown, and stood up to go, putting on her coat.

Mikesh felt uneasy. Another hunch, added to all he already heard, about my brother not dying by accident, with not the slightest shred of hard evidence at its base as proof. It was like the theory of a trained army of killers providing support to Lee Harvey Oswald when he pulled the trigger on Kennedy from an empty warehouse: no army ever proven, no conspiracy revealed, just every other man or woman on a barstool from Boca Raton to Fresno ready to swear under oath they knew the murder of the dashing young president was a group effort. Mikesh wasn't taking the bait.

"I'm sorry I couldn't be more help, Evelyn."

"No, you've helped. You let me know that it was really Ralph's car, and you let me know that you looked into this, thought it might be fishy, too. And I know you don't want to think about it anymore. But if you learn something, you let me know. Ralph wasn't wrong about much. In fact, my Ralph was never wrong."

Mikesh told her he'd think about it.

"Thanks, Arnie. I feel like Ralph's reputation has a mark against it and, you know me; I won't rest easy until that mark's been cleared."

That night, as Mikesh's truck sloshed through the rain, wipers marking time, Mikesh wondered again where my brother was going when his car left the road. He thought of the fatherless boy wandering dreamily with me along the Turkey, the decision to leave college to step onto the bleak plains, the man who walked into a New Hampton bar to tell a tired Linda Schmidt she would become Sister Naomi, the thirty-year-old who would take the old world apart and put it back together rotated to a whole new angle. What was Josh seeking in that thick fog? "*You* are here," he told Mikesh.

Mikesh might not ever know where Josh was going, but for Evelyn's sake, and for Ralph's, as well as his offer to my mother, he would find out what happened to the old Buick that was the instrument of my brother's death.

CHAPTER 23

THE NEXT DAY MIKESH called the sheriff's office and reached Seegmiller. When Mikesh made his request, Jimmy got quiet, and then asked for his number. A few minutes later, the phone rang

"Hey Arnie, I decided I'd step outside and call you on my personal phone. I know the coroner's report went out, but Fox still says the case is 'under investigation,' and you know by the law of this state that means Sheriff doesn't have to give you diddly. I don't have to either. Fox hasn't done anything on the case, but he isn't closing it either. Between you and me, I think someone higher up asked him to just sit on it until it goes away. So I'm not even going to ask him about an information request. It's not as if you couldn't drive around to the half dozen garages in town asking about a crumpled up Buick and figure it out in less than an hour anyway. The car has been at Mel's."

"Thanks, Jimmy."

Mikesh let his eyes adjust to the interior when he stepped into the work area of Mel's OK Auto Works during their coffee break. He heard voices and laughter in another room. The one man in the body shop turned off his grinder and lifted up his safety glasses when he saw Mikesh waiting. Mikesh didn't recognize him.

"I'm Arnie Mikesh. I'm the person who found Joshua King when he died in a car crash in March. And I'm a friend of a friend of King's, Mary Towers. She and I keep talking about that crash. It shook me up a bit, because I keep re-living that moment. And I heard you guys had the car. I wondered if I could take a look at it right side up and in daylight, thinking it might put some ghosts to rest."

The auto body repairman studied his face. "Arnie Mikesh. Didn't you wrestle varsity for Calmar at 167 back in '84 and '85?"

"I gave it a shot."

The body repairman laughed. "I like that! Well, I guess you got to have humility when Spanky Dirks, the Turkey Valley wrestler in your weight class, took either first or second at state four years running."

"They're still proud of Spanky down there." Mikesh thought of the wrestler to whom the man referred: now a feed company rep with six children, a man who boasted a six-pack set of abs that he invited people to punch.

"I live over near Waucoma now. They take their wrestling seriously."

"Damn! You can say that again. I wrestled 167 for Decorah just a few years after that. In middle school I watched you take the mat a few times. Turkey Valley's guy beat my butt once, but only once, and not at conference. He didn't make winning easy, though. He knew every dirty trick in the book. I still got some skin scars from the way that scumbag dug his stubble into my shoulder. That kid had a two-day beard that felt like broken glass." He was rubbing his shoulder through his shirt as if to demonstrate.

The man surveyed Mikesh. "You said you live over there? What do you do for fun these days?"

"Just try to stay out of trouble, that's all. I got a farm. I take care of that."

"Farming, huh? Well, you got plenty of farm neighbors over in that part of the world."

"It's okay. It's not a bad place to live."

"Suit yourself."

"So that Buick, like I was saying, I heard you guys have it."

"*Had* it. We had it 'til a week ago. But it's gone. At the car crushers."

"That seems strange. I heard the case was still under investigation."

"Investigation? Ain't nobody looked at that car since the morning they brought it in. High time they got it out of here, take it off the state's dime."

"Didn't they check it over? Check to see if there was anything wrong with it?"

"That car came in here on a weekend. I wasn't here. Mel took care of it. He told me state police emptied out the glove compartment and the trunk, looked around under the seats. So we figured they were checking for drugs, if that's what you mean."

"Nothing else?"

"Nope. Mel laughed about how fast they were outta here. You know how it is with guys on a government payroll. Don't like to let their coffee go cold. Who knows, maybe the guys had a lot on their plate. It was after that bad foggy night we had." The man caught himself. "I guess if you found the car you probably remember all about that."

Mikesh didn't reply.

"It's too bad what happened to that man, King. I never seen him myself. But he sure turned around the crooked used car dealer over in Cresco."

"Who's that?"

"Guy name of Hammon, Shorty Hammon. Hammon's Quality Used Cars. Quality my ass! The guy used to sell absolute junk. But to talk to Shorty, every car on the lot was a dream on four tires. The main thing about Shorty Hammon, though, was the way he worked financing. The guy was the master of the low monthly payment. Lowest down payment, lowest monthly payment, that's what you heard. And it got in the people who couldn't afford a car in the first place. And he'd get 'em in his office and jerk them around, mess with them until they didn't know the difference between a twelve-month and a seventy-two-month loan. Next thing they knew they were walking out of there with the papers for a worthless pile of junk that was going to cost them for the next six years, when they'd be lucky to get six months of driving out of it. I'm talking poor families. Single moms with kids. Eighteen-year-old guy trying to deliver pizza to pay the rent."

The repairman continued, "Seems King's people had a rally or meeting in the park across the street and old Shorty gets interested. All these people gathered and listening, all looking at the same man. So Shorty leaves the secretary in charge and goes over there, but there's a big crowd, and it's flat, and he can't see a thing, cause I'm telling you, the guy really is short. Well, he sees this kiddie slide, and he climbs up the ladder and he's standing on the kiddie slide listening to the last part of what King is saying. And when the meeting breaks up, King goes right over to Shorty, 'cause he has seen him up there, higher than everyone else, and before Shorty even has time to leave, he says, 'I been watching you, Hammon. Take me to your place for dinner. We've got things to talk about.'"

"Did the used car man take him up on that?" Mikesh asked.

"It's like Shorty was hypnotized. He says 'sure thing.' Brings King and a couple of his people over to his house and they have Chinese takeout. Next thing you know, Shorty Hammon has become a straight shooter.

Not only that, he calls in some of the people with the worst loans, and he writes them off: gives them the papers to their cars free and clear. I couldn't believe it when I heard that. That's a real miracle there. Shorty Hammon on the up and up!"

The body repairman paused.

"Anyway, that's the one thing I heard about King. So if even if that was the only good thing he did in his life, that's something. But I guess you wanted to know about that busted-up old Buick. Like I said, it just collected dust 'til about a week ago. Then we got word to haul it down to Waterloo."

Mikesh asked for details on the place it was sent—a junkyard near the airport, on the north edge of the city. The repairman said it was likely to sit around there for a while if they wanted to strip any of it out for parts. But given its age and seriousness of the damages, they might not bother. Mikesh thanked him for his help.

After Mikesh turned, but before he could leave, the body repairman asked, "You said you were a friend of Mary Towers. How's she doing?"

"Okay, I guess. Why?" Mikesh turned back.

"Nothin' really. I don't really know her except from being a few years ahead of her in high school. I might have been out with her a few times way back when. I just wondered if her old man has been leaving her alone."

"Her old man? Someone she lives with?" Mikesh stumbled. He was trying to think of some hint Mary might have dropped about someone in her life. Something at her apartment that would show a man lived there too.

"Not lives with. But used to. I'm talking about her dad."

Relief splashed over Mikesh. "She's never mentioned her parents."

"I don't blame her. Gus Towers used to live around here, but he got into some trouble and moved on down to Missouri."

"What kind of trouble?"

The man puzzled for a moment before he spoke. "Gus is a trucker, contracted out his own rig. Got in trouble with one of them big pork companies that had him do a lot of their hog hauling. And you may know how they are. Own them hogs from piglet to pork cutlet. Well, Gus was protective of that rig. Didn't like the way a load of worked-up market-weight hogs nosed around the racks on it, bending things up. So if Gus loaded up those hogs on his own, he'd fix 'em, so they didn't mess around with his truck."

"How did he do that?"

"Up in his cab he had a Little League bat, maybe twenty ounces or so. And Gus, he'd stand at the loading chute and hit every pig over the snout with that bat as it came through. Took real pride in his aim and had just the right touch to maybe just crack a bone, soften it up like. Whacked every damn hog in the whole truckload! Those porkers let Gus's truck alone." The man snorted a laugh.

Mikesh's stomach felt suddenly hollow. "Sounds like a person you wouldn't want to mess with."

"Well, you or me, no. You wouldn't want to cross Gus if you didn't have to. But a big pork company, they feel different. Gus can let booze get the best of him. One time he handled a load of hogs when he'd been on the bottle. Shows up at the meat packer with a whole lot of hogs got bad nosebleeds, plenty of broken skin. The meat packer found out it had to be Gus messed with the hogs. And then it turns out there were other pigs before that showed up at the plant with busted noses, just that it didn't much matter to the ham or the bacon, so no one had said or done anything about it."

"And this is Mary's dad?" Mikesh asked.

"Yup. Hog processer was ready to press charges 'til Gus points out to them he's hauled a lot of their hogs and busted a lot of pig snouts over the years, and no one has said a thing. Maybe that wouldn't look so good for them if it came out in public, so they didn't prosecute. But he'd made them mad. They put out the word and made sure no one in the pork business hired him again."

Mikesh said, "You asked if he'd been leaving Mary alone. What did you mean by that?"

The repairman studied Mikesh again. "Well, at the time he had this trouble with the meat packers, Mary was living in town, like she does now. Gus started drinking worse, and one night he showed up at her place with that bat of his. Went right after her. I don't think he busted any bones, but from what I hear, he treated her a way a daddy ain't supposed to treat his girl."

Bile rose into Mikesh's throat. "What happened?"

"I said you don't want to cross Gus, but once he left her place, she called the cops, went right after him. And she would have sent him to prison, except that the district attorney accepted a plea bargain. I think in the end Mary didn't want to have it go to a public trial either. I think there was some past with her and Gus and that bat of his she just didn't want to talk about in a room full of people and press. But it canned old Gus's ass. He spent a couple of years on parole, and he's under a lifetime restraining order. He goes anywhere within a mile of his daughter, they'll lock him up for real. The lady judge on the case wanted to tack Gus Towers's sorry hide to her wall and spit on it."

The repairman gave a dry snort and continued. "Gus moved down to Missouri maybe four, five years ago, after he'd finished that parole, and works for an outfit down there, doesn't have his own rig anymore. But not too long ago I heard someone say Gus was thinking of moving back up to these parts. Don't really see how he could. I just wondered if there was anything to it."

Mikesh said he'd only met Mary after the car crash.

"So you don't know about her mother then, either. Mary Towers moved away from home while she was still in high school. Her mom died when she was in junior high. And they say Gus started messing with her even back then, once her mom was gone. Mary turned seventeen, she was out of there!"

"That's terrible!" Mikesh could feel his breath go short.

"Well, there's all kinds in the world." The bodywork man smiled, as if to continue his story, but Mikesh was gone.

CHAPTER 24

MARY WASN'T SURE ABOUT Arnie Mikesh. After the Saturday where she stayed to nurse his bumped head, he saw her for lunch, full of news about the Big House, with plenty to say about his trip to Des Moines. She liked the enthusiastic way he talked about his discoveries. She had the sense that he was, in part, making these inquiries for her sake, chasing down leads and hunches to see if they paid out. Mikesh promised to come by the next week to fix a drip he noticed in her kitchen sink. He came, but when she was working, so they hardly talked. Then silence. Later, he did not return the call she made to try to re-connect. She wondered if he was sensitive enough that he grudged that she was working the day he fixed her sink.

Then today he called. She agreed to a late lunch at her apartment. He brought what she could only assume was a food offering: a beginning-of-June picnic. Fresh-baked brown bread, local lettuce, cheese, smoky slices of roast beef, marinated asparagus, dark chocolate. As he unpacked the food he explained that not long after he'd seen her last he decided to take a break from looking into Josh. That made him hesitant to see her. But Mary surmised from the food that he'd had a powerful change of heart.

Mikesh talked about his work. It was only as they were eating that he mentioned her father. Mary couldn't tell if he felt hurt that she did not speak about it before.

"Listen, Arnie," she began, "I don't like to talk about my dad. I don't want to waste a minute more of my life thinking about him, if I can help it. He's a pig. I wouldn't want to give him the pleasure of knowing he was on my mind."

Mary doubted Mikesh could understand her absolute desire to forget every brutal thing her father had done. How could Mikesh know how it felt when the trapdoor opened beneath her feet and she dropped into a gloom so thick she lost her will to climb out?

"My mother kept him somewhat contained. I don't know how she took it, or why she married him. I never got old enough with her to have that kind of talk. She had a way of dealing with him, though, that tamed him. When she got sick he drank more. Instead of helping her, he became hopeless, really bad. That's when other stuff began. I was in junior high. Momma was sick, and . . . ." she trailed off. Only the women in the support group she found, years later, and the counselor she settled on could understand what words could not frame.

"After I moved out and was living with other girls, my father left me alone. I met Josh. The time Dad came after me again was years later, when it all went bad with his business and I was living on my own. It was just after Dad's plea agreement that Josh came back."

"Back from where?"

"That's when he'd been in Mexico. I hadn't seen him for three years. Suddenly there he was, kind of like the way you turned up here today." She gave Mikesh a searching look. "Josh heard about the business with Dad. I think his mother wrote. He didn't say that's why he came back, exactly, but there he was. Josh told me he was moving back to the States to work in Denver. He said if I wanted to get away from here, I could move out there, too."

"What was he proposing?"

"Proposing that I could move to Colorado, get further away from my dad, be closer to him if anything happened. Not proposing marriage, if that's what you mean."

Mikesh couldn't tell if the edge in Mary's voice was resentment at him for the question or at Josh for what he suggested.

"What did you tell him?"

"I told him I didn't need his help with my dad. I'd taken care of him. That if I needed any other help it was going to be from the law, and this was the place where the police and the courts knew all about my father and had made arrangements—where they had my back. Also that I was seeing a counselor who was helping me. Josh looked deflated. He found it hard to believe I'd want to stay here. It could be that my going to Denver might have been part of his plan in moving back, but I wasn't interested. I said, 'Josh, you did your part for me when I was twenty, a girl who'd lost her mom, whose dad was evil, and who'd had to grow up fast by living on my own in high school. I'm not going to take anything else from my dad, ever again, and it's not going to help me deal with it any better if I'm in Denver."

"He let it go at that?"

"He said if I ever needed him, he would come."

"And he never mentioned it again?"

"He did. The last time I saw him, just last year, we talked about it. He and Maria went from the Big House to Elkader for one of his house gatherings, but Maria wanted to visit people, so Josh had some extra time. He asked me to meet him in Elkader, have lunch. We walked below town along the river, where Josh and Tom messed around growing up.

"Josh seemed a whole lot older. He wasn't excited about life like he was back in those early days. He had a lot on his mind, sending out missionaries to start up house meetings in new places. He talked about how he was eventually going to Des Moines. He said there was talk of sending out his people to Detroit, Kansas City, Denver, maybe even New York. In one way he was excited, but in another he seemed to know he was losing control. He was anxious about who he could trust."

"Did he mention anybody in particular?"

Mary laughed. "You're still trying to work that all out, aren't you!" She didn't tell him she'd been thinking too, trying to remember what Josh revealed.

"No. He didn't mention anyone. He just said that there were more pastors coming to the first house meetings in new towns. Asking him tough, tricky questions, trying to trip him up, show the good Christians in the room that he was evil, fake. Now that his following was getting bigger, the righteous had him in their radar. A radio preacher challenged him to a debate on Christian talk radio where every caller would make him a target. He had to decide about that."

Mary thought again of the heat of that August day, almost a year ago. The track along the river was dirt. As she and Josh walked they kicked up dust. Across the river locusts buzzed in the trees. No clouds, a sky half white with haze. Josh showed her the rock on the bank where he and I fished, the bend where we swam, the point where early on we sent rafts of twigs out into the current and watched them disappear. Mary figured Josh was picturing those fragile boats getting smaller in the distance as he stood looking downstream from the town, his face pensive. "I might not have long," Josh said. He licked his finger, drew it through the dust of the riverbank, and put his finger in his mouth, as if he wanted to taste the earth.

What should she tell Mikesh about all of that?

"Josh said the world was turning against him," she said. "He said, 'I might not have long.' Josh also said that with his new mission work he would travel even more. He would rarely have the same roof over his head, but he still worried about me, that if I just said the word he'd get me to the Big House. There were people at the Big House he trusted, who would take care of me, no matter what happened to him. He said his mother was there, and she cared for me. And Sister Naomi was a better and stronger person than he was in lots of ways. He said he'd talked to Simon Peña about me too. What he didn't say is, that Peña would rather scratch my eyes out than give me the time of day!"

Mary and Mikesh both laughed.

"I'm used to people considering me trouble," Mary told him, thinking Mikesh could never imagine, given her history in this town, and her work as a massage therapist, a job some people would never understand.

"But years ago I got help and worked myself to a place where I could live with what my father did to me. That history doesn't go away; you learn to live with it, just like you might learn to live with an accident victim, a child, say, or a wife, who can no longer talk or feed herself. You learn to manage. Arnie, when my dad used to do bad stuff to me I found a place I could go; it may have been inside my head, but it felt like going someplace quiet, someplace outside my body that was safe. I was expert at that.

"To heal," she continued, "I had to learn not to separate my mind from my body that way. I learned to face what had happened to my body. And I learned to make my body a safe, familiar place where I would be comfortable, not to ever let myself leave it. Everything Josh said about the Spirit: that's too much like that place I used go. My dad sent me there. I won't go back, no matter how much I ever loved Josh."

Mikesh told her about Evelyn's visit, and how he was determined to do her the favor of tracking down her husband's car. When Mikesh left after lunch, in fact, he was driving to Waterloo to the place that had it. Mikesh seemed like himself, and Mary liked that. She offered no encouragement or advice, but was touched by his peace offering and concern. She told herself with a measure of pride, that she read kindness in his eyes the first time he appeared. She hugged him at the door as he left.

Mary Towers's past, and Gus Towers's continuing distant threat were the dark energy of her life, bending the course of her days, the path of her thought. To her credit, Mary untwisted her path, found some happiness.

She accepted ownership of the life she'd been given, made choices, and lived by them. She decided as she talked with Mikesh, that if he wished to pursue the answer to Josh's mystery, he had to do it for himself, maybe for the woman named Evelyn with whom he worked, for my mom, but not for her. By his own volition and his own power, he'd have to contend with the energy my brother's death weighed against the constricted orbit of Arnie Mikesh's life.

CHAPTER 25

WHEN MIKESH HAD CALLED the car crusher, saying he'd been a friend of
the deceased, the woman at the other end explained that by arrangement
with the selling party, neither he nor anyone else would be allowed to
examine the vehicle. When he asked if he could look at any other vehicles, the woman hung up. After he left Mary, Mikesh drove to a Black
Hawk county parking lot across from the auto recycler, and watched traffic that went in and out. The last car drove out at five thirty and the gate
of the crushing plant shut, with no sign of activity. At six Mikesh nosed
his pickup to an access drive along a corrugated metal fence. The road
quickly became grass. Mikesh kicked into four-wheel drive, heading for
a corner where the fence jogged west. Pulling in, as close as his sideview
mirror would allow, he cut the engine. There was no gate. It was quiet. If
he went over the fence right away he would have two-and-a-half hours
before sunset to look for the Buick and clear out.

The only person who might approve of his reckless adventure would
be Evelyn, whose heart would warm to his getting a second look at Ralph's
comfort car, even if it meant illegally scrambling over an imposing fence.
Standing on the roof of his truck, Mikesh did a chin lift from the fence
top and swung his legs, missing on the first try. The second time he made
a pendulum swing and dug the sole of his boot sideways when his foot
cleared the top. There was nothing but the thin edge of metal there, but
that was enough purchase to allow him to pull the rest of his heavy frame
into a straddle of the fence top that threatened to slice his groin and abdomen like a crinkle-cut fry. Shifting his hand position, he dropped to
hang against the other side, still gripping the top of the corrugated metal
with his gloves. He kicked back and fell sideways when his feet landed on
the uneven ground, panting with his exertion.

Picking himself up from the weeds and dirt, Mikesh looked for a way out. To his relief there were stacks of cubed cars along the whole opposing side of the lot, between a rail line and the fence. Getting out from the top of those should be easier than getting in. He saw several long metal buildings, probably parts storage sheds. By the lift and crusher were a few stripped-out wrecks sitting where they had been deposited, rusted and bent in odd angles. Mikesh scanned this cluster of vehicles for the Buick. This was the last stop for cars and trucks too badly obliterated to stand on a salvage lot. These had the rumpled look of sleepers lost in their dreams. A few unstripped cars were parked in a short row near the building at the front. Mikesh walked in their direction.

Though it rained earlier in the day, the sun cracked below the clouds and lit the west-facing buildings and fence. The air smelled of grass. On three sides of the salvage yard were greening pastures and freshly-planted fields. Just yesterday Mikesh had ridden Ziska to the third of his paddocks, to drive the cows and their calves into the yet-to-be-grazed meadow of the fourth. For several days, the animals had been smelling that meadow, succulent and tempting. Once Mikesh opened the gate it took no coaxing to nudge the cows that direction. Only the calves were oblivious. They planted thin legs and looked at him with dense faces, heads cocked half sideways, and then bolted, kicking up their hind legs, or wheeled half around in play. Their mothers knew better and walked toward the opened gate, calling to their wayward young. Rosie, who had no calf to manage, was one of the first handful of cows into the new pasture, pushing her nose into the turf, giving her head a twist, and kicking out with both hind quarters as if she was a calf herself. Spring was giving way to summer.

Mikesh felt his venture would turn out all right. He seemed to have the place to himself. The fence was meant more to block the junkyard off from the neighborhood view than to shut out intruders. The closest of the newly arrived cars was a pickup, the same model as his own, though older. The truck must have been rear-ended by a semi-trailer. It tipped back as if sitting on its haunches, absolutely flattened from just behind the cab to the back bumper. As he approached it, the soppy ground beneath his left shoe shifted: a loose piece of chrome trim flashed to his left as an extension of it lifted, making a whoosh and a clink as it dropped back down against a rock.

Suddenly a dog barked from the control office: a dog moving his way. All Mikesh had for defense was a small flashlight. He could see a black streak coming at him, its bark guttural and deep. He would never make it to the fence. He ran to the abandoned truck and tried the door. The handle clicked, but seemed jammed. He put his weight into his next pull. The door swung free and he leaped in, the big animal hitting the outside panel, pushing the door closed behind Mikesh as it snarled outside. The dog's paws were on the window ledge, its white fangs bared as it barked in a frenzy outside the cab. The big Rottweiler wasn't about to let him go anywhere.

No one came to investigate. Alone with over two hours of daylight and only his thoughts, Mikesh imagined elaborate scenarios where he kept the dog at bay with his gloved hands while he scaled the pile of metal and leapt over the fence, where he tricked the angry dog into the cab and shut it inside, where he outran the dog to the entrance, opened the gate, and ran through, laughing as he pushed the gate shut between himself and the animal. Sober reflection told him that staying free from the dog's teeth seemed unlikely in these escape plans unless he killed the animal with a makeshift weapon. He weighed this against the alternatives: arrest for trespass, a felony or misdemeanor conviction, the fine and maybe jail time, and losing his security job again. His profession was to keep people from doing what he had just done. Who would say anything in his defense? The people who knew him best would ask themselves, "What in the world snapped in Arnie Mikesh?"

As night came on it grew colder in the truck cab: the outside temperature around fifty. Mikesh was not wearing a jacket. He chided himself for leaving his cell phone in his glove compartment. Every time he shifted or moved the dog barked. The marks of the Rottweiler's slobber matted the windows on the passenger and driver sides. From what he saw earlier, the Buick didn't seem to be in the line of uncrushed cars, and may not have been in the group with this pickup either, which meant this adventure was of no help in the first place. With the quiet and the loss of light he had plenty of time for his own thoughts: that he was hungry, needed a toilet, and wished he was home, sitting in his favorite chair. Better yet that he might be with Mary, the woman whose hands read his thoughts, who made her way forward each day from an orphaned and violated past. Mikesh laid on the seat and pulled his knees up close to get warm. Looking through the upward-tilting windshield he saw cloudless sky and stars. Mary told him that at nineteen or twenty my brother made her feel like she had been touched by starlight. Mikesh wondered what made her say that. When Josh spent his last night on earth the windows of his car were shattered out. Josh lacked Mikesh's bubble of insulation. The ground that night was covered in snow. The fog was so thick Josh could only have seen a wedge of gray that flickered on the road side of his vehicle as headlights passed above him. Mikesh closed his eyes and tucked his head under an arm as he recalled my brother's injuries. For the first time it struck him why my brother had been singing his "Coming Together" song in his solitude, the answer finally clear. Josh heard the approach of Mikesh's truck and maybe even his footsteps: every sound magnified by his solitude, even if he was only partially conscious. For my brother, who greeted the light of the Spirit in the faces of those who greeted him, Arnold Mikesh was Shekinah, there to help him come home. "Is anyone *else* with you?" "You," my brother said. "Stay with me. Enter . . . infinity."

On the cold truck seat, Mikesh could feel the dizzy rush of his world shifting around 180 degrees, from the place of the guilty party Paul Fox had suspected of vehicular homicide to the cameo appearance of the light, untangling the twisted trajectory that dark material put on my brother's life. Mikesh hung on to the thought. He relished it while he could, because tomorrow morning he was going to find himself back in the place of the accused, and this time the charges would stick.

Balled up on the car seat to keep warm, Mikesh slept intermittently until he woke for good to the barking of the dog after sunrise. Mikesh must have shifted while dreaming. Even though it drove the Rottweiler into a frenzy, Mikesh stretched as well as he could to get the cold night of kinks from his back. Mary could take care of those and speak in his defense. He knew that if a phone call would have brought anyone to his rescue, it would have been her. He thought about her hug. She would laugh if she could see him, safe but at the mercy of the big black dog, just as she had laughed at the thought of his horse's mother's maiden name.

The first man through the gate found him sitting upright, unsmiling, in the middle of the truck seat. The man in khaki-colored shirt, jeans, and a St. Louis Cardinals baseball cap, was black, pushing retirement age if not past it. "Well, look what the cat dragged in!" Mikesh heard him say in a voice muffled by the windows and over the renewed barking of the dog. The man put a leash on the dog, and asked Mikesh his business.

As it turned out, the man ran the crane that lifted vehicles into the crusher. "No one to love that old dog, unless it's me," he eventually told Mikesh as they walked back to the operator's shack.

"My wife, she likes to sleep late. I come early to give this old boy a little playtime to keep him from goin' crazy. We give each other company. Dog be the owner's idea of security, but the owner, he ain't here much."

The man's name was Galen. He softened toward Mikesh when he heard, through a partly rolled-down window, that Mikesh came looking for the Buick and explained his connection to it.

"I crushed what was left of that car last Friday," Galen said as he opened up the modest concrete block office building and made coffee. "Set of wheels so banged up I don't think they bothered to strip it, old model like it was." The dog, which kept Mikesh fearful all night, was quiet and paid him no attention as he chewed at a disappearing strip of rawhide.

"Didn't know it was the car killed Joshua King, though." Galen looked meditative as he stood at the door of the shack and tossed a big piece of knotted rope that the Rottweiler bounded to fetch.

"Joshua King the friend of a friend of mine."

After Mikesh, at long last, relieved himself and sipped the hot, weak coffee, he heard from the old man who tossed the rope, in between sips from his own mug of coffee, about a man named Lazaro, employed at the plant, a short man, good at the careful and demanding work of stripping out vehicles. Lazaro was from Mexico but had lived in the U.S. for over ten years. He had a house in Waterloo where he lived with his wife and her sister. Their house served as home to one of Josh's regular meetings.

Lazaro and the two women were transformed by the Spirit to which Josh introduced them. But they were not trustful enough of gringos to move into the Big House. Lazaro discussed this with Galen, who agreed that it would be crazy for Lazaro's family to give up their home. Nor did they want to split up from each other under the regime of that place. But each was a devoted follower of my brother.

I know Lazaro. Because of that, I know the story Galen related to Mikesh, a much-circulated story from before the time I joined my brother. It began with a healing. A man from their home village in San Luis Potosi came with his wife and two children to get away from trouble with a drug cartel. They occupied a room of the house. But the older of the children, a girl four years of age, was subject to seizures: grim spectacles where she would fall to the ground as if dead, tremble and convulse, stuttering and crying out horrible noises. The mother blamed it on herbicide exposure while she worked in the fields, pregnant and nursing, on their slow way north. She had seen similar cases in other families where the women worked the fields, and she knew how to protect the girl, using a strip of cloth to restrain her through the fits. But Lazaro's sister-in-law, Maria, felt it was a demon possession. There was no medical care available to the new family; they had neither insurance, nor money, nor legal residence. But a man Maria knew, who agreed with her diagnosis, said he knew a *curandero*, and he would bring him. When he arrived at Lazaro's house, the *curandero* turned out to be Josh.

The people of the household were alarmed. They had not expected a white man. But as Lazaro told it, they gave Josh their trust because the *curandero* had three great recommendations in addition to that of the friend who brought him. He spoke "the language." Not just Spanish, but the mountain village Nahua of Lazaro and his neighbors. Second, he immediately spoke to the girl in a way that engaged her and showed respect. And finally, he had "the great quietness," something Lazaro would not explain.

Josh asked that the kitchen table be cleared, and that the girl sit on it with pillows placed behind her. He conversed with her about her parents' village, a place she had never been. He repeated an old story people in the village told about the highest peak visible from their homes: how ants climbed up to the garden of heaven on a pillar of stone and ruined the plantings, until the pillar broke into the mountain shape. Josh told the girl about how her ancestors lived in that place in a great empire long before the arrival of the first ships from across the sea. And he asked her about her grandparents, about whom she had heard much. She happily chattered about this, but eventually her manner became distracted and her features twisted and twitched. She fell backward, rigid, on the pillows, and arched her belly toward the ceiling. Words came from her in a low voice. The mother restrained her with one arm while Josh passed his hand above the surface of her body. As his hand passed over the ribs, just below the girl's heart, the deep voice came from her again in what sounded like words that Lazaro said were neither Spanish nor Nahua nor English. Josh's hand dropped to the ribs and his fist closed as if grabbing something as he spoke, again in words none could understand. Suddenly the girl convulsed again, the horrible voice crying out from her. Josh turned his clenched fist, fingers upward, and then opened the hand with a tossing motion, as if throwing what had been there into the air. "Leave her!" he shouted in English. The girl made a final cry in the terrifying voice and grew still. Lazaro was afraid she was dead. But she breathed softly, and opened her eyes, and sat up. She asked Josh to tell her the story again about the mountain and the ants. After that, she had no attacks.

The child's mother spoke with the Catholic priest. He said they should stay away from Josh, that such things as demons like this rarely, if ever, existed. If they did, then the man who spoke in the language of demons must be one himself. But Josh returned to see the girl and said nothing about what happened before. He brought her a *dulce* and complimented her parents on her health. When offered money for his help, he refused. Persuaded to stay for dinner, he enjoyed the food far beyond any measure of politeness, and he talked knowledgeably about the country of their home, taking their side against the corrupt local *presidente* and judge and the cartels: those persons whose cruelty and greed drove Lazaro, Marta, Maria, and their friends to make the long and dangerous journey north, and forced them to live in this place of harsh winters and strange customs, away from those people they loved. Josh called each person in the household either "brother" or "sister" or "child." He talked about the life of the Spirit.

The family invited him to return and others came, first for healing, but then to listen and to ask questions. Few people in this place had been able to answer the heartfelt questions of Lazaro's friends with such sympathy and knowledge. Soon their meetings were regular and filled the house. Lazaro told of how, at one of these, his wife Marta came with whispered, angry words to get Maria, who sat with the others, listening and speaking to Josh. Josh stopped and asked what she wanted. Marta answered that her sister was forgetting that he and their other guests would soon need something to eat. Josh said, "But who is showing me the greater courtesy: your sister who attends to my words, or you who fret about my hunger?" Lazaro laughed at how this had flustered his wife. He told Galen this story several times, always concluding with, "Pretty good question, don't you think, my brother?"

That led Galen to give his other reason for respecting Josh. Lazaro always called him "brother." Galen explained to Lazaro that usually that term was reserved for one black man speaking to another. And Lazaro told him that Josh liked to tell a story exactly about this custom. Josh told Lazaro and his household to honor every one of their brothers and sisters. And when asked who *were* their brothers and sisters, Josh told them a story like one from the Bible. He said a man newly arrived from Mexico was beaten and robbed in the park of the section of a city where Hispanic gangs had more power than police. The man was left bleeding and unconscious, wearing only his jeans. A leading businessman saw him as his cab passed the park, and he looked the other way. A bishop drove by on his way to the city headquarters of the church and he thought to himself how sad that people drink themselves drunk, and drove on. But a black man, a brother, who did not have a car and who was walking through the neighborhood to get to a place where he was going to apply for a job, saw the man in the park and stopped. He asked for directions and carried the man to a hospital, where they treated the brother rudely, assuming he was the person who injured the Mexican. He had to give his name, address, and leave a check, signed over to the hospital, because the man from Mexico had no identification. Josh told the old Bible story in this new way and asked, "So who really understood who their brother was? The businessman? The bishop? Or *the brother*?"

"I'm not sure I could be that brother," Galen said, as he finished the story, "but I *do* like the thought."

Galen said he thought about that story when he heard about Josh's death on the road, telling Mikesh, "Looks like you turned out to be the brother that night!" and smiled.

They spoke about the accident scene. "Anything you can think of that would make a car miss a curve like that after making several sharper ones just before?" Mikesh asked, the nosy terrier in him back again on the track.

"You say he spent the night in jail. A night in jail will tire a man out, 'specially if they treat him bad. Don't forget that. Could just have been all wore out and fell asleep at the wheel." Galen paused. "But it *might* not have been the man. Could even be his brakes give out."

Mikesh asked Galen to remind him of what could cause that to happen. "Brakes get too hot, they give out. Steep grade, lotta curves, that will make brakes get hot. Low fluid, air or water in the lines: brakes will quit working with that, too. That crusher out there, it works that way. You give it enough hydraulic pressure, it'll flatten a semi. But that pressure fail and you couldn't crush a beer can with it." Galen was sitting, patting the big head of the dog.

"What's the most common cause of that?"

"Usually it's a hole somewhere: lets the fluid out of the lines, lets condensation in. Any time you get water in the lines instead of fluid, heat turn into steam. System's not built for steam pressure, just hydraulic. Overwork the pedal when you got water in the lines, your brakes go all mushy."

Suddenly Mikesh was restless. Twenty-five miles north, on his way home, was the Big House, and he had some questions to ask there. For the first time in the hour since his rescue from the pickup cab, he was thinking of being someplace else, but didn't know if he was going home or to jail.

Galen laughed when Mikesh asked what he was going to do with him. "You done your jail time on that truck seat, man, with this old dog as your keeper. You ask me, there's too many doin' prison time in this country already. You didn't steal no junk. Far as I can see you didn't *come* to steal no junk. Just glad this brother of mine finally earned his keep."

CHAPTER 26

"He who looks, finds"

CZECH PROVERB

THE BIG HOUSE WAS on Mikesh's way back home. He phoned to see if Barbara and Dale could take care of his place, telling Barbara that if last night was an indicator, he might be gone the whole day, might even have to call in sick for work. He wanted to have his new questions answered.

He found the door of the Big House open. Two people chatting in the hallway directed him to me, sitting at my computer. I was happy to see Mikesh, gave him a welcoming hug, and gestured for him to take a chair. The small white room housed two desktop computers, a printer and not much else: the Big House tech lab.

I was excited because I was near completion on a small book of sayings: the teachings of my brother Josh as I heard them during the time I spent with him. When I explained to Mikesh what I was doing he said this seemed like a good idea.

"Do you think so, Arnie? I must admit, I'm thinking largely of people like you who never got the chance to see Josh. You were the final one, the last to see him alive. From then on, anyone who gets interested in Josh's work is going to hear about it from someone else. Josh wrote nothing."

I closed the door, beginning again in a lowered voice.

"There are people who think this a waste of community time. For them . . . how can I say this? They want to promote Josh and the *idea* of Josh without really teaching Josh's ideas. I'm hoping this gathering of his core teachings will act as a balance. I'm planning to get it printed to hand out to people at new house meetings."

As I looked down at the computer, it occurred to me that there was one teaching Mikesh would like particularly. I searched the computer file for "cattleman" and read aloud from the screen: 'Once, as Joshua finished speaking at Greene, a Catholic priest stood up and asked, 'If, as you say, you follow in the work of Christ. Why don't you call yourself a Christian?' Joshua said to him, 'A man who owned two large cattle farms needed to travel abroad for a year. He placed an ad for a cattleman. Two men applied. The first said he was an excellent cattleman, bragging of his abilities herding and managing animals. The second said he could not call himself a cattleman, but he worked a lot with hogs, loved animals, and tried his best to see they did well. The farm owner was worried about what he heard the second man say, but he needed to leave the country immediately, so he hired both and gave each charge of one of the farms. When he returned a year later he was horrified to find that the first man sold the whole herd for slaughter, each and every animal, pocketing the money, then leaving the country himself. The other man ran the second farm even better than the owner, and returned it to him with more cattle and better soil than when he left it. Which was the better cattleman? The man who bragged of the name or the man who hesitated to accept it?'"

Mikesh shook his head. "That one's okay by me."

"These sayings will speak to people now that Josh is dead: help them hear the voice the people who knew him heard."

"Speaking of the voice you heard," Mikesh replied, "I'm wondering if you could tell me more about that last afternoon you saw Joshua alive. I know we've been over this before, but did he say or do anything that would explain why he got in that car and drove?"

I couldn't see why Mikesh needed to revisit this. We had talked about that afternoon before. "All that came up after Josh got back from the jail, besides our meal, were Shekinah's future in Des Moines and the weather."

"Maybe you could just describe to me what happened after Josh got back from the police station."

"We had a meeting scheduled for the house where we were staying. First we had a meal together. Josh broke bread. Then we talked: a mix of discussion, teaching, business. We had been in Des Moines for ten days, enough to get a feel for the city, and we only had four days left in our stay. We wanted to help establish a base and promote the work there. We talked about Des Moines, a program for single mothers, the community we hoped to establish. Josh talked about hungers of the body, hunger for the Spirit."

I studied the ceiling, trying to remember details. "The meeting ended earlier than it might have because of the fog. It was getting noticeably thick, and people were worried about driving. And I was mindful of Josh being tired. As the meeting was breaking up a sister stayed behind talking to Josh. She was intent on some sort of free clinic for women being part of the work. She wanted to make sure he heard her. I left and went to the kitchen to get something to eat. I heard the sister go out. I was staying in a basement room and thought I might lie down for a few minutes. As I came into the hallway I saw Josh coming back in the front door of the house. Randy was with him. I think Josh saw the sister out, and outside Randy met them and gave her advice about that fog."

"Do you know that's what happened outside?"

"I saw and heard Josh talking as he and Randy came in. Josh said, 'Has it come to that, Randy?' and Randy kind of wrinkled his brow and said, 'Yes, Josh, I'm afraid so.'

"Josh replied, 'Okay. I wanted to know. Thanks.' Then they went to their rooms."

"Why do you think that Randy had been talking about the fog?"

"Because Randy told me that. I asked him about it later. While I'd been having my snack he'd put gas in the cars and been out driving in that fog, so he knew what it was like. He told the woman the fog was bad enough that she would have trouble getting home."

"Is it possible that Randy might have been giving information to Josh that was different than what he told you? Or that Randy and Josh might have stepped out and talked after the woman left?"

"I suppose. I don't think anyone else was outside then. But like I said, that's not what Randy told me."

Just then the room door opened and Peña looked in. "Mikesh, I didn't expect to see you. It's a coincidence you're here. I wanted to talk to you this morning."

Peña took the other chair in the room. "We've been going through a bit of a shakeup around here lately," he explained. "Sister Naomi sat down with me last night to talk about one part of it, and it has to do with you."

"Randy left us. He came to us close to two years ago. He had that fire in the belly. Really wanted to make things happen for Shekinah. The Spirit was alive and working in him in a powerful way. He had lots of church experience, and he was practical, good at getting things done. He wasn't much for words, but he became the man who kept this place going: plumbing, electricity, and cars—he was good at all of that, and at setting a place up for a service, figuring out if we needed sound. Within a few months, I can tell you, I couldn't manage without him.

"And it wasn't just that he was a practical help. He believed in Joshua. Randy was one of those in Shekinah, and not the only one, who believed Joshua might be a new Messiah, might be Jesus come again. And to tell you, Mikesh, I've had those thoughts myself. They got stronger as I worked with Randy, and he and I would talk. But here's where I need information from you. A few months back I noticed that a woman who worked in the bakery, a woman named Sister Julie, started to pay an un-usual amount of attention to Randy. When I finally asked him about it, he said it was because she shared his view of Joshua as Lord, and she and him were talking about that. I wasn't happy about that kind of involve-ment but I decided to let it pass. But Sister Naomi tells me that not long after your visit here, Julie paid a visit to you, and told you that Randy was maybe interested in her in an improper way, maybe threatening her. Is that true?"

Mikesh described Julie's visit, how she said a man gave her prob-lems, and that what Naomi said made him believe it was Randy. Peña's brow clouded.

"Well, that's hard for me to believe," he said when Mikesh finished. "I tell you, that's just not the kind of thing I ever saw. But since then, things have happened that make me wonder. You see, not long after Joshua's funeral, Randy became a different person. We planned for over a year to start sending out people from the Big House and from some of the stronger home meetings to new towns and cities, to help Shekinah grow. Early on, while Joshua was alive, you couldn't find a bigger supporter of that idea than Randy. He helped us with every step."

Peña looked up at me to see if I agreed, and saw that I did.

"But once Joshua was dead," he continued, "Randy dragged his feet, asked questions. If it came to a matter of expanding Shekinah he put up roadblocks. 'But Joshua is dead, Simon,' he'd say. 'That *was* the plan, but Joshua is dead. Don't you see it isn't the same. Him dying means it was never meant to be.' So he and I began to have our disagreements, our fights. Not long after your visit here, less than two weeks after Joshua's passing, Sister Julie left. Sister Naomi said she told you about that."

Mikesh nodded.

"After that, Randy got more agitated and impatient. 'But Simon, can't you see that people are leaving. Shekinah is not going to go any further.' Or worse yet, 'Don't you see it's proven that Joshua wasn't what he said? He's dead. He wasn't what he said. The brothers and sisters need to get back to their old ways.' Two weeks ago, Randy started on something else. Had I taken care of the car Joshua wrecked? That wasn't unusual in a way, because those were the kind of details Randy always thought about: cars, their motors, their oil changes. It had been some time since we'd heard anything about that car. It was just sitting up there."

Mikesh guessed what came next.

"I didn't do anything at first," Peña said, "and he got agitated. He asked again, then really pushed me on it, so I called the sheriff up there, and got the okay. Randy took care of all the details, sold the car to a junkyard he'd found, made the arrangements. And I guess they took the car. But he'd made such a big deal of it, he caught Sister Naomi's attention. That car belonged to her at one time, and now she found out we made the title over to the junkyard. She asked him about it, and he got nasty with her.

"That was a bit over a week ago. At the start of last week, Randy said we should start selling off some other things: appliances, furniture. That there was no use planning to keep this place together. We felt insulted. When Randy saw that, something snapped. He got quiet, didn't seem well. Last Thursday he stayed in bed all day. Then Friday he said he was leaving, that he no longer had any interest in a group that wouldn't listen to him.

"He insisted on my signing over a car to him, said it was the least that was due to him after all his work here. The least we could do to show our gratitude. He was insistent. Saturday he was gone. He took one of our cars with him. I hadn't signed it over to him, and we haven't heard from him. Even so, I might not have thought or said anything, hoping he'd blow off some steam, reconsider, maybe come back with a new attitude. But yesterday on our bread truck's early Monday morning run into Waterloo the driver was stopped by engine problems. We had to hurry to rent a new truck. In the afternoon the mechanic from the towing company called and said the engine failed because someone put sugar in the gas tank and that truck is going to need a new fuel filter, fuel pump, and carburetor.

"Normally I would have said vandals, or someone antagonistic to our work did that. It wouldn't be the first time we were a target. But now

I'm wondering if it could have been Randy. He was an upright, clean person. I find it hard to believe. Do you think there was something I missed that happened between Randy and that woman?"

Mikesh wondered where to begin. "Julie was trying to get on my good side too," he said. "She could be very persuasive. She was looking into what I knew about Josh's death, maybe trying to make me suspicious of you folks down here. She's now on the payroll of Senator Cornish. I think she was working for him or his associates while she was here. But what her real connection to Randy was, I couldn't say. She might have put him up to something."

Peña looked baffled.

"Simon, what happened the last afternoon of Joshua's life, that might have involved Randy?" Mikesh asked. "Anything you can think of?"

"Randy was there. He put gas in the cars. He came back from his errands warning that the fog was not safe for driving."

"Who did he warn?" Mikesh said.

"He warned all of us there at the house, a sister who was leaving later than the rest. I heard him tell Tom about that."

"And where would the keys for the cars have been after he was done with them?"

"In the hallway, on a table. We'd agreed they would be there."

"So Joshua later could have easily picked them up?"

"Yes. It looks like he did."

"What if Randy told Joshua something different than what he said to you—that he had just been out filling up the tank of the Buick, just the Buick. Would that have made Joshua use that car?" Mikesh wondered if Peña would see where the logic of the scene was leading.

"I suppose," Peña said, "but first he would *want* to have to use the car. Joshua didn't like to drive. He wasn't a good driver. We always encouraged him to let someone else drive."

"What could someone say to Joshua that might make him leave on a foggy day and drive immediately in the direction of Northeast Iowa without talking to you, who were managing so much of his business in Des Moines?" Mikesh probed.

Peña's face contracted. He said nothing.

"Did you ever talk to Randy about Mary Towers? Have you ever told him about any Decorah gossip relating to her that you might have heard from Jude Bailey? Did you ever discuss Joshua's feelings for her or his concerns about her father?"

Peña was quiet for a few heartbeats before he spoke: "Last summer Joshua brought all that *mierda* up again. He was concerned about the future in case he would not be around. He told me he wanted that woman to be able to come to live in the Big House if she ever feared anything from her father, even if he, Joshua, was no longer here."

"Did you say anything about this to Randy?"

"I guess I did. Tom here, and his mother, they have a weak spot for that woman. And Sister Naomi, she would be soft too. Just think. Joshua gone and *la bruja* in his place! Right here at the center of things, rubbing her hands all over us, and all the while denying everything Joshua stood for. You bet I talked to Randy about it. I didn't like it, and I let Randy know that. Randy understood." Peña was panting with anger.

"So let's just imagine that Randy had some of those feelings he's lately been telling to you. That he had his doubts about Joshua and thought he was a fraud. Let's just imagine Julie, who got on Randy's good side by talking about Joshua being divine, now encouraged Randy in thinking that was a lie. What would happen if, on that afternoon outside the house in Des Moines Randy took Joshua aside and said he had just been filling up the tank of the Buick and heard from somebody that Gus Towers had returned to Decorah, aiming to get back at his daughter?"

"Josh would have gone to her right away." Peña was shouting now. "He would have gone to her!" Then he lowered his voice. "Even though she never expressed the slightest interest in what he taught, Joshua had a weakness. He couldn't see through her like I could. I knew it would destroy him: and destroy Shekinah. And now, you tell me it did destroy him, so you see, I saw it coming. But listen, Mikesh. If Randy had those evil feelings, if he wanted to kill Joshua, like you suggest, what made him think the drive would do that?"

"I think Randy knew very well all the turns and corners between Northeast Iowa and Des Moines, whatever route Joshua would take," Mikesh said. "And I think he knew there were ways to make a fast driver, which Tom told me the very first morning Joshua was, get into a dangerous situation on that long drive. He just had to compromise the brakes: drain away some fluid, or more likely to extract fluid and replace it in the lines with water. That would not be a problem right away, but it could turn into one on the long drive. With the fog, that was even more likely. A trained mechanic, with the Buick in the garage, could have managed that quickly, either before or after he talked to Joshua, with none of the rest of you the wiser."

CHAPTER 27

"dig a trap for someone, you fall into it yourself"

CZECH PROVERB

SIMON AND I WERE skeptical that Randy could have done what Mikesh suggested, but Peña gave him Brother Randy's full name: Randall Deegan, and his address. Mikesh drove between the green roadside ditches and fields of young corn seedlings in a drizzle, his wipers sweeping intermittently. It was out of his way: a drive almost to Cedar Rapids. The address turned out to be a rural garage near a crossroads. *Deegan's Repairs* was painted above the overhead door of the cement block building that served as the garage. Further back from the road, on an overgrown lot, stood the house and farm buildings, none looking like they were in use.

But there was a car in the driveway. Walking nearer the house beneath the dripping trees Mikesh saw the porch door was open. He walked up a wooden ramp. The afternoon was quiet and warm, even steamy.

When he knocked on the inside door he heard a voice. "Yeah?"

In the kitchen he entered Mikesh saw an old man in a wheelchair, pulled up next to a table. A television was turned on to a game show. From its speakers Mikesh heard, "you are the winner of today's preliminary round jackpot!" a burst of audience applause, and a fanfare of synthesized music. The old man who turned from the television was heavy, looking pinched in his chair, his face unshaven and almost as gray as his hair. Mikesh could see that he was not going to speak, that he was waiting for Mikesh to state his business.

Mikesh explained that he had just come from the Big House.

"That place! Well, if you come lookin' for Randy, I can't tell you for sure where he is."

Mikesh said Randy left the Big House Saturday with one of their cars, and they hadn't heard from him since.

"One of *their* cars!" the old man huffed. "What did those people leave Randy, I want to know? What did they do for my boy in the two years he gave them? *Their* car!" The old man snorted and shook his head. A new musical jingle came from the television and a repeating bell that made it clear the clock was ticking down for a contestant. Plates were piled in the kitchen sink. Two plastic carrier bags of groceries sat half unloaded on the counter. The walls were dim with years of accumulated grease, the smell of which was creeping up on Mikesh.

"Randy's always been a good, clean-living boy," the man was telling him. "Only problem was he couldn't take his religion at any other than a full dose. Religion, it's almost like a disease with Randy, he's got it so strong."

"Action Fellowship. Sabbatarians. Then this Spirit Church stuff, where the man in charge can heal, speaks from authority, has power over demons, just has to be Christ come again!"

"I'm not with Shekirah," Mikesh explained. "I got interested in Joshua King. I happened upon the wreck where he died."

"Joshua King!" the old man snorted. "I checked that Joshua of Randy's out. My sister-in-law brought me over to a meeting they had in these parts. My legs is gone bad with diabetes. The way I figured, if the man was what Randy said he is, then maybe he could help me walk. But we come to that meeting. It was just in a little place, someone's house. And no ramp for the wheelchair, and three steps to get in. How was that gonna work? But my boy Randy, he was there. I didn't get to talk to him much when he was living in that Big House, but I let him know we was coming. And he had three fellas help him with the chair. They lifted me up them steps and into that house. But when I got a look at the man, I simply could not believe my eyes. Long hair. Messy. I know my ministers and this fella wasn't one. We're crammed in there, and I had to sit up front on account of my wheelchair, so everyone's eyes are on me, while this Joshua's saying 'Spirit' this and 'Spirit' that."

Mikesh could tell that the old man had been waiting to unburden himself. "I'll tell you, sir, I just wanted outta there. Came to the time of healing and I wished I hadn't of come. That Joshua, he lays his hands on my shoulders and looks me straight in the eyes, which was hard, I can tell you, cause what I really wanted to tell him was 'give me back my boy!' But there's Randy in the room, and there's the man lookin' into me. 'There's a power in the Spirit makes all things possible,' he says to me, real quiet like. And then he cries, 'A power in you!' And he lifts his hands away and looks at me. But I didn't feel no power. He could see it didn't work. Puts his hand on my head and says, 'May the power of the Spirit work in you, Brother, and make you well.' You can use your own eyes and see that I'm sittin' here today without the good use of my legs."

Mikesh was touched by the bitterness in the old man's voice.

"I can't even tell you if my own son is in this house or not. I called upstairs four or five times since morning, but got no answer. Maybe he went out in the night. I don't know. My hearing ain't good. I can go down that wooden ramp and out the sidewalk to the drive, but don't expect me to get this chair anywhere else in all this muck! I get into a soft spot out there and I might as well drown. If it was dry I could get out around a bit and holler for him. I see the car he came in is out there. But where my son is, mister, I don't know."

Beneath the anger of the man, Mikesh could see the fright. He asked him if Randy said anything about his plans.

"Plans! Randy ain't got plans. Randy come back from that church of his, and told me what I knew already, that this King joker was a fake, not the God my son thought. That he denied Jesus, accepted homosexuals, lets the girlies run half his operation, that his plans weren't nothing if not downright dangerous, but that he was dead, and all that business was over. And it's left Randy with nothin'. 'Back to runnin' the garage,' I told him. 'It's a square and decent business, and people still know you from before.' Randy, he's a good mechanic. Word of mouth is already there for the boy. But it was as if my Randy was deaf. He wasn't listening. Sunday he moped around this kitchen and didn't go out. Yesterday he didn't get out of his bed upstairs all day. Only came down here at suppertime. Still up when I went to sleep last night. Today I ain't seen him."

Mikesh asked if he might look upstairs to see if Randy was all right. The man in the wheelchair seemed to welcome the idea, looking to the door at the base of the steps. The rumpled bed in the room Mikesh found at the top of the narrow stairs was empty. There were racing posters on the wall, a Bible on the bedside stand. The other bedroom and the storage closet were empty too. Randy Deegan was not there. After speaking again with the old man, Mikesh looked in the musty-smelling cellar. Cobwebs, an empty chest freezer with its lid up, old wooden chairs and stacks of magazines and parts supply catalogs were all he found.

Mikesh said he would look outside. The old man wheeled his chair through the porch and out onto the platform at the top of the ramp to watch him, saying nothing. The garage was locked. Through the window it looked quiet and unused. The barn had an empty hayloft upstairs, and empty animal stalls downstairs; these housed two lawnmowers and boxes of empty motor oil bottles. When Mikesh emerged from the lower door he looked up and saw the old man still watching, though it was spitting rain. Mikesh gave him a timid wave.

Mikesh walked behind the barn and into what had been the animal yard. The lot was overgrown with trash trees and buckthorn, young ones coming up everywhere. But a cleared lane went through it and down along a fence at the edge of a windbreak. He turned to walk out along the lane and stopped.

The body hung like a nearly-empty sack from a gnarled and bent tree that shaded what had once been the watering tank for stock. The dead man looked stiff, with arms at his side, shifting only slightly with the breeze. Deegan had shimmied his way up the huge, bending trunk of the hollow box elder until he was at a point where it ran almost parallel to the ground. Here he fixed one end of the rope to the tree and the other, at a short distance, to his neck. Then he must have jumped. Since he had such a slight build, he could not have broken his neck with the fall. It had to have been a long and agonizing death.

The contorted face was not far above Mikesh's own. A damp note was pinned to the chest of the shirt, the same plaid button-down, perhaps, Mikesh saw in the online video. The note was close enough to Mikesh's eyes that he could look up and read it even though the blue ink had blurred in the mist.

"I thought he would die. He did. I took no money but his blood is on my hands. He was not what he said. I just can't live with my self. May God forgive me."

After he made the 9–1–1 call, Mikesh called my mom with the news.

CHAPTER 28

"She who waits, lives to see."

Czech proverb

Mikesh showed up at the top of Mary's step between dealing with the investigators at the scene of Deegan's suicide and going on to his job. He had the same awkward look he wore the first time she had seen him there. When he told her about finding the body of Randy Deegan, Mary was surprised. She ached to believe Josh's death had been the simple accident most people first believed, an idea less disturbing than his betrayal by someone close to him, and a conspiracy of the wealthy and powerful putting the man up to it through the woman called Julie. When Mikesh told her about the elder Deegan's conversation, sorrow paired with her pity. She tried to remember if she had seen Randy Deegan at the funeral of the man whose death he orchestrated and whose work he carried on for several months after he had killed him. But when Mikesh told her the likely role a story about her played in getting Josh onto the road, grief and rage consumed her. Gus Towers was once again a blunt instrument, battering a ragged path through her heart. She felt more sorrow now than when Josh had died, an empty familiar loneliness. Once again she found herself cut off from the person who could best comfort her.

Except for Mikesh. He could see the gloom in which he left her, so he returned the next day, a Thursday, with a casserole. He kept her quiet company while, outside, the sky seemed to open in thunder and rain. After he left to attend to his farm, she found an odd consolation in the raging of the weather. It fit her mood. Off and on the rain continued for the next four days, pouring down on Saturday in a steady curtain. By

Saturday night there was a flood watch. Water burbled up from storm drains. Municipal sewers crept or broke upwards in geysers into streets and basements. In every house in the lower sections of town, people hauled the contents of their basements up to the main floor. Dusty remnants of their grandparents' estates or their grown-up childrens' youth perched in unstable stacks on couches or kitchen tables. Neighbors banded together to empty what remained of last summer's vegetables or last fall's venison, carrying the freezers up to a dining room where the floor was still dry, and the electrical circuits safe, where they could be plugged in and safely refilled. When the Upper Iowa River rose to near the top of the dike, running level with the rooflines of houses on the other side, the whole lower portion of the town was ordered to evacuate. A married pair of women Mary knew, along with their cat, arrived at her door. On Monday the main bridge in Decorah was closed and several of the roads in and out of town were made impassable by standing water or raging streams.

Mary had company. Her need to comfort her friends distracted her from her grief. She cooked chili. She helped her friends carry their valuables and photo albums into her apartment. She made sure the guest cat stayed a door away from Safie. Monday noon she stood with the two women on the dike just above their home and watched the Upper Iowa River, fifty times its normal size, and several times its normal speed, stretching across the valley, carrying newly leafed-out trees along like sticks, end-to-ending slabs of concrete and sodden logs. The river raged, nearer and nearer to bringing complete catastrophe to the houses, businesses, and public buildings that stretched out behind the three of them as they stood in wet grass.

Her friends shouted to make themselves heard, but Mary was too overwhelmed to speak. The roar of the swollen river spoke to her; the world was a brutal thing that ate, and cut, and raged. She felt the impulse to step forward into the chaos. But she did not. On Tuesday she helped, as the waters receded and the neighborhood reopened, to salvage, sort, and throw the household goods from her friends' basement. By Wednesday she was rebooked solidly with clients whose appointments had been disrupted and people who had thrown out their backs carrying buckets of water from their basements or lifting to a chest-high perch the portable pumps that emptied their cellars of water. Her last appointment ended well after seven o'clock. She talked on the phone to Mikesh, who was at his job and chasing leaks as she made herself a dinner of toast. This she ate on the couch in her very quiet big room. Unable to lift herself off to bed, she fell asleep.

Mary must have slept deeply through the first part of the night, but after midnight she had a dream. In the dream she awoke to the sound of a familiar voice speaking to her. Mary's dream self pretended to sleep to keep the voice alive. That voice gave her such a pleasant feeling. But then the voice became sharp and commanding: "Mary!" Her dream self opened her eyes and saw a man kneeling by her. Who was it? His face was shaded. But then she knew it was Josh with the sandy head of wavy hair he'd had when he first met her. "Mary!" he said again. "Josh!" she replied, taking his hand, relieved to feel its bones, its muscle, the taut, familiar skin firm against her grip.

"I was so sad!"

"Why sad, Mary?"

"Josh, you were gone! And it was my fault! All my fault!"

"No Mary. That wasn't your fault. You're perfect. You were made that way. That is why I have always loved you."

"But Josh, I'm not perfect. I failed you!"

"Mary, you never failed me."

"I was not good enough."

"No. You're mistaken. Wait here."

Mary wanted to follow, but she was paralyzed, as if her limbs were hung with 60-pound dumbbells. Josh walked away from her down a hill. As he walked she realized she was in a deep green room created by the shade of a cedar. Josh was walking through a field of grass. She grew alarmed because she saw that at its base a river was raging. She wanted to warn Josh but her voice was unresponsive. Suddenly Josh stepped into the water, but instead of sinking in and being carried away he walked across its surface, reaching down and picking something out of the flood. He walked back towards her carrying what looked like the branch of a tree.

As he got closer she cried out, "Josh. You frightened me. I thought you were gone. I thought you were dead."

"I was never gone, Mary. Look."

He then raised the branch towards her. She could see it was a perfect miniature oak tree that had been caught in the flood. The end he raised towards her was its base, and nestled at the very heart of the roots, glowing as softly as an ivory *netsuke*, was a perfect acorn. Mary was touched by its beauty. She could not look away from it. But as she stared, the acorn changed its shape until it was a tiny, curled up human being. She looked closer, mesmerized. The person was her, down in the roots of the tree, and no bigger than a thumbnail, glowing like the flame in a birthday candle. Suddenly she knew Josh was right. She was perfect. She could not take her eyes from her beautiful self. But as she stared, her shape changed once again into different small person, curled into a perfect ball.

She looked up: "Josh, it's you!"

"I was there all along. You just couldn't see me." He set the tree on the grass, and it leafed out immediately. "The world and its pieces are one. Each will be resolved to its root."

"Don't give up heart, Mary. The Spirit restores. She glows in everything you see."

"Why couldn't I see that?"

Josh looked steadily at her and held up his right hand with its fingers splayed.

"Five powers are against you: the powers of lightlessness, ignorance, desire, the flesh, and anger." As he numbered them off, he slowly lowered a finger for each power he named. Having named them all he stood with his fist clenched. "This is the power that remains when each of those has been overcome."

In her dream, Mary stared at Josh's compact hand, but she missed those beautiful, pointing fingers.

"Josh," she complained, angry, "why do you always insist on overcoming the flesh?"

"Because the part of me in you that never passes away can only be seen by your mind, which exists between the soul and the Spirit. If you look for me, look for me in your mind. I am no longer in the flesh."

He walked down the hill from the cedar tree toward the flood. She wanted to stop him, but again she could only watch. This time he stopped short of the river, but the flood rose higher, lifting him as he stood, turned around so that he looked at her. And it carried him, standing, out of sight.

She was alone, though the small oak tree remained, green and leafy. She looked up again at the cedar and down the hill to the flood, and she remembered this place. She had been here before!

With that Mary woke up. This time she was truly awake. It was not a dream. She was in her apartment, and the lamp by her couch was still on. It was night. But each piece of the dream was vivid in her mind. When had she ever had a vision like that before? And where was the place she had been? One part of her worked hard not to forget or lose any part of the dream, while another worked to think of the place, the real-world place where the unsettling dream was set. Then it came to her.

She jumped up from the couch. The clock read 3:45. She needed to get to the graveyard. The place she had seen Josh was Communia cemetery.

The drive through the night was as strange as her dream. She had to take a detour out of town. The culvert in an area inundated by mud still had to be tested by state engineers before the road above it could be reopened. Once on the hilltop of the Middle Calmar Road, winding her way to Federal Highway 52 south she thought about flooding elsewhere, and remembered that one of her clients spoke about the Turkey River having even worse flooding than the Upper Iowa. She thought of Mikesh. Did his creek flow into the Turkey? It was the Turkey she and Josh watched and walked along that afternoon last July and toward which she was driving. She pulled over and took out her map. In the Honda's dome light she made out where the Turkey flowed and chose a route that would keep her on high ground until just before Elkader. She hoped the low country from there to the cemetery would be clear to drive. She turned on her radio and moved the dial through Minnesota and Wisconsin channels, through all-night oldies and country, until she found an Iowa news station. The stories were about flooding. All the rivers north of Des Moines were out of their banks, their names familiar but their locations vague to her: Raccoon, Skunk, Wapsipinicon, Cedar, Volga, Turkey. As she drove, it rained again: a pelting rain that her wipers at their fastest speed could not outpace. She slowed to a crawl and through water cascading down her windshield could only guess at the outline of the road. She lost all sense of how far she had come down the highway. She ran over the small parts of a limb before she could stop, back up the car, and maneuver around the bigger pieces of a fallen tree.

Mary missed the turnoff she needed to make at Froelich because she could not see the houses. Fortunately, the rain let up enough to see the sign for Giard. She checked the map, turned around, and this time found the road she needed. As she descended into Elkader she could see that, even though the air was still filled with rain, the sky was lightening.

As she passed into the edge of Elkader Mary saw signs of terrible flooding. The entrances to roads were blocked with barricades. Water filled the ditches. She saw, with rising panic, orange-flashing emergency lights several places in the town at her left: disaster zones.

Continuing on the road that skirted Elkader, near the bottom of the valley that had been the site of Communia she saw, again, orange-flashing lights. The road ahead was blocked. Illuminated patches cast by similar lights flashed on the uphill stretch at the other side of the valley. She pulled onto the shoulder. The place was deserted. She seemed to be the only person in the region who failed to get the message that roads were closed. She picked up the flashlight she'd remembered to bring. Sitting in the quiet of her car, she could hear the rain gently hitting the roof, and could tell that the morning had lightened even further. She pulled a cheap orange rain poncho over her head and climbed into the cold.

The gravel of the shoulder was sloppy after the rain, so she walked on the pavement. She had it to herself. With her ears attuned to the quiet, she noticed, above the rain, the sound of the creek that flooded over the road. It raised prickles of fear. She had seen Josh walk on top of that flood. She carried a memory of the terrain from the late-March funeral. Up the rise on her left was the entrance to the cemetery. She left the pavement, and again felt her sandals squishing in the gravel, but there was no standing water. The way to the cemetery gate was clear, though she slipped once and fell to her knees, dropping the flashlight. She stood up, wiped the flashlight lens on her jeans and continued. The sound of the creek in the valley grew louder as she crested the embankment and walked into the graveyard. She made out the flood, a wide smear of reflected sky at the bottom of the hill. As she walked toward the water a shiver passed through her and she stopped. She was taking the path Josh took in her dream, when she had been unable to move. She saw behind her at the top of the hill the cedars below which she stood at the funeral, and which made the protective room of her dream. She walked further down the slope. The flashlight was becoming less necessary. Landscape outlines were clearly defined: the wooded hill on the other side of the creek, the strip of rushing water, the ground of the cemetery falling toward it. She passed the last of the stones of the graveyard into a more open stretch of slope. It hadn't registered at the time of the funeral because of all the people. There were no stones near the grave. Josh was buried by himself in the lowest portion of the cemetery toward the creek, near a fence, and away from any other graves. She stopped, uncertain of her ground. She was less than one hundred feet from where she believed the grave to be. She saw debris left by the flood as it climbed and then receded down the slope. In that margin of debris, this side of the rushing water, she believed Josh was buried, but the fence behind the grave was gone. No, there it was, bending out toward the road. And there it was again, climbing the hill toward the cemetery shed. Between, it disappeared. She stepped slowly, testing the ground with the toe of her sandal before she trusted weight to her foot. She shone the light toward the ground ahead of her.

Something wasn't right. She could see what happened. The flood ate into the base of the hill, cutting away its bank, tearing away dirt. This gash pushed far into what had been cemetery. The whole area had been under rushing water. It cut through as far as the grave. She could see distinctly where the hole had been dug. The flood had torn away the earth and sod. She trod carefully, testing the grass that only hours before must have been flattened beneath tons of pummeling water. But she could clearly see the stream edge, the new bank, the expanse of sod, and the cut-out edge of what must have been the grave.

She shined her light over the edge into the depression that remained of the grave. What she saw was a yellow eye looking back at her: the reflection of her flashlight in water that still pooled below. She needed to know what was down in that hole.

Mary made her way back to her car to look for an instrument with which to fathom the hole. A pickup with a stock rack had pulled beside her car. The driver, a middle-aged woman in a headscarf, milking clothes, and green raincoat, stood in the road to survey the progress of the flood. When Mary asked if she had a long stick or pole the woman pulled a pitchfork from the bed of the truck. Asked whether Mary could use it to test the water in the hole the older woman at first said they should go get her husband. She finally agreed to let Mary take the pitchfork only if she could go along, to see that Mary didn't disappear into the flood. They walked gingerly, the farm wife clutching the pitchfork, testing the ground before her with its tines as they entered the washed-out area. She insisted on holding Mary's ankles to keep her anchored as Mary lay flat in the debris and mud at the edge of the grave and extended the fork down to the full reach of her arm. The tines disappeared into the water, the progress slowing as they met resistance beyond mere water, but down, down, down, through the silt until Mary could barely still make a fist around the blunt end of the handle.

The coffin was gone. The grave was empty of all but silt.

The other woman was named Marion Koester, a childhood neighbor of my mom. Looking for the coffin, she and Mary walked several hundred feet down along the creek bottom past shrubs half leveled and hung with grass and cornstalks and around pools lit by the morning sky.

In their long muddy scramble through increasingly ample light they couldn't find the coffin. Finally it rained hard again, and they gave up. Mary thanked Marion and watched her pickup drive slowly away as she dialed her flip phone. She called us—or, rather, she called my mother.

"I'm at the cemetery in Communia. There's been a flood. Joshua is not here."

AFTERWORD

THE STORY OF JOSH'S death ends here.

Since Josh's life culminated in an invitation, "join me in infinity," I collected his most important teachings in a work that I titled *Good News of the Spirit*. I was finishing that collection when Mikesh stopped by the Big House the day he found Randy. You can find *Good News* online and in print.

What you are reading now is the record of the months between Josh's car crash and the discovery of his murderer, including many different testimonies about his life and work, events leading up to his death on March 21, 2008, and the lives of several people since that date. Some of you will not like this chronicle, dealing as it does with persons who do not believe they advance Josh's work, many of them scornful of my brother's whole mission. But hatred, scorn, and misunderstanding were part of the soil into which my brother chose to plant himself. As I said in starting out, if you do not know the grit of my brother's environment, you will never really know my brother or what he was trying to do, how he stood out from his surroundings.

To catch you up, the work of the Spirit goes on in spite of us. Though Josh is dead, people continue to seek and follow him, and in doing that, to find the life of the Spirit. This chronicle has detailed the inner experience of several of them.

You may remember that in Mary's dream Josh told her, "the part of me in you that never passes away can only be seen by your mind, which exists between the soul and the Spirit." No matter how much we might be creatures of flesh, sinew, blood, and bone, consulting our watches throughout the workday, our most intimate selves dwell in a place beyond time. The Spirit fills that space with life, just as the Spirit fills the world of fact with its color and energy. To tell Josh's story, I've recorded what went through the minds of those who pursued him in his life and in his death, chronicling as best I could what transpired "between the soul and the Spirit." If I could say there was one lesson, above all others, I learned from my brother it is this: what is beyond time in you, what lives on, is what you give of yourself to others. Josh gave so much of himself, that in the end, as I saw his body lying in that hospital, the green sheet peeled away, it seemed that there was nothing left. But his life, his words, and the Josh to whom this story gives witness, show that I was mistaken. His final sacrifice of himself for Mary completed the Spirit's full birth process; Josh's body passing away, Josh passed into the rest of us.

The pages on which you rest your thumbs, the black print on your lit screen, the words that pour through the buds in your ears are the book I wasn't sure I had the resources to record. Frail clay container of my untrained art, it is now finished.

You may want to hear more about the main people I chose to include in this account.

Josh's death was the result of one doubtful believer's test whether he could die. It proved that Josh was just as breakable as you or me. It also showed that Joshua could be fooled, that he was maybe a little foolish, at least where Mary was concerned. Those cracks in my brother's human character let the Spirit's light shine through. Contrary to Brother Randy's plan, my brother's status as teacher and healer has been boosted by his dying, the victim of a friend's betrayal, and by having his body disappear. When I spoke with Arnie Mikesh that first morning after Josh's death, I warned him that many in the church would not believe that Josh was dead. The flood, and the disappearance of Josh's coffin that it effected, made my prediction accurate beyond anything I imagined.

As for Mary's dream, the one that sent her to the cemetery that morning, it has met with wildly different receptions. Simon was at first angry. He asked, "Why would he single her out for a revelation, and keep it from each of the rest of us who worked so closely with him?"

My mother pointed out that Josh knew Mary and he loved her, perhaps more than he loved any one of the rest of us, as his last act on earth testified.

But Mary's experience precipitated a rash of other visitations. Though it has not proven true for me, the last year has been a time when young and old alike dream dreams and have visions. Josh and the Spirit live on.

Simon's feelings eased when he saw that Mary wanted no more to do with the faithful followers now than she ever had.

Just last month Simon started a house in the Bronx, in New York, where some brothers and sisters already live. He hopes to do great work, though at present the numbers who know the Spirit there are few. Simon remembers the early days in Waterloo, when Josh was simply working with a handful of kids, and my brother gave Simon advice about angling for bass, and then told him to start fishing for souls. Though he now lives in a very dangerous neighborhood, Simon takes Josh's progress as a model for what he might accomplish in his new home. Of *this* narrative you have just finished, however, Simon does *not* approve. He considers it neither the full story, nor in good taste, nor showing a true understanding of Josh. I am content with that. Simon has his own story to tell.

Sister Naomi, still distanced from Evelyn, decided that she would take up the work my brother started in Des Moines with a women's free clinic, shelter, and food pantry. Sister Naomi went to Mary once she learned her story. Sister Naomi knows what it feels like to have had Josh reach out and redirect her life. Other than my mother, she has become Mary's best friend among my brother's followers, though she lives far away.

Brother Gary leads the work of bringing Bremer County soil back to life and running the CSA. My mother, the farm girl in her fifties my brother ordered Mikesh to help, leads the community at the Big House, where the bread has won awards. Mikesh has paid her several visits to help out in the garden, always bringing home a couple dozen eggs for his trouble. Where my mother is, the Spirit's presence is strong. If I have a second home, it is with her at the Big House.

But my mission is elsewhere. I plan to travel first to Pattanam, in the Kerala province of India, where a leader in the Christian church has invited me to come and teach. In that land, the followers of the one goddess, Shakti, have an ancient home. I have a hunch it is my destiny to spread Josh's message in ashrams, in churches, or along roadways clogged with bicycle rickshaws and water buffalo as well as big red passenger sedans. Because Joshua spent his adult life seeking the Spirit in far-flung places, I believe he would approve of that.

Jude Bailey has moved to Chicago, where he has found work in a truckers' union.

Julie, whose vague complaints in the hope of shifting Mikesh's attention Randy's way led to Mikesh asking about Deegan in the first place, continues as "community answer person" for Senator Cornish's office. By report, she also has a boyfriend in the person of a high-placed executive in the ethanol industry, a man whose tastes when it comes to having a good time, are very like those of the *ex*-boyfriend Julie described to Mikesh.

In October 2008 a Winneshiek County judge ruled that Josh's death was the result of criminal acts confessed to by Randall Deegan in his suicide note. After investigation, the county prosecutor determined that these acts were Deegan's own and no one else's, premeditated in Deegan's disordered way of thinking as a way of testing whether Josh was immortal. The law, in its wisdom, saw no way of proving that any planning or encouragement could be attributed to Julie, or the senator for whom she now works, or the large agricultural interests represented by her boyfriend. The law also, in investigating the crime, found a money-green stash of cleome leaves, carefully dried the previous September, along with a box of sandwich bags in Randy's drawer of automotive tools in the Big House garage. With less deadly intent than he trained on Josh, Randy tried in his sad way to put Mikesh of commission on the highway, too.

In closing the case, the sheriff's office contacted Mikesh about the blood-soaked cotton coat he had pushed around my brother to keep him warm. When Mikesh stopped in Decorah to collect the coat, he threw the bag containing it in the back of his truck, thinking he would take the coat home and burn it. But when he stopped at Mary's place and she found out about his errand, she asked if she could have the jacket. Washed, but still stained, she keeps the coat in a drawer in her living room, and sometimes, when time stops, when blackness descends on her, or when she simply feels cold, she pulls the coat around her, pulls her feet to her on the couch, and cuddles into Mikesh's jacket, watching the light change on hill out the window of her apartment.

The various houses and meetings move in their own ways. There are those houses, those brothers and sisters, who want more of Josh and less of the Spirit. Their gatherings and their work have become more worshipful but less Spirit-filled. Brother Simon's Bronx following, if he has his way, will go in this direction. He has exchanged the name Joshuite Church for Shekinah. He fears that without Josh in the flesh, the work of the Spirit is threatened. Among his followers, the sharing of the bread is believed to be a physical visitation of Josh among the members. As Josh's brother, I find this morbid, Simon's own way of keeping up with Mary and her dream. But Simon condemns me as the eternal doubter.

Arnold Mikesh could not be called an apostle, but the Spirit works even in the most skeptical, as I have tried to show in the details of this story. Arnold Mikesh may have started this story as only a silhouette even his mother might not recognize in a truck cab, but in the eye of the Spirit Mikesh loomed large and vibrant, even in the heaviest early Saturday morning fog Northeast Iowa could manage. The Spirit registered the tiredness that weighed down Mikesh's elbows, as well as the slight buzz of adrenalin he felt from the late-night mix of Warren Hayes guitar riffs and anxiety about driving off the road. The Spirit registered Mikesh's solitude. Josh King, my six-minute-older brother, entering fully into the Spirit, willed Mikesh toward him. My brother needed to see Mikesh's flashlight, needed the warmth of his borrowed jacket, needed the dim sight of his face joining him in the tent of light that filled the tiny space between the heavy car and the cold earth, needed the sound of his voice, and the warmth of his hand against his face. He needed to direct Mikesh on to my mother, and in doing that, to set in process the enquiry that would reveal the truth about my brother's death. Though Mikesh did not know it at the time, as he gave my brother his coat and placed his finger on my brother's neck to find a pulse, he entered in with him to infinity.

From now forward, no new converts will meet Josh in the flesh. Mikesh was the first to tell the news that Josh is dead. This chronicle, so much touching on Mikesh, is a way of saying that the Spirit lives. "Honor the Spirit as it burns in those you greet," my brother told us. Deceived by a traitor, tricked by a lie, Josh drove off into the fog because of his honor for the Spirit in one of his closest friends. In stopping to help my brother and in tracking down the true story of his death, Mikesh, too, was honoring the Spirit after his own fashion.

I spoke untruly to Mikesh that morning of our first March meeting in a Decorah parking lot. I said I only wanted him to tell the story of his encounter with Josh once. Little did either of us know that his "encounter" would stretch out into an involvement of closer to three months, and that the story he would end up telling would be this book, ultimately written down by me, but chronicling the way my brother worked his way into Mikesh's mind, the way Josh continued to work in his friend Mary's mind and heart, and the way the Spirit lives on not only in spite of my brother's death, but also because of it.

Mikesh and Mary talked it over when I made my request that they share their whole stories with me. They decided they owed it to Josh, as long as the story I told stayed truthful. We all agreed on the issue of truth.

So we met: at their places, or in the coffee shop. I learned the names of Mikesh's cows and how not to frighten Mary's cat, Safie. I asked them questions only a therapist might ask. I convinced them to let me put my explanations into the story, as long as my acknowledgment of the working of the Spirit didn't go too far beyond what either of them might claim.

Those two remain close. Mikesh hangs on to his computer but has gotten rid of his television so he will spend more time listening to people, like Mary, who expect him to talk back.

The two of them consider mine an odd project. And as I told you on page one, it certainly is an unlikely one.

Is it foolish?

I hope by the ring Dr. Razavi gave my mother when Josh and I were born that it is not. And from this last stage appearance, I, Tom-Tom, make my exit.

And in the absence that remains . . . Shekinah.

www.ingramcontent.com/pod-product-compliance
Lightning Source LLC
Chambersburg PA
CBHW070223030726
47505CB00006B/1800